# In the Dark of the Grove

## by

## Jon Wesley Huff

**In the Dark of the Grove**
**By Jon Wesley Huff**

**Third Edition**
**Published by Oblivion House**



Cover design, interior Illustrations by Jon Wesley Huff





Into The Dark of the Grove was first published in 2021.

Paperback ISBN 979-8-9907598-2-4

Jon Wesley Huff

*To everyone who read this and helped shape it, most especially my ever-faithful beta reader Laura.*

*And to my love, Paul, for all the support and laughter.*

# IV

# Prologue

ying ended up being more difficult than Herb Thomas had anticipated. He'd assumed the build-up to it would be the worst part. The drive to Silver Cove had been an uncomfortable mix of familiar and foreign. He hadn't been up this way in nearly a decade. The once charming lakeside town had taken on a commercialized feel, with tall condos now partially blocking the view of Lake Michigan. He drove into the familiar parking lot of Silver Cove Beach, though he preferred the free parking along the roads of the quaint downtown. His wife, however, had always insisted on paying to park in this lot, since it was closer to the beach. She could spend twelve hours working in the fields, but she hated walking on sand. He smiled at the memory of her and their son, Kyle, running as fast as they could to the shoreline and the cool wet sand that awaited. The smile didn't last long.

Herb's wife had been gone a long time now, and he hadn't seen his son in fifteen years. This time, he parked in the lot because he wanted his car to be easy to find. He snuffed his cigarette out into an overflowing ashtray—the result of picking the bad habit up again in the two years he'd been planning all of this. The build-up to this moment had been hard. The uncertainty of whether this was an act of bravery or cowardice plagued him. He never thought of himself as a brave man. Even the book, the greatest act of bravery he'd ever managed, was masked in illusion and art. He looked at the passenger seat, where his comp copy of Dunbar's Grove sat. His last book, and his most important one.

Herb thought of his life. He thought of the series of mistakes and blunders that had left him with a family he hadn't wanted, and finally to this moment. Why was it that now—just as he was ready for it to be over—it suddenly felt precious? One last time he allowed his mind to wander. What if he'd told his father he wasn't going to take over the farm? What if he'd been able to write full time, instead of at night, when it rained, or when the fields were dead and frosted over? He put those thoughts away, as he slid Dunbar's Grove into his jacket. It was long past time for that sort of daydreaming.

He mentally went over every detail again, craving the solace of knowing he'd done everything he could do. The agony of the last two years of planning had left him utterly exhausted. He'd spent so many sleepless nights trying to figure out how to get his message across, but in a way that they wouldn't know what he'd done. This kind of exhaustion wasn't cured by even days of sleep. This kind of exhaustion crept straight to the bone and then rested heavy like a lead weight. He was only alive because his death would draw too much attention, given the talk that had started to swirl around the book. But his suicide? That would be a nice bow wrapped around everything. They'd put their guard down, at least at first.

The fact this entire plan hinged on someone—who had every reason to hate him—piecing together clues that were designed to be vague at best didn't fill him with much confidence. That was, of course, assuming Kyle even bothered to return home. There was always the chance his son could leave it to the lawyers, and Herb wouldn't have blamed him.

All of this, however, was just a prelude to the annoyance of dying itself. He walked a half hour down the shoreline, away from the lights of the condos. Here there were just a smattering of lake houses. The last of the sunlight disappeared as the dusty amber of the horizon faded to gray. At last, he came to a stretch where all of the houses were dark, and the calls of the gulls faint in the distance. Hopefully that meant he'd have privacy. The last thing he needed was some well-meaning witness trying to stop him. He walked out into the lake, but its waves battered him away as though he were an infection it wanted rid of. His annoyance turned to rage as he kicked his legs and thrashed his arms to get further away from the shore. How had anyone ever managed to drown themselves? He had a memory—from a movie or a book, he couldn't remember which—of someone weighing themselves down before walking into the water. That would have been smart. For all his planning, he hadn't really thought this part would be so difficult. With one last, determined surge of power, he dove further into the murky depths of the lake. Finally, the undertow took him.

This death wasn't like he'd imagined it would be. It was no gentle descent into oblivion's embrace. He choked and sputtered. His body rebelled against his intentions, tried to claw back to the surface of the water and back towards life. Even as he whirled in confusion and terror in the lake's depths, he cursed himself. He cursed himself—ever the writer—for trying to write his own ending. His last thought was of the cruelty of reality. A world he could not control. Full of people with their own thoughts and desires. Narratives he could not weave.

# 1

## *Essen*

I t was a perfect summer day, and Kyle Thomas resented the hell out of it. He rolled his window down, and the perfect sweetness of fresh-cut grass stewing in sunshine washed over him. It mixed with the more earthy scent of the sweetcorn, standing proud (if a little stunted, thanks to the lack of rain) and ready for harvest. The late afternoon sun washed everything in a slightly golden haze and caused the crops to cast long dark shadows that stretched over the newly cut road-side grass and onto the mottled surface of the road. The effect was dream-like and nostalgia-inducing.

It reminded Kyle of the summer drives he and his mom used to take in the country. Sometimes they had a destination, and sometimes they didn't. Sometimes it was just a reason to get out, listen to some music, and collect some of the wild grasses from the side of the road. His mom used the grasses to create fragile bouquets to decorate their home. Bouquets that would inevitably be destroyed by his dad's fumbling.

This was exactly what Kyle wanted to avoid. The false comfort of sunlit days only made the harsh reality of what came after more painful. He was coming back to the town he had grown up in—he refused to think of it as home—in protest. He was the last Thomas. The last in a long line that stretched back to the town's founding. He passed a low sign made of polished stone that read:

**Essen, Indiana**
**Population: 4,500**
**A Good Place to Live**

He could see the faint outline of white spray paint—the last remnants of some sort of graffiti that'd been scrubbed away—and found this strangely reassuring. When he was young, a wooden welcome sign had been posted here. The kids in town had frequently made a game out of vandalizing it in new and creative ways. He was glad to see this small act of rebellion had continued.

Other than some soulless new housing developments on the outskirts of town, Essen, Indiana, looked unchanged even after all these years. The twin towers of the Baker Farm's grain silos still glimmered weakly in the sunlight as he entered town along Mills Road. The road curved past a small industrial park that used to house a microwave popcorn manufacturer, an aluminum siding plant, and a tool and die shop. All those businesses were gone now, but new tenants occupied the buildings. The general shape of it was the same, with only the signs having changed. This gave way to the stretches of tree-shaded houses that lined the streets in a ring around downtown.

In the darkest part of Kyle's heart, he'd hoped Essen, Indiana might be a sad ruin. A meth-riddled shell of its former glory. But there were still kids playing at Faraday Park. Outside of Kessinger's Grocery, two older women parked their carts—primarily there to hold their gigantic purses—side by side as they gabbled. They stopped to gape at the unfamiliar car that passed them by. Everything was much as he remembered it. The roles were the same. Only the actors had changed.

Kyle turned right before he reached downtown and headed toward the East side of town. The 'newer' shops were out this way, lining Mint Run Street before it wound over the bridge and out of town. He was sad to see Perry's General Store was gone and had been replaced by a generic dollar store. Perry's was his favorite haunt as a kid. He'd gotten his first cassettes in the Radio Shack housed within the building. This was where Kyle had bought the fabric to make a pillow in his home economics class. Where he'd seen his first men's workout magazine, and realized that the muscular man in the purple speedo intrigued him in ways he didn't understand. This was also where he'd purchased (and, yes, sometimes stolen) Teenage Mutant Ninja Turtle figures and a vast array of comic books.

As he turned into the pot-hole riddled parking lot of the AllCare Insurance office, Kyle shook the memories away. He didn't want to dwell on the fact that most of his fondest memories of Essen were in that store. It was too sad a thought, and he wanted to be in a decent mood for what came next. He stepped out of his car and stretched his back. It'd been a five-hour drive, and he hadn't bothered to stop at any of the rest areas along the way.

The insurance office was a modest little brick building with a glass front. Through the glass, he could see a young woman—barely out of high school—sitting at the front desk, staring intently at a laptop. She had dark lipstick, the curve of her right ear was covered in small earrings from top to bottom, and her blonde hair was dyed shades of blue and pink on the ends. Behind her were three posters, all of which looked a little faded, touting the benefits of going with AllCare for your insurance needs. In his youth, the building had been a local video rental place. There were still holes bored into the brick where a neon sign had once flashed "video" in brilliant purple letters at passersby.

"You actually did it," said a deep rumbling voice the instant Kyle walked into the office. Kyle was startled for a moment, before realizing the sound was coming from a hallway to his right. At the far end of it, he saw Max Williams walking down the hall. "You actually came back."

"Hey, I'm as surprised as you are," Kyle said. "It's weird."

"It'll be fine. Essen has changed a little since you've been gone."

"Has it, though? I think I saw the Thompson sisters outside of Kessinger's. They were giving me the stink eye. It certainly felt like old times."

"You're always gonna have assholes," said Max. "And old biddies who act like they're the town's watchdogs. On the bright side, if you get any weird looks this time, it won't be because you're the town's resident homo."

The young woman at the front desk cleared her throat loudly, although she didn't look away from her work. Kyle noticed, next to her computer, was a dog-eared script for some sort of play, heavy with highlights and notes in its margins.

"Homosexual, I mean," corrected Max. He paused a moment,

his brown eyes narrowing, before turning to the young woman at the desk. "That better, Lissie?"

"Somehow, not when you say it," Lissie murmured to her computer screen.

"It's okay. Max kicked more than a few asses back in high school defending this 'homo,'" Kyle said. Lissie looked dubious but shrugged her shoulders.

"Asses that you'd rather have done other things to, if I remember correctly."

"The pretty ones were always the cruelest."

"Speaking of pretty, look at you! It's like you lost half of you," said Max.

"The gays are merciless," Kyle joked. Max cocked his head to the side quizzically. Kyle tried to fill in the blanks. "I couldn't get laid. It was good motivation to get in shape."

At this, Max grinned and nodded his head in understanding. It was a cute way of summing up a dark period in his life. But that's what you did when you caught up with someone you hadn't seen in over a decade. No one wanted to hear your life story. Not really.

Standing next to the man again, Kyle was struck by how unlikely their friendship might have been anywhere but Essen. Max was a popular football player. Not the star quarterback or anything, but he was well-liked, and there were few institutions more beloved in Essen than football. Max had been part of the team that took Essen to state for the fourth time in its history. But he was still a black kid in a town where you could count the number of families of color on your fingers. His family had been the only black family in town when Kyle was growing up. Their shared outsider status helped sustain their friendship in the beginning.

"Well, that's why I've got my sexy 'dad bod.' Getting laid these days requires way less effort," said Max, proudly slapping the paunch around his waist.

"You in a play?" Kyle asked Lissie, hoping to change the subject.

"Nah, I do the lighting. Local community theater. It's going to be terrible," Lissie said.

"This is why we don't let you sell the insurance," Max groaned.

"I mean, the lighting will be good?" This elicited a groan from Max, which seemed to please Lissie. Kyle couldn't help but smirk.

"Come on, let's shoot the shit in my office away from the studio audience."

Kyle followed Max back into his office. It was a reasonably tidy place, with a white wooden desk with silver legs he recognized from a trip to IKEA a few years ago. An older model MacBook was connected to an octopus of wiring that linked it to a mess of various peripheral devices. The plush black leather chair Max settled into felt out of place in comparison—a relic from a different age. As Kyle seated himself in an uncomfortable clear plastic chair across from Max's desk, he noticed the many framed photographs surrounding the AllCare logo painted on the center of the wall.

"Still amazed you didn't end up with Betty Clark," Kyle remarked. Max's expression darkened.

"Well, Betty died a couple years after high school," said Max.

"Oh man. Sorry." Kyle felt a churn in his stomach.

"It's okay. It was a long time ago. We'd split up by then. She went off to Purdue, and I was stuck here. So that didn't last long. A drunk driver t-boned her car while she was driving home for Spring Break."

"Damn."

"Yeah. I mean, don't get me wrong. I was broken up about it at the time. But life keeps chugging along for the rest of us." Max got up and took one of the portraits off the wall. "And eventually I met Heather." He and Heather were grasping each other and staring into the camera lens. They both had high-wattage smiles that showed off their incredibly white teeth. Nestled between them was a little girl with brown skin, kinky reddish-brown hair, and freckles. Kyle was terrible at guessing children's ages, but he was thinking she looked four or five. Heather Williams was skinny and tall—a few inches taller than Max. She had pale skin, freckles to match her daughter, and curly red hair gathered up on top of her head.

"A kid too?" asked Kyle. "So respectable."

"Yep, that's Azura. Although this is an old pic. She's nine now and insisting we call her 'Zee.'"

"That's kinda cool." Kyle looked closer at the picture. Zee had her father's grin.

"Maybe," Max said. "But we try to give kids these interesting names to make up for the fact we're all called Sam and Joe and John, and they go off and decide what they want to be called anyway."

"You sound like an old man."

"Speaking of old men. Your dad's last book…"

"Yeah." Kyle tried to slump back in his chair, but the sound of straining plastic caused him to sit upright again. "You read it?"

"No. Not a ton of extra time, to be honest. But I think everyone else in town's read it. Once people figured out the town in the book was a thinly disguised version of Essen, and… well, you know the rest."

"Dunbar's Grove by Herbert Thomas," Kyle said, holding out

an imaginary book as if reading its title. "About a grove, next to a lake, outside of a small town in northern Indiana. Doesn't take a genius to put two and two together, I guess."

"Want to know something funny? I live out at the Lake of the Grove now," said Max. Kyle shot him a confused look.

"I thought you were doing okay. I mean, it looks—"

"No, no, I'm doing fine," said Max with a laugh. "In fact, I've got some opportunities coming up that might get me up the ladder. But Lake of the Grove isn't like when we were kids. They've cleaned it all up. They figured out people with money want to live by water, so the old guard got bought out or pushed out."

"People want to live by that old swamp?"

"They cleaned that up too. I mean, it's still murky with tons of algae lining the bottom, but you can swim in it. Even take out a paddle boat. You should come by sometime while you're in town," suggested Max.

"Sounds fun," Kyle said absently. It was strange to think of the lake that adjoined The Grove as some destination for the well-to-do of Essen. The town had always had money. The school was a testament to that. Even though the town was tiny, it boasted a first-class football field, Olympic-sized pool, computer labs with the latest equipment, and other amenities schools in much larger cities didn't have. But when Kyle lived in Essen, most of the people with money lived in the large old houses on the brick-paved roads around Faraday Park. Eventually they started migrating to one of the many new housing additions popping up on the edges of town.

A kid he knew at school, Justin Miller, moved into one of the sprawling McMansions with his family. Kids at school got wind of the fact that only three of the rooms in the house were actually furnished because the family couldn't afford any more right away. The teasing that followed was merciless.

The Lake of the Grove, in contrast, had been surrounded by trailer homes. Home-made docks of plywood and two-by-fours dotted the slushy green waters. You were more likely to find trash floating in the lake than you were people. The local kids did build tire swings and hung them from the branches of the tall trees surrounding the lake. But the fun there was the thrill of danger should you fall into the murky, stagnant water. The Grove itself was technically separated from the Lake by a country road, but they were basically part of the same stand of trees. Both were surrounded by farmland. The reason the farmers of decades past left the trees around the lake was understandable. But why they left The Grove had always been more of a mystery.

When he was twelve, Kyle had read an article about it in the paper. In fact, that article was part of what had inspired him to become an investigative journalist. It mentioned there was an old forgotten graveyard there, but even the earliest dates on the stones were after the land was cleared for farming. So, the cemetery wasn't the reason The Grove was left standing. Most of the old stones were pushed over or smashed by the delinquents who'd frequented The Grove since the 60s. That was what The Grove was most known for when Kyle was growing up. It was where teenagers snuck off to go drink, smoke pot, make out, and even have full on sex. There had been whisperings that Lane Bradford and half the football team ran a train on Gale Phillips out there. Max, his lone source for football team gossip back in the day, said he didn't see anything like that happen, but he'd left early because of his parents' strict curfew—which was probably for the best, since Gale ended up getting pregnant and there was no small amount of scandal surrounding the whole affair.

Now, The Grove cultivated a new sort of infamy, all thanks to his father's final book.

"You said in your email you were coming to sort out the property?" Max asked. "Are you—I'm not sure how to put this—you thinking about looking into the stuff in the book? Whether it's true or not?"

"No. I mean, it's not true, right? It can't be," Kyle said. Looking further into everything the book had churned up had crossed his mind, but he'd been ambivalent at best about the prospect. "You know I wasn't my dad's biggest fan. And I hadn't seen either of them in twelve years. But even I can't imagine him doing that."

Max nodded and stared off into the distance thoughtfully for a moment.

"For what it's worth. I didn't think so either," said Max. Kyle nodded because it did make him feel happier to have someone else confirm his gut feeling.

"Look, I don't want to keep you too long. We can catch up later," said Kyle.

"Want to grab a drink? The office closes in a few minutes."

"I'll take a rain-check. I definitely plan on seeing whatever fancy house you've set yourself up in. But it was a long drive, and I want to take a shower."

"How long you think you'll be in town?"inquired Max as Kyle got up out of the uncomfortable chair. "I'll ask Heather which night would be good for us to have you over."

"Not sure. Probably a couple weeks. Maybe less," he said.

And so, they began the long Midwestern ritual of parting. Max told him that was plenty of time to get in a couple visits. He mentioned the town fair was coming up, too, if Kyle stayed around long enough. Kyle nodded his head, but was getting more and more tired, and was trying to leave as quickly as was polite.

It was at least another five minutes before he'd been able to leave Max's office and was in the short corridor heading toward the exit. Enough time had passed that the sign on the door was turned to 'closed' and Lissie was packing up her script, books, notebook, and multi-colored gel pens into a small black backpack adorned with a variety of buttons and pins. She was so engrossed in her packing that Kyle felt awkward interrupting her to say goodbye. But as he opened the door, Lissie spoke. As before, she did not look at him but kept her focus on her task.

"I listened to your podcast. It was pretty good," she said.

"Ah, so you're the one," joked Kyle, worrying it sounded more bitter than funny. He'd spent a year researching and making the podcast, and barely anyone had listened to it. It was the beginning and end of his podcast career.

"I like that you made the girl an actual human," said Lissie. "People either make the victims saints or treat them like they're basically a prop in the killer's story. You going to do another one?"

"Thanks. That… that means a lot to me," Kyle said. "But I mostly keep to shorter-term investigative pieces for magazines or sites now."

"You're not going to do one on your dad? And his book?" Lissie surprised Kyle by finally looking directly at him. She had shockingly aqua-colored irises. Kyle realized they were contacts, but they gave her gaze an effectively eerie quality. She was hard to read because of them, but here was a hint of genuine concern at the corner of her eyes.

"I guess I'm going to get that question a lot," said Kyle, shifting uncomfortably. "But, no. I'm here to figure out what to do with the farm. That's it."

"Good." Lissie said it so emphatically, Kyle couldn't help his face scrunching up in confusion. Her face softened, and for the first time, the steely confidence the young woman radiated faltered. "If you do decide to look into it, don't tell anyone. Word travels fast around here and people are being really weird about it."

A cold tingle started midway up Kyle's spine. It crawled slowly up his back and made the hairs on his neck stand on end. Was it her eyes? The tone of her voice? He couldn't be certain why he felt so unsettled. He gave her a quick, awkward nod and stepped out of the door and into the warm summer night. A shiver pulsed through him. As he got into his car, he scolded himself for letting Lissie get to him. She reminded him of a lot of the theater kids he'd known in high school, even if the look had changed since then. Theater kids were just dramatic, right? With that thought, he pushed the strange mood away.

# 2
# *Baker Hall*

"What's wrong, Hot Topic?" asked Trevor Hill in his gratingly whiny voice, shouting from the driver's seat of his BMW. Lissie stopped, gave him a look of casual disinterest, then kept on walking. Trevor's cronies snickered in the back seat.

"Aw, come on. Don't be like that. We're just kiddin'," Zach Halloway called out to her. "You're kinda sexy."

"Give me a brown paper bag and I might consider it," said Trevor. This drew another round of laughs from his friends.

"I'm sure you boys have something better to do," said a tall stern woman who emerged from the shadow of a tree just ahead of Lissie. The faces of the three men went pale.

"Yeah, of—of course Mrs. Baker," Trevor managed to stammer, before shifting his car into gear and speeding off down the red brick street. The tall woman strode beside Lissie. Her short blonde bob practically glowed in the streetlamps. She held her black-gloved hands behind her back.

"I wish you'd just take the Benz. Or have Samuel drive you," said the woman.

"You know why I won't, mother," muttered Lissie, looking up at the woman with her aqua eyes. Angelina Baker had always towered over Lissie and her father. When Lissie was eight, her parents had taken her to an exhibit at the Art Institute in Chicago. There'd been a statue there, chiseled from some sort of smooth stone. It had reminded her so much of her mother. It looked down upon her with blank, cold eyes—secure in its beauty and purpose. An insane desire to push the statue had gripped Lissie. It was so powerful, she'd faked a stomach ache so they could leave early, even though the trip had been her idea.

"Yes. Definitely not a conversation I need to have again," said Angelina.

"I just don't get why they listen to you."

"Well, I'm sure me being the mayor has something to do with it," Angelina quipped.

"Then why even mess with me in the first place?" asked Lissie. They both stopped before the familiar iron gate, set in the brown brick of the wall that lined the street. Before her mother could answer, their manservant, Samuel—waiting for his mistress's return—opened the gate.

"Welcome home Mrs. Baker. Lissie," said Samuel in his slight Kentucky drawl. Samuel was in his mid-40s, with dark black hair that turned silver at the temples. He had a thin face with sharp cheekbones, but his tanned and lined face kept him from appearing delicate. There was a ruggedness to him that felt out of place in a manservant, Lissie thought. About as out of place as the concept of a manservant felt in the modern world. But that's how her mom had always referred to him.

"Thank you, Samuel," said Angelina. "Is dinner still on schedule for eight?"

"Yes, Ma'am."

"Excellent. Can you please grab some sheers and trim the top of the western hedge before then? There is a stray branch near the southern corner that is terribly distracting."

"Yes. Of course, Ma'am. My apologies," said Samuel before turning on his heels and heading toward the garden shed at the rear of the house.

Lissie and Angelina continued walking the long stone stairway up the hill on which Baker Hall sat. The mansion was nearly as old as the town, a two-story brick structure in Italianate style. The original coloring of it was quite plain in comparison to the Victorians that popped up around it, but eventually the Baker's had it decorated in creams and muted yellows to complement the red brick.

"As for your question, my dear daughter," said Angelina, "you'll find boys like to test their boundaries. You're a challenge to them. You make yourself such an easy target with the way you carry yourself and what you wear. They just can't help seeing what they can get away with."

"Got it. So, I'm the problem, and they're just doing what comes naturally?" Lissie's neutral tone was meant to accentuate, not hide, the sarcasm dripping from every word. Her mother refused to acknowledge it.

"Just so. Now be a good girl and try to make yourself look presentable for dinner." Her mother took off her long black gloves, revealing the vitiligo-mottled skin underneath. Everyone in town knew about Mayor Angelina Baker's condition. But she still insisted on always wearing gloves outside of the house. It was an open secret, and it was hardly the only one in Essen. Lissie decided to pretend to ignore her, and instead silently made her way up the stairs. But her mother was not done with her yet.

"Soon you'll find a man. Have a child. The world will make more sense. I promise," Angelina assured her.

Lissie couldn't shrug this off. She stopped mid-way up the stairs and shot her mother a look of pure contempt. As always, her mother was unfazed, draining all pleasure or triumph in Lissie's defiant silence. Lissie looked away and clambered up the steps to the upper hallway. She did not pause to look at the door of what had once been her bedroom. She'd not been into it since a little after her sixteenth birthday, over three years ago. It was a year after her father's operation had gone wrong. She'd had all she could stand of her mother's unflappable pragmatism in the face of the horror they'd endured after that. So, she announced she no longer wanted a part in the life her parents had given her. She wanted to live as independently as she could, even if she still had to live at home for practical reasons. It was a bratty, impulsive rebellion. She'd expected it to last a day or two before her mom finally broke and begged her to return to her room. That never happened.

Lissie kept going past three other closed doors—a bathroom and two other bedrooms—until she got to the last door before the attic stairs. Her father's room. She knocked, although there wasn't really any need. It wasn't like her father would be otherwise engaged. She turned the knob slowly, and peeked in. The room was mostly dark, only illuminated by a dim and ancient lamp with a green shade.

It cast her father's form in shadow as he lay on his bed, his breath coming in shallow rattles.

"Hey dad, just thought I'd come say hi," Lissie said as she crept nearer to him.

As usual, he stared forward at the blank wall across from him. She'd argued with her mother so many times about getting him a TV. Angelina insisted he preferred the blank wall, as if there were any way to tell.

"I had a brush with celebrity today. Well, celebrity adjacent, I guess. Kyle Thomas—he's Herb Thomas's son—actually came into my job at AllCare."

Her father stared forward, his irises a strange dove gray color to match his skin. Doctor Otto had never been able to identify his condition. And Lissie's own internet searches hadn't amounted to anything. She grabbed her father's hand in hers. It was so strangely cold.

She hadn't even known anything was wrong with him, until the night she woke to the sound of heavy footsteps in the hall. She saw the men come, in their white coats. They followed Doctor Otto into her parent's bedroom and came out again with their dad strapped to a gurney. She tried to run to her dad's side. But her mom stopped her. She said her dad was sick, and they were taking him for an operation to make him well. But something went horribly wrong and when her dad came back, he looked like he did now. Somehow much lesser than he used to be.

"I'd better get going. If I don't get down in time for dinner, mom will have my head," Lissie said, giving her dad's hand one final pat.

She closed the door to his room gently and climbed the smaller set of stairs at the back of the hall up to the attic. This is where she'd fled when she abandoned her room, and the life Angelina Baker had given her. The rebellion seemed fairly minor to her now. She was too afraid to run away. But she'd found an old mattress in the attic. She got a couple part-time jobs around town and started to buy her own things. Her mom assumed she'd be the one to break and return to her laptop, phone, and expensive shoes. When that never happened, her mom begrudgingly accepted it, even though she made it very clear she thought the whole thing was silly. Lissie had been saving for years so she could finally move out. She only had six more months until she'd have enough for a down payment on an apartment in South Bend. She'd be free of Essen, this house, and her mom.

She hated to leave her dad alone with her mom, but over the last few years she'd slowly come to the realization that she had her own life to lead. It wasn't that her mom would ever hurt her dad. She loved him, in her own way. But Angelina never spent time with him. Samuel fed him, bathed him, and changed his bedpan. Only Lissie ever talked to him or treated him like a human being. It was as if her mom was too embarrassed by his brokenness to even look at him. It was this cruelty that eventually led Lissie to reject her mother. But she did still live under her roof. And her mother expected her at every dinner when she wasn't working late.

Lissie sat on a wooden crate and quickly brushed a comb through her hair, looking miserably into an old oval mirror she'd propped up against the wall. Behind her, strange irregular black shapes filled the attic—the jagged, forgotten, and dust cloth-covered remnants of decades of Bakers. She was determined not to become a permanent part of the collection.

# 3

# *The Man by the Door*

As Kyle drove the country roads to his childhood home, the sun completely deserted him—dwindled to a slit of orange in the west. Kyle purposefully put off going to the house. After he'd left Max's office, he had stopped by the dollar store to use the restroom and to pick up a few supplies he thought he might need for his stay—toilet paper, paper cups and plates, some plastic silverware, and a few snacks to tide him over for the night. Kyle planned to make a proper visit to the grocery store later but didn't want to deal with that yet. Just the thought of running into more faces he recognized and having to go through the same basic conversation over and over exhausted him.

Now, Kyle regretted the decision. After fifteen years of living in a decently sized city, he'd forgotten how dark the country could get. Essen itself did not put off much light pollution, except when the lights of the high school football field were on full blast for game night. He navigated the roads as if from muscle memory. Every sharp curve was anticipated. The streets that were gravel when he was a kid were mostly still that way. The only real surprise was that someone had finally put guard rails up on "Deadman's Hook." Though, the guardrail on one side was mangled, indicating teenagers and lost out-of-towners still took the curve too fast. The nickname wasn't particularly accurate. No one had died that he knew of on the curve. Usually, they plowed into Randall Baker's corn fields. That wasn't great for the car or the corn, but it wasn't fatal either.

Small towns liked their ominous names and legends, and Essen was no different. Unlike their counterparts in the South, who seemed to treat such legends with hushed reverence, people in the North of the country tended to approach such tales with a wink and a wry grin. But they kept telling the stories.

Despite the comfortable familiarity of the drive, Kyle did not like the darkness. He'd been easy to scare as a kid. Growing up in the country with its pitch-blackness and the never-ending chorus of night sounds didn't help. At one point, his dad had threatened to use his belt on him if he didn't "man up." This got his father a sharp slap from his mother. He'd imagined he'd grown past all that. He was in his mid-thirties, agnostic to the point of being just shy of atheism, and he certainly didn't believe in things that went bump in the night. But here he was, the dread he'd felt in Max's office spread to his whole body. He knew his discomfort was more than the vague fears darkness can bring. He realized how eerie it would be to see his childhood home completely empty of the people he used to call his family.

When his mother had passed, the trauma had been blunt and painful but also distant. When he'd heard his dad was gone, he'd been surprised at how little he had felt. Now, the closer he got to the old farmhouse, the more the reality of it all sank in. He found himself dreading pulling up to that dark house. However, as he turned onto the gravel road that led to the farmhouse, he found something eerier.

In the distance, the farmhouse was alive with light. Kyle thought, for a moment, it was the wrong house. There hadn't been any other houses for miles when he was a kid. But it was possible a family bought some of his mom and dad's land. The farms in the region had been hit hard by a run of bad weather a decade back. Maybe they'd sold some of the land to raise funds? Except, the last time he'd seen his parents, they'd looked like they were doing exceptionally well. The disorientation passed, and Kyle could see this was indeed his family's farmhouse. The two-story structure's white coloring was ghostly thanks to the ambient light spilling out of every window. The curtains were drawn back so a passerby could see clearly inside.

It reminded Kyle of a tiny house he'd seen last Christmas when he was shopping with his ex in Saugatuck. It was part of a set that formed a whole Christmas village. Each building was lit from the inside, and you could stare into all the little rooms. Perfect little rooms devoid of people. There was nothing particularly festive about this sight, however. The porch light was on, spotlighting the two rocking chairs sitting motionless and empty on the gray stone.

Kyle drove up slowly onto the gravel circle drive that curved behind the house and then back onto the street. He stopped his Prius near the shed and got out slowly. He looked at the backdoor of the house, thinking of all the times his mom had told him not to let it slam shut. He watched the light spill out of the door and imagined another universe where his mom walked out of the kitchen and onto the landing of the small staircase. Her brown hair would be gray, swept back into a ponytail. She'd smile at him, the way she used to smile at him when he was a boy. The warm smell of vanilla waffles, made just for his visit, would waft out with her. She'd tell him his father was upstairs, working on his book. He'd be down in a little while. Kyle gritted his teeth and shook the thought away. This had all been a mistake. He should have hired people to take care of this. If he'd been better off financially, he would have. But he was here now.

He walked up the stairs and jiggled the metal handle, cooled in the darkness of the summer night, and found it was locked. Which was to be expected. He fished the key he'd been mailed from out of his pocket and unlocked it. But he hesitated to open it. He felt like an intruder—breaking and entering.

"Fuck it," he said to no one, and entered.

He tried to force his mind to become more professional and detached. He was an investigative reporter. He could approach this task with that same mindset. He noted the décor had barely changed since he was a kid. This did not strike him as strange, though. His mom was the decorator, and she'd been dead for over ten years. His dad obviously kept the place up. Or he'd gotten someone to come in and clean. But he'd left everything pretty much the same. The window over the sink still sported the tiny yellow curtains with their cheerful pattern of bright red ladybugs. The green ceramic frog on the windowsill still held a pink sponge in its mouth and a scrubbing wand in the top of its head. The small metal-edged circular table was on the far left, with three orange plastic chairs around it. Kyle saw a framed portrait of the three of them hung over the table, but he turned away from it quickly. He could feel his detachment slipping.

That's when he noticed the plate of chocolate chip cookies wrapped in plastic wrap on the mottled white and gray counter. There was a little note on it.

**Wanted to make sure you didn't come home to
a dark house. Let me know if you need anything.
– Nancy Kirby**

The Kirby's—who'd moved to town after Kyle was out of the picture—were the ones looking after the farm after his dad's death. Kyle laughed at himself for being unnerved by what was—it turns out—a neighborly gesture. With that tension relieved, he suddenly felt exhausted. It had been a long day. He sat the bag from the dollar store on the counter, no longer feeling hungry. Mostly he wanted to sleep.

He locked the back door and then began going from room to room in the house, shutting off the lights as he did. The first stop was the formal dining room, that more often served as his mother's sewing room. Her old Singer was still in the corner, hidden by a dust cover. Kyle used to sit for hours playing with his LEGO at his mom's feet as the gentle whir of the machine's motor whined on. Next to it was the gargantuan display cabinet that held silver-rimmed china Kyle had never seen in use. Then there was the living room, with the same gray carpet and hideous hunter green couch. On top of the ancient console television stood a large flat screen model. Kyle wondered if that was his dad's first purchase after his mom died. His mom would have never approved of such a behemoth blocking the view out the front window, and his dad did like his football games. He walked up the narrow staircase, purposefully not looking at the many framed photographs lining it. He turned off the light of the bathroom at the end of the upstairs hall, before he passed by his old bedroom, which had been converted into a blandly cheery guest room.

And then, he came to his parents' room. Strangely, unlike

all the other doors in the house, this one was shut. The windows on the upper floor were open to let the cool night air in. He supposed a change in air pressure could have closed the door. But as he reached for the knob, he felt a light, hollow feeling in his stomach. He scolded his own foolishness, but as he opened the door a small crack, he realized he did not want to look inside. He could not look inside. Not yet. Not fully.

Through the crack, he could see one of his mom's prized possessions. It was a picture of Jesus, standing outside a wooden door. He'd hated that painting since he was three. The door reminded him too much of the wooden door to their shed out back. Jesus was glowing and was meant to look peaceful and beneficent. But his skin was so white, and his irises so dark—a brown that was almost black—he'd seemed more like a lost ghost than anything else. It had terrified Kyle as a kid. He had nightmares about this ghostly specter of God's only son appearing out back by their shed. His head turning slowly. His eyes vacant. His mouth opening to whisper something, but all that came out was the raspy release of air.

With shaking hands, Kyle reached through the crack of the door and fumbled blindly for the light switch. He was sure it was just to the left. Kyle looked downward, trying not to look at the painting anymore. His fumbling to find the switch became more frantic. His face was flush with annoyance and embarrassment, letting this old fear under his skin again. Finally, his fingers grazed the light switch, and he clicked it off. He withdrew his hand and shut the door quickly and more firmly than necessary so the hard wood-on-wood thwack it made echoed through the empty house.

Kyle intended to sleep in the guest bedroom, but the sight of it made him angry. And he wasn't sure he wanted to stay on the second floor. Even with the windows open, it felt a little stuffy and hot. He walked quickly down the stairs and opened one of the windows facing the road. He closed the curtains, stripped off his jeans and t-shirt, and laid heavily on the ugly green couch. It was pleasantly cool and soft, and in no time he was asleep.

# 4
# *Patrick*

Kyle awoke to the delicate crunch of tires on driveway stones. He blinked his eyes at the sunshine filtering through the gauzy curtains in the windows. The morning air was crisp as it wafted in, and Kyle enjoyed the freshness of it immensely even though there was the slight fruity smell of dung mingled with it. A dull pain throbbed on the right side of his neck from where he'd rested his head awkwardly against the arm of the couch, but a few gentle stretches made it feel better. In the light of the morning, the old farmhouse took on an air of inviting, if generic, hominess. It wasn't his style of decoration, of course. And it didn't feel like home to him anymore, but it held the trappings of it. It made his fears from the night before seem even more foolish.

With bleary eyes, Kyle shuffled toward the kitchen, suddenly wishing he'd picked up some coffee at the dollar store. He had the vague notion he should check to see who had pulled up in the driveway, but he was more immediately concerned about getting some water. Kyle found the glasses where they'd always been kept. He recognized the one he grabbed, with its yellow-tinted glass and smooth circular indentations around its circumference. After filling it at the sink, he took a great gulp of the cold water, and it tasted just as he remembered it. Well water could be a mixed bag, but the water here was fresh with a pleasant mineral tang. He was so caught up in drinking it, gulping noisily on a second glass, he did not fully register the back door opening until it was too late.

"Oh, damn! Sorry," said a voice behind him.

Kyle whirled and found himself face to face with a man who could only be described as beautiful; close-cropped black hair, brilliantly green-yellow eyes, and a hint of stubble. His skin was tanned and beaded with sweat that started at his brow and trickled along the strong line of his chin and then down the nape of his neck. He wore an old A Rush of Blood to the Head-era Coldplay shirt. The sides of the shirt were cut off, giving a good view of his well-muscled arms and torso. They were not the well-defined and chiseled muscles of a bodybuilder though. They were softer than that, in a pleasing way. They looked more like practical muscle developed through hard work. Kyle could see a hint of the pectoral muscles that flowed into a thick torso. He took all of this in seconds, before returning his gaze to the stranger's face, which held an apologetic smile. Lines crinkled at the corners of his eyes.

"Don't worry about it. I'm, uh, Kyle. Kyle Thomas." Kyle reached out his hand, and then became acutely aware that he wasn't wearing anything other than a slightly ratty pair of gray Hanes. To make matters worse, there was slight tightening of his underwear. It was his turn to smile apologetically. "Let me get some clothes on."

"Don't worry about it. I'll be out of your hair in a second. Besides, nothing I haven't seen before," said the man, waving Kyle's concern away. "My name's Patrick by the way. Patrick Kirby." Instead of a handshake, Patrick handed Kyle the casserole dish he'd been carrying. Kyle hadn't even noticed it in the man's hands.

"Well, nice to meet you. For some reason I pictured someone… older?"

"Ah, you might be thinking of my dad, Pat. I'm Patrick Kirby Jr. People call me Patrick to keep it straight. And this is my mom's breakfast casserole. It's pretty great. The crust is loaded with butter, though. Fair warning."

"Probably why it smells so good," said Kyle as he placed the casserole dish on the counter. He wasn't lying either. A heady mix of eggs, cheese, and bacon defied the tin foil wrapping covering the dish and snaked through the air. Patrick's butter comment made Kyle hyper-aware of his own body, which was currently very much on display. Kyle tried to take care of himself, especially after being bigger most of his childhood and into his twenties. But his midsection remained stubbornly soft. "First cookies and now this?"

Patrick chuckled. His laugh, like his voice, had a pleasingly boyish quality to it. Kyle guessed he was probably in his mid-to-late twenties. Kyle felt the tightness in his lower extremities increase and turned away from Patrick to get a pair of forks out of the box of plastic utensils he'd purchased. He grabbed the casserole dish and tried to glide over to the kitchen table as naturally as he could, all while trying to face away from the man.

"Want some? There's more here than I could eat in a week," said Kyle. Patrick shook his head, and then absent-mindedly reached for the bottom of his shirt and pulled it up to mop some of the sweat from his forehead. He revealed a set of softly sculpted abs that made Kyle grateful he was now sitting at the table. He nervously plunged his plastic fork into the casserole dish, grabbed a bite, and stuffed it into his mouth.

"No thanks. My mom made one for us too, and I've already had some. Besides, I've got work to do. I was going to do some weeding until you got up, but I did bring our mower. I might go ahead and start on that and take advantage of the cool morning if it won't bother you? Mom said you probably got in late last night, so I was trying not to wake you," explained Patrick.

"Yeah, no problem," said Kyle, who could not seem to stop himself from stuffing casserole into his mouth between sentences. "I ended up sleeping downstairs. Otherwise, I'm sure you wouldn't have."

"Why downstairs?"

"That's hard to explain. I haven't been back here in a long time..." Kyle had no clue where to go with this sentence. He didn't feel like talking about it, and he doubted this guy wanted to hear it. "Honestly, I don't know if I have a good answer for you."

"Hey, I don't need one. That's me being nosey. My mom says it's a bad habit," said Patrick.

"Hey, I won't knock it. It's sort of what I do for a living," said Kyle.

"You a writer like your dad was?"

"I'm a writer. But not fiction. I write investigative pieces for websites, magazines, and podcasts—that sort of thing." Kyle hoped he wasn't sounding completely pretentious. He took what ended up being way too large of a bite.

"Wow, nice! Look, I better get going, but we should hang out sometime. I'd love to hear more about what you do," said Patrick as he extended his hand. Kyle swallowed the casserole down so quickly it almost hurt.

"Sounds great. I'm going to need something to do the next couple weeks," Kyle agreed. He grasped the man's hand. The strength of it sent a tingle of pleasure through him, and even as he enjoyed it, he silently cursed himself for acting like some dumb kid getting giddy in front of a school crush. Patrick shook his hand and turned toward the door. Right before he was going to exit, he turned back toward Kyle.

"One word of warning, though," Patrick said, his voice suddenly serious. "Don't be fooled by my mom's cookies and casserole."

"What do you mean?" asked Kyle, slowing the fork as it traveled toward his mouth to deliver another delicious mouthful.

"My mom's not a bad sort, but she's not exactly being altruistic. She wants you to sell your land to her and dad," Patrick said with a wink. With that, he was out the door, leaving Kyle with a forkful of casserole and some time to cool off.

# 5

# *A Complicated Thing*

Kyle felt off as he drove through the fields toward town to stock up on some decent food at Kessinger's Grocery. He'd forgotten how awful the water pressure was in the old farmhouse. The shower-head was ridiculously low as well, coming to right above his clavicle, so he had to stoop to get the pathetic stream to douse his hair. The house had been in his family for generations, so Kyle could only surmise his great grandparents were elves—the Keebler kind, not The Lord of the Rings kind.

To make matters worse, he'd forgotten to pack his usual hair products. He tried to use the stuff his dad had in the shower, which was a combination shampoo, conditioner, and body wash that smelled like a vague amalgam of pine air freshener and coconut. It left his hair feeling both limp and greasy. Kyle put way too much pride into his hair; he knew it. But even when he was bigger and felt insecure about his body, he'd gotten compliments on his hair. When his hair was having an off day, like today, the rest of him felt off. It didn't help that he was a little worried about running into Patrick Kirby with his hair looking the way it did.

As he pulled into Kessinger's parking lot, he tried to let the feeling go and recover some of his confidence. He wanted his wits about him in case he ran into any of his old classmates. The truth was since he'd left home at seventeen, he'd not kept up with anyone from Essen. He'd made fleeting attempts at keeping in contact with a select few, but eventually that all faded away. Also, he could count on one hand the people he'd like to see in Essen. And he knew two of those people had moved away.

He knew he'd have to field more questions about Dunbar's Grove. It wasn't a topic he cared to discuss or think about much. It was the first of his father's books he'd read since he left home, though he kept up with his father's work in a vague way. Mostly, he hated to admit, it was with the hope the critics might tear the latest novel apart. As much as he'd tried to let his anger with his father dissipate, it was always there in the background. In the end, the reviews were incredibly positive for Dunbar's Grove. It was once readers noticed the strong parallels between the main character and the book's author that the questions started. Kyle still remembered the first time he'd seen a headline on the web questioning whether his father's last novel was autobiographical; including all the details it provided about how the main character murdered his wife.

It had unearthed a strange cycle of feelings within Kyle. He'd felt nauseous as he read the article. Then he got angry some asshole writer looking for clicks was accusing his dad of being a murderer. Then he got mad at himself for defending his dad.

He was so lost in thought; Kyle didn't notice the first shopping cart he grabbed from the corral next to the entrance of the brown-bricked building had a problem. Namely, there was a runny, smelly, yellow-green substance leaking from a puddle in the front basket and dripping down the back of the cart. A hesitant sniff confirmed Kyle's worst fears. It was probably from a child that was placed on top of the little plastic flap that converted the basket into a seat. Kyle checked his hands and was grateful to see none of it was on him, but he was still grossed out. He grabbed another cart and took one of the pre-moistened anti-bacterial towelettes from the dispenser near the door and rubbed down not only his hands, but also his newly selected cart thoroughly. As soon as he finished, he noticed a short older woman was staring at him. Her thinning gray hair was cut short and hung limply around her face. Her eyes were two dark coals and seemed too small in proportion to the rest of her face. They glittered at him impassively. Kyle realized then she probably wanted a cart, and he was blocking her way.

"Sorry about that," he said, stepping out of the way. "I wouldn't grab—"

Before he could explain, the woman wordlessly grabbed the cart with the mess on it. She slapped her purse heavily onto the basket and pushed her way into the store. Kyle quickly grabbed his cart and followed her. But she was already on the other side of the store.

"Quick little thing," he said to himself, deciding that trying to let the woman know about the cart at this point would be more awkward than letting her discover it for herself. He looked around and saw the old grocery store was somewhat updated inside. The store's signage was new. He missed the vibrant orange and red ones from his youth. There were even some automated checkouts. But the lighting still seemed a little low. And the wheels of his cart squeaked over the waxed and polished beige-gray tile floors in the same rakkety-takkety way they always had as they traveled over the grout.

Kyle started to run through the shopping list in his head when he saw someone he didn't expect to see. Janie Alvarez was looking through the juices in the refrigerated case in the produce department. She wasn't on his list of people he wanted to see from high school. But the sight of her wasn't unwelcome, either. It was complicated, and he wasn't ready to deal with it. He panicked—unsure of whether he should say hi or not—when the choice was taken away from him. She looked up from the juice bottle she'd been studying, trying to read the small-print ingredients, and saw him. The look on her face instantly turned from surprise to practiced ambivalence. They awkwardly guided their carts toward each other.

"Kyle. It's been forever," said Janie. The words themselves might have implied a warm greeting, except her tone was more neutral than that. It was more like she was stating an undeniable fact than anything else.

"Yeah. I'm in town for a couple weeks. Out at the old farmhouse. Checking on the place and deciding whether to sell it or not. Although everyone keeps asking about the book. Which I get," said Kyle. He realized he was babbling out of nervousness, so he cut himself off before letting the thought come to any sort of natural resolution.

"Right," she said, her face relaxing into a genuine frown. "I was sorry to hear about your dad."

"Yeah, me too," Kyle said noncommittally. It wasn't that he wasn't sad about his dad's death. But it wasn't an easy-flowing grief. It kept getting caught up and rerouted by all the stones of resentment and anger he and his dad had dropped along the way. "So, what're you up to these days? Last I'd heard, you'd moved to San Jose?"

"San Diego," Janie corrected. "Sean and I moved out there for a while for his job. But with all my family being here, and me getting a little homesick, we moved back five years ago when he started working from home."

"How's Sean doing these days?" Even as he said it, Kyle wished he could transport himself somewhere else. He listened to her reply without hearing as she explained what Sean's new work from home role was like. He did not want to have this conversation. He suspected Janie didn't want to have it either.

He and Janie had been childhood sweethearts. The way their parents told the story, they met in preschool. Janie was one year older than Kyle so she was in a different class. But every day during breaks they would stand on either side of the chain-linked fence that separated the play areas and talk to each other. Neither Kyle nor Janie could recall what was said, and their parents and teachers were always watching from afar. What did four or five-year-olds discuss with one another? Their favorite colors? The relative merits of eating your own boogers? The latest episode of Mr. Rogers? Kyle had no clue. But this connection was a legend between the two families. It was a legend Janie and Kyle grew up believing in.

Janie's actual name was Jacinta Isabella Alvarez. And she went by Jacinta until third grade, when a particularly uninterested and young substitute teacher had gone through the class roll call. He butchered her name and pronounced it yak-nita. And Jacinta was mercilessly called Yak Nita through the rest of third grade. The summer between third and fourth grade, she escaped to summer camp and took on the name Janie. Enough of the girls went to the camp with her—and used it when they got back—that the new name stuck from fourth grade on. The only rule was you couldn't call her Janie in front of her parents, who thought the name was disrespectful to her heritage. Her grandparents had immigrated to America and suffered many hardships (her mom was fond of reciting them all when needed) to secure the comfortable life Janie enjoyed.

Kyle and Janie grew up together. Their friendship turned into something else by the time they were in sixth grade when they started 'going out' in the way kids do. This meant they held hands in the school halls and passed notes, mostly. Kyle loved being Janie's boyfriend. He'd started hanging out with a new crowd around that time. He'd abandoned his friend, Henry, who he suddenly deemed too geeky for his tastes, and started hanging out with Chad, David, and Dustin. They talked about the previous night's episode of Seinfeld. They started the practice of 'shunning' the people whom they decided were no longer worth their time (including Henry), and generally acted like assholes. One of the side effects of being Janie's boyfriend was that the guys seemed more relaxed around Kyle. There was some tension that had been released that Kyle didn't even realize was there until it was gone. Something was 'safe' about Kyle now, and Chad, David, and Dustin could relax more around him.

It wasn't meant to last, though. Between his eighth grade and freshman years, he realized he didn't like himself the way he was. He didn't care much for Chad, David, and Dustin either. Janie ended up a casualty of all the changes Kyle made after that, although not for a couple years after. They tried to keep their friendship going. Janie even invited Kyle to her wedding, which was the last time he'd been to Essen and the only time he'd seen his parents since he'd left home. That ended up a mess in the end.

"Kyle? You okay?" asked Janie. Kyle's eyes widened in embarrassment as he realized Janie was finished speaking and he'd been too lost in thought to notice.

"Sorry, Janie. I'm out of it. I got in late last night, the water pressure sucks at the farmhouse, and I've been kind of off all day," said Kyle. Janie's mask of pleasant neutrality broke, and a slightly mischievous grin flashed across her face.

"You haven't changed that much, have you?" she asked. But she said it with fondness and not accusatorially.

"You know, I'd like to think I have. But the more I'm back here, the more I wonder. At least this time it wasn't because I was up too late playing Diablo."

"Well, anyway you should come and see Sean and the kids."

"You have kids?" asked Kyle. Janie rolled her eyes.

"Yes, I mentioned them while you were daydreaming. I've got three kids, actually," she said.

"Wow, you've been busy."

"Well, yes. Being a mom to three kids is extremely busy work. But not the way you mean. They're all adopted. We adopted them from different countries as part of a program through Higher Faith," said Janie. Kyle tried to hide his cringe at the mention of her church, but Janie picked up on it immediately. Even after all these years, he was an open book to her. Her eyes narrowed.

"We'll definitely have to plan something," Kyle said quickly, stopping the conversation he feared was going to follow before it could even start. Kyle was as involved in the church as Janie for most of their lives. They drove forty-five minutes to Josiah Milton's Higher Faith megachurch in South Bend every Sunday. But as time wore on, Kyle found it harder to reconcile his faith with the feelings he was having as a gay man. The year before he moved out of his parents' house and left town, he'd stopped attending. He and Janie fought about it more than once.

"Good. I'll give you my number. Tuesdays and Thursdays our oldest, Chunhua, has piano practice but any other day is good," Janie said, apparently content with letting the old argument go as well. She handed him the slip of paper on which she'd hastily written her number. This was followed by a few awkward seconds where they tried to decide what the proper goodbye between them might be, before settling on a half-hearted hug. As Janie's cart rattled over the gray tile floors away from him, Kyle decided to get enough groceries for the next two weeks so he didn't have to come back to Kessinger's again.

# 6
# *Janie*

"Honey, that you?" Sean Hackett asked from the other room, his fingers clicking away at his laptop keyboard. "Nope, just your mistress, coming over for a little action," said Janie as she closed and locked the front door of the little duplex she called home.

"Henrietta? But you don't usually come until Wednesdays." Sean walked in, took the grocery bags from Janie's hands, and gave her a quick peck on the cheek before hustling them back into the kitchen.

"Why is your mistress's name Henrietta? That is the least sexy name ever."

"That's the point! I have a sexy wife, so to be really kinky, I'd need to have my mistress be the exact opposite," said Sean.

"I'm disturbed by how much thought you've put into this,"

Janie said.

"Hey, I work from home and only have two 10-month-olds for company nine hours a day. I get bored."

"Where are the Twin Terrors by the way?"

"Hard to believe, but they're actually down for a nap. Which is a blessing because I've got a good four hours of work still to do. Chunhua's at her play date with Emily until dinner," said Sean.

"Good," Janie said, although she only half-heard him. A framed photo of her wedding party had caught her eye and distracted her. Had it really been over twelve years now? Sean sidled up against her.

"What's wrong? You've got that crinkle in your forehead that usually means you're thinking too hard about something."

"It's not a big deal." Janie turned away from the photo and walked to the kitchen. She had the smallest glimmer of hope that Sean might leave it at that. She started to unpack the groceries. As she suspected, he joined her just a few seconds later.

"I want to help," Sean said. Janie sighed and put the box of mac n' cheese down, heavily, on the counter.

"I know you do. It really isn't a big deal. Kyle is back in town." Janie looked directly into his eyes as she said this, wanting to gauge his reaction. She was surprised to see nothing but pure relief.

"That is amazing news. Maybe you can finally talk to him and get this chip you've been carrying around for twelve years off your shoulder."

"Ha. That's not happening," Janie scoffed, suddenly swiveling toward the cabinets to put away the rest of the groceries. She heard Sean groan in frustration behind her.

"Why not? How many times have you drafted emails and

Facebook messages you never sent? You bought a Christmas card for three years in a row you never mailed, too. Now he's back in town. It's like fate!"

"Except, he's in town because his dad killed himself… after writing a book that made it seem like he murdered his wife. I don't think I need to lay all my stuff on him right now." Janie took all the plastic bags and mangled them into one compressed ball, which she absentmindedly threw into the cabinet. Sean moved close to her, pressing his body into her back and wrapping his arms around her. He crouched down slightly and laid his head gently on her shoulder.

"Look. I'm not saying you have to do anything," Sean said softly. "I'm just saying give it some thought. If the moment feels right."

"What if I sound like an idiot? What if I am an idiot?"

"You won't and you aren't."

"I guess I'm just never sure how to start. How do you tell someone they were the center of your universe? That they ripped your heart out when they disappeared and shut you out of their life?" asked Janie. Sean didn't answer. He just pulled her closer to him. Janie knew why. They'd had a variation of the same discussion many times over the years. There was nothing complex about the answer. You just said the words.

# 7

# *Max*

Kyle was sitting on the living room floor of the farmhouse. He was drinking a Guinness and sorting through the boxes of pictures he'd pulled up from the basement. It was a hot day, and the air conditioning didn't work well, so Kyle enjoyed the smooth thickness of the ice-cold liquid down his throat. He was also enjoying the slight buzz he had. He'd been disappointed Patrick wasn't still around when he got back. He wouldn't have minded another look or two at him. Kyle had put the groceries away, loaded up a cooler with ice and the case of Guinness he'd purchased, and figured he needed a plan of attack. He had to go through his parents' personal effects. Then he needed to decide what to keep, what to sell, and what to throw away. He was not looking forward to it. The farmhouse was not huge, but he knew from childhood experience searching for Christmas gifts that it held all sorts of nooks and crannies to shove stuff into.

He decided to tackle the basement first, as it was sure to be the most time-consuming part. As he sorted through the pictures, he started to regret the decision. In this one, the family was at the water park at the Dells. Here they were at Oldham Mill festival, making candles by dipping string in wax. Here they were in the cavern in Kentucky with its strange golden pools. He found out later the color came from the gelled lights in the cavern, but at the time he'd been convinced they were pools of liquid gold. He was riding on his dad's shoulders in the picture, smiling for the camera as his mom took the picture. It all made him sad. Which made him angry at himself. Which made him mad at his parents all over again for throwing it all away.

Kyle threw the pile of photos down on the floor, finally giving up, when his cell phone rang. It was Max.

"Hey, I didn't interrupt anything did I? You don't have a hot piece of ass from Grinding, do you?" asked Max.

"It's Grindr, for one thing. Although it's cute you're pretending you don't know. And there's surprisingly not a lot of gay action in the middle of Indiana farmland," said Kyle.

"Well, good. Because it turns out the best night to have you over is tonight!"

"I don't want to be any trouble."

"No trouble. He's no trouble, right honey?" Max asked, his voice getting softer as he turned away from the phone. There was a muffled noise that sounded a little like no trouble at all from the other end, although it was hard to tell. "See? If it makes you feel better, you're plan B anyway. Another couple canceled on us. Heather is making a pot of her famous peanut chicken stew. There's enough to feed an army."

"That sounds good, actually. But uh… I've got a buzz going

on."

"Shit, is that all? I'll come pick you up," said Max, before quickly adding, "it's no problem."

"Well…" Kyle looked at the piles of photos all around him. He thought of the closed door upstairs, and the creepy Jesus painting. He thought of the general unease that seemed to fill him again now that it was dark. "Fuck it. Might as well."

Max showed up fifteen minutes later in a slick-looking Jeep that was such a bright electric green, Kyle saw it coming from miles away as he waited for him on the house's porch. The Jeep was blaring some sort of classical music, which amused Kyle to no end.

"What the hell are you listening to?" Kyle asked with a slight laugh as he clambered into the Jeep.

"You don't recognize it?" Max asked.

"I'm sure I've heard it before. Maybe. I don't know, all this music blends together for me," said Kyle. The Jeep's tires squealed and sent some of the loose rocks of the drive flying as Max hit the gas pedal and they rocketed down the road.

"It's Bach's Unaccompanied Cello Suite No. 1 in G Major," said Max. He had to shout over the sound of the music and wind as it howled through the topless Jeep.

"Classical music, huh? You are getting old."

"I'm only a few months older than you, and I'll still be looking fine after you're a wrinkly old white grape. Besides, it relaxes me. Helps with my anxiety. Well, that and this," said Max, reaching into his inside coat pocket and pulling out a small vaporizer pen. "Want some?"

"I don't know. Alcohol and pot can be a bad mix for me," Kyle replied, looking at the vaporizer, and weighing his options. He was tempted. The truth was his anxiety was flaring up too. He used to have a prescription for some pills to help with it, but it'd been years since he'd needed them.

"Now who's sounding old?" asked Max. That was all the convincing Kyle needed. He took the vaporizer pen and took a hit, and there was a pleasant smoothness to it. He'd never been a smoker and preferred his weed in edible form when he decided to partake. But this wasn't bad either. "There we go. That's it." Max swayed his head to the music, which changed to another piece Kyle didn't recognize. Kyle smiled and closed his eyes as he handed Max back the vaporizer. He let the cool June air wash over him as he exhaled. It'd take a moment for the effect to hit him, of course, but he already felt more relaxed being out of the house and knowing the high was coming.

In what seemed like no time at all, Max was driving down the winding road that led to the Lake of the Grove. Even from this far away, Kyle could tell it was a changed place. The tightly-packed trees were glowing from within. What looked like hundreds of windows, glaring a brilliant orange, were nestled amongst the shadows of the trees. The lake was surrounded by two-story houses. As they got nearer, Kyle saw the neatly manicured backyards. Some were obscured by high wooden fences. But others were not, and many of these had groups of people enjoying the summer night. They sat on long outdoor couches and high-backed wicker chairs. They sat around copper-finished fire pits or square, silver fire tables as neat, narrow flames jetted out of the rocks on top of them. One backyard even featured a live jazz band, and people were dancing in the yard.

This was a far cry from the one time Kyle had gone to the Lake of the Grove when he was younger. He'd slept over at Dustin and Chad's, and the latter's older brother Charlie was supposed to be watching them. Well, technically Charlie was only supposed to be watching Chad, but neither Dustin nor Kyle's parents knew that was the case. Around ten at night, the group finished watching a rented VHS of Infra-Man, when Charlie's friends called him and convinced him to go out to the lake. Chad insisted Charlie take the three of them or he'd tell. With great reluctance, Charlie loaded them into his car and found himself carting three twelve-year-old boys to the most debauched place in the whole town. The three of them were sure they were going to get to see actual, real-life boobs and couldn't wait. Even though Kyle felt a hint of ambivalence about seeing boobs, he was still curious.

Back then, the Lake of the Grove was a far wilder place. The woods around the lake had seemed to swallow all the light. Only hints of the dull amber glow of the interior lights of the trailers had broken through here and there in a scattered and chaotic fashion. There was the occasional bonfire—sometimes directly on the ground, but more often than not emanating from an old rusted-out barrel. Gray smoke had risen from the fires and mixed with the cigarette and pot smoke to form a sort of permanent haze.

Charlie pulled his car up to one of the makeshift docks that circled the lake, and Kyle could see the beams cutting through the smoke. For what must have only been a second—but felt much longer to Kyle—the light fell upon the glistening, wet form of Tyler Baron. Tyler was a senior, and one of the Baron twins. They were both on the swim team and the wrestling team, with the bodies to match. The memory of Tyler's firm white buttocks was permanently seared into Kyle's brain. As was his floppy blackish-brown hair that clung to the sides of his face, and the smile he flashed at the car along with his behind. The entire scene took on a hazy dream-like quality due to the smoke, and when Charlie turned off the lights of the vehicle, it was like someone had turned off a movie projector. Tyler disappeared into the night, a vaguely defined wet glimmer.

Kyle did not see Tyler Baron for the rest of the night. He must have left shortly after, but he certainly left an impression. Kyle didn't understand his fascination with what he'd seen. Everything back then remotely sexual held some interest, after all. But a seed was planted that would only bear fruit a couple years later.

This Lake of the Grove was far from the dream-like, magical, and danger-tinged place of his youth. It had been tamed, gentrified, and thoroughly civilized. Nostalgia made Kyle sad for a moment before he remembered how that night had ended. Charlie's friends plied his younger brother with drinks because they thought it was funny to see a twelve-year-old drunk. And it was entertaining. Dustin and Kyle both turned down the drinks they'd been offered, to a chorus of boos. But it meant they got to enjoy Chad making an ass of himself. It became much less fun for everyone when, on the ride home, Chad got violently ill and started puking up globby pink blobs of congealed Snapple and vodka all over the interior of Charlie's car. It was probably for the best the old Lake of the Grove was gone, although Kyle suspected today's teenagers had found other places to be idiots.

Heather Williams had a high, musical voice and laugh, and welcomed Kyle into her home with a tight hug. Azura (aka Zee) was on the couch, lying with her back on the seat of it and kicking her legs absent-mindedly into the air as they rested against the back of the couch. She was playing a game on her phone and seemed to be bouncing along to some sort of music.

"Zee, come say hi to your dad's friend," Heather said. She

tried three variations of the same line as she, Max, and Kyle stood around the kitchen and she put the finishing touches on the stew. She was squeezing lime on the top of it when she started to call for her daughter again, and then gave up mid-sentence. "She's not even a teenager yet, and we've lost her. I think I was at least twelve or thirteen before I began ignoring my mother."

"She needs a good swat on the behind," said Max as he grabbed a bowl of crushed peanuts and torn cilantro leaves that were meant to be used as a garnish and put them on the dining room table.

"Except, I'd rather not leave our children with emotional scars," said Heather with no small amount of sarcasm.

"Better that than raising a brat." Max shrugged his shoulder and looked to Kyle for backup. Kyle turned away quickly, being no authority on children, and admired their home. Heather said something about there being a happy medium, but Kyle purposefully tuned them out now.

"You've got a beautiful home," he finally said. It was a far cry from the McMansions Kyle remembered popping up around Essen. Someone in the family had modern tastes and an eye for decoration. As the three adults sat down for their dinner, he said as much.

"That would be Heather," Max said proudly.

"To be fair, Max has the good sense to get out of the way and let me do my thing." Heather winked at her husband, and he went in for a kiss. Heather's freckled face reddened, but she accepted it eagerly.

"You two act like you got married a week ago." Kyle took his first experimental sip of the stew. He blew on it to cool it down and found it smooth, creamy, and surprisingly spicy. It was delicious.

"Oh, we're putting on a show for company," said Heather.

"Stick around long enough, and you'll see the real horror show soon enough."

"Don't say things like that! He'll think you're serious," said Max with a laugh.

"I do have a poorly developed sense of humor," Kyle said, which made Heather burst into more of her musical laughter.

Zee came to the table, drawn there by the rumbling of her stomach and the smell of the food. She put her phone down and looked around at the three adults. The look on her face could only be described as that of an alien sent to study the strange, primitive inhabitants of another planet. Because of a mix of Guinness, pot, and wine, the three adults began laughing in unison. Zee rolled her eyes hard and scooped out stew into her bowl. She whispered something under her breath, but it was lost amidst the laughter.

"Oh, guess who I ran into," Kyle said after the laughter subsided and everyone was enjoying the meal in relative silence. Max shrugged his shoulder. "Janie Alvarez." Max's eyes widened.

"Janie! I like her. I've seen her at some of the fundraisers at school. You know her from the old days?" asked Heather.

"Oh, shit. Sorry, man, I totally should have warned you she moved back into town," said Max.

"Yeah, we have a history," said Kyle somewhat enigmatically.

"Janie and Kyle were childhood sweethearts. Until he broke her heart by being G-A-Y." This last part Max mostly mouthed, although a slight whisper did escape his lips.

"Dad, I don't have my headphones on, I can spell, and I know what gay people are," said Zee as she thrust her spoon into the bowl of stew.

"Well. Yeah. Of course, you do," Max said. He looked slightly embarrassed.

"There are, like, a couple lesbians and one gay guy in my class," said Zee.

"In fourth grade? Here in Essen?" asked Max, incredulous. Heather closed her eyes as if willing herself elsewhere. Zee shrugged her shoulders. Max turned to Kyle as if he was supposed to be the authority here. Kyle mimicked Zee and shrugged his shoulders too.

Hours later, after Kyle's belly was full and hurt from laughing, and Zee went to bed, he joined the Williams on their back patio. A comfy L-shaped couch surrounded a cast-iron fire pit. A tall fence hid the backyard from the neighbors on either side, but the view of the lake was unobstructed. Max excused himself to get some wood for the fire.

"He's excited you're here," said Heather, sipping on her red wine.

"Really? I mean, that's great. Just we haven't talked much since high school. I was afraid it might be awkward. But it's kinda like old times," said Kyle.

"He's been buzzing with energy. I needed to see who this guy was my husband was so excited about. See if I needed to be jealous." Kyle practically spat out his wine. He was about to say something when Heather waved her hand and smiled. "I'm kidding. And, between you and me, I think it'd be hot to see. But Max is so vanilla."

"Yeah, sounds like Max," Kyle said, not daring to mention the couple of times Max had gotten drunk with him and tried expanding his horizons.

"He's been really down lately."

"Why's that?"

"I probably shouldn't say." Heather downed the rest of her

wine and continued anyway. "He's hit a wall at work. He's worked so hard to get us where we are. I mean, we both have. But he can't seem to expand his client base anymore. All because of that damned club."

"Club?" asked Kyle, before the pieces clicked into place. "Wait, you mean Minty Green? That old place is still creaking along?"

"Oh, is it ever. And it's not creaking," Heather said ruefully. "It's doing better than ever, I guess. People drive from South Bend to attend their private parties."

"So… he can't get the club members to buy insurance?"

"Oh, I'm sure he could if he was a member."

"Why isn't he, then? It, uh, looks like you guys could pay the dues," said Kyle.

"I'll give you one guess," said Heather, cocking one eyebrow. Kyle should not have been shocked. Especially here in Essen. Heather continued before he could even properly react. "I mean, it's not like they say that's the reason. But it is. It's bullshit. Ever since Manchester took over, that b—"

"Uh, oh. I see my lovely wife has launched into her patented Minty Green screed," said Max as he emerged from the shed hefting three large logs.

"The mystery, dear husband, is why you are not as mad as I am."

"Well, to start with, I've been black my whole life. And I've lived in Essen most of that now. None of this is a surprise. Tell her, Kyle," said Max.

"Yeah, it wasn't fun," Kyle commented, trying to figure out how to elaborate.

"Kyle and I used to have a game where we tried to figure out who was more screwed—a black guy in Essen or a gay guy in Essen.

Spoiler alert, I almost always won."

"Yeah, although you did lose some points in the game because you were a burly football player and I was a pudgy artsy weirdo," said Kyle.

"Until I pointed out being a useful tool wasn't exactly an advantage."

"Sounds like a real fun game," said Heather.

"It was a boring town to live in, and… wait, a minute, did you say Manchester?" asked Kyle.

"I was hoping you wouldn't catch that," said Max with a sigh. Heather looked at the two men, confused.

"Yeah, Alice Manchester. She used to be a teacher at your school, right?" asked Heather. Kyle's face reddened, and he scowled. He'd hoped the old bat would have been dead by now. Heather noticed the change in his mood and silently asked her husband what was wrong with a look.

"Alice Manchester—Mrs. Manchester, as we knew her, was… well, basically Kyle's archenemy," said Max.

"Yes," said Kyle. "Yes, I'd say that's as good a description as any."

# 8
## *Curdled Cream*

rs. Alice Manchester taught the honors English class for both the seventh and eighth grade, and there was little in those early days to indicate any problems might arise. The woman was heavier set, with a mop of stringy brown hair falling around her round face. Her skin was pale, and there were brownish-purple circles under her eyes. She wore round, orange-tinged glasses that sat on her small nose. She had a mouth that was usually taught and turtle-like, but that could expand into a wide grin when it needed to. Kyle saw her smile a lot at first.

Mrs. Manchester was into speeches. She would stand in front of the class, after the day's lesson on The Great Gatsby, or Shakespeare, or The Canterbury Tales was done, and speak passionately about the future. More specifically, she'd talk excitedly about how they— her class—were the future. Kyle was not sure how many times she'd used the phrase, "and the cream will rise," but it was enough to make him flinch later in life whenever anyone else used it. Kyle had liked English class. He loved writing and creative writing. Having a father as a writer—even if he was a part-time writer during the farm's downtime—helped. But he'd also been an avid comic book reader at a young age. He'd learned all sorts of new words in The Silver Surfer, The Fantastic Four, and What If? and this eventually led to reading Choose Your Own Adventure books. And this led to reading Dune and so on and so forth. Because of all of this, he'd found Mrs. Manchester's speeches inspiring… at first.

Eventually, however, he discovered that while her inspirational speeches were meant to lift them up, she had no problem dropping the hammer on them when she was angry. If she'd felt the class performed below expectations—let's say their essays were too superficial in their analysis of Romeo and Juliet—she would rage at them. She was personally insulted by their failures. Her face would grow red. Her turtle mouth would pucker into an impossibly small thing as she practically vibrated with disappointment. As much as Kyle loved writing, he struggled with the mechanics of it at times. He'd find out much later about his dyslexia, which no doubt impacted his schoolwork as well. He would sometimes feel Manchester's emotional hammer on a more personal level. Mrs. Manchester habitually degraded the entire class for the low scores of one of them. That one person would sometimes be Kyle, and he'd never feel so low as when that happened.

Dustin, Chad, and David were all in the honors English class, too. It was part of the reason he'd fully embraced them as friends, with all their casual snark and cruelty, after starting to hang out with them in sixth grade. He felt like he belonged with them. He liked feeling better than other people, after all the years of being the underdog. If the group's ire turned toward Henry or some other former friend, he would feel a little bad. But only a little. The feeling of belonging helped ease his guilt. And so did Janie. Janie did not approve of his new friends. But she tolerated them because she loved Kyle. He mistook tolerance as acceptance, and at the time there was no more accurate moral barometer than Janie. As a unit, he and his friends became Mrs. Manchester's disciples. Their self-worth hinged on her happiness. When she was proud of them, they felt invincible. They believed in their superiority. They believed that, yes, they were the cream of the crop. They believed they would mold the future. All they had to do was do an excellent job interpreting three Edgar Allen Poe poems before next Tuesday. The idiocy of all of this would not hit Kyle until much, much later.

The four boys were also a part of an even more select group than the honors English class. They were on Mrs. Manchester's Academic Challengers team, along with Leanne Brookes and Cindy Baker. It was a chance to ingratiate themselves to the woman further. It was another way for her to be proud of them. They traveled from school to school all around the region, and mostly trounced the competition as they answered trivia questions across a wide variety of disciplines. Each of them had their areas of expertise, although they were expected to study hard in all the areas of the challenge. Kyle was an alternate, and rarely competed. His specialty was spelling, with a decently sized knowledge of literature. But these subjects were covered by David and Leanne already, so he only competed if one of them was sick. But he traveled to every practice and every game. He joined them at Pizza Hut to celebrate when they won. He wasn't into sports, so it was his first taste of being a part of a team, and he liked it. Of course, if the team lost, then they weathered the storms of Mrs. Manchester's deep disappointment. But overall, they were usually able to use the guilt and shame they felt as fuel for the next competition. However, it was because of the Academic Challengers Club that Kyle began to notice Mrs. Manchester didn't treat him quite the same as the others.

The first incident started at pretty much the beginning, although he was eventually able to shrug it off. All the team members were to get matching blue polos embroidered with the team logo and their last name, purchased from a trophy shop in town. Kyle ran into two issues. First, they did not have polos in his size. He was wearing an extra-large shirt at the time, but the polos were in child sizes, and only went up to large. The trophy shop found a similar blue polo in an adult size, but it was a slightly different shade and make, with a rough-textured collar instead of a smooth one. The second issue was more significant, though. The polos came to a cost of nearly thirty dollars because of all the embroidering. It was not widely known at the time, but the Thomas farm had been suffering for years. Kyle's grandfather made some bad investments, and a prolonged drought had destroyed a lot of their crops when Kyle was in sixth grade. The next year brought too much rain, which was nearly as ruinous. The Thomas family did not have a lot of money, and thirty dollars was a lot to them at the time.

Kyle begged and pleaded with his mom and dad, but they said it wasn't possible. Kyle's mom was already stretching their budget to feed them and was probably going to take a part-time job at the new Burger King to make ends meet while the farm recovered. His mom looked a little sorry she had to say no. But his dad seemed to take pleasure in it.

"Tell Alice Manchester I said she can take her blue polos and shove them up her—" his dad started, before being cut off abruptly by his mother. The next day in school, Kyle waited until after the last class of the day and walked into Mrs. Manchester's room. Her head was down, grading papers. He could feel the heat in his cheeks as he approached her desk.

"Hi. Uh, Mrs. Manchester… sorry to interrupt," he said. The red pen in her hand stopped scratching across the paper, and her head turned slightly. For a strange moment, her eyes narrowed as she looked at him. And then, her lips creased into a slight and stiff smile.

"Not at all, Kyle. What can I do for you?" she asked. But she did not stop grading the paper. For a moment it seemed like she was crossing out words without even looking at the paper, but Kyle realized she must have been finishing the thought process he'd interrupted. She returned her gaze to the paper and kept writing as he spoke.

"I'm sorry to do this. But my parents can't afford my polo. My polo for the Academic Challengers team," said Kyle. He paused briefly to see if Mrs. Manchester might react. When she didn't, and the red pen kept scratching on down the page, he decided to press on. "My mom found a polo I already own that's a pretty close match. She wondered if I could wear that for a while? For the first couple of competitions. I'm getting a paper route. And my mom's getting a part-time job. I'm sure in a few months I can get the polo."

Mrs. Manchester kept marking up the paper until she got to the bottom of the page. She finally sat the red pen down, and then turned her head toward Kyle and smiled at him again. The grin was wider this time—much more like the one she wore when giving her "cream will rise" speeches. But her eyes were hard and gray.

"Your family owns a million dollars' worth of land. I'm sure your mother and father can afford thirty dollars, Kyle," she said. Without another word, she picked her pen back up and started on the next paper.

Kyle was too shocked to react immediately. The many times he'd played out this scenario in his head over the weekend, his worst fear was keeping the tears choked back after Mrs. Manchester said it was fine. Or, at his most optimistic, she agreed to pay for the polo shirt herself. There was never, ever any scenario he'd imagined where she'd shut him down so thoroughly. He could think of nothing to say, so he drifted out of the classroom. He waited until he reached the hallway before the tears started flowing freely. He'd tried to compose himself before he saw Janie, running into the bathroom and splashing cold water on his face. But she knew instantly he'd been crying.

"That… that… witch," Janie spat out, her faith not allowing her to say what she wanted to say.

"I don't know, she has a point. I mean, my parents must have some sort of savings at least, right? Extracurriculars take money," said Kyle as he sat beside her on the cold stone steps of the middle school.

"Yeah, and most of them have fundraisers or spare equipment or whatever if parents can't pay for it. And it's not like your team needs polos!"

"I should quit the team. Say I don't have time for it or something."

"No. No, you can't do that," said Janie. Kyle knew Janie didn't like the amount of time he spent with the Academic Challengers Club because it was more time with friends she considered a bad influence. So, her insistence woke him a little from his self-pity.

"Why not?"

"Because you're happy. I think? I don't get the appeal—at all—but that's not the point." Janie wrapped an arm around him and rested her head on his shoulder. His shoulders had grown broad over the summer as he'd gotten taller. The fat on his body was now more spread out, and Kyle was sure that was part of the reason people didn't call him names anymore. He liked Janie resting her head on him. Her hair smelled like strawberries, and she knew exactly what to say to him.

Janie had paid for his polo out of her own savings. Kyle paid her back with money from his paper route, but he was still eternally grateful for what Janie did for him at the time. It was only later he thought about how much hurt he might have avoided if he'd stayed off the team.

# 9

## *Lissie*

issie stared up at the exposed rafters of the attic, unable to will herself to sleep. An hour later, just as her eyelids began to get heavy, she started to feel it. There was little warning. One moment she was fine, and the next she felt a sharp and sudden need to urinate.

"Oh, come on," she said into the claustrophobic confines of the attic. Her body had the worst timing when it came to these things. Yes, she'd had that last cup of coffee a little too late. But that's why she'd tried to go before she made her way up to the attic. Sighing, she forced herself out of bed and fumbled her feet into her slippers. Lissie was eager to avoid her mother, so she tried to be as quiet as possible as she descended the attic stairs. Ahead of her, she could see the door to her mother's room was open a crack, and light spilled out. Her mother had always been a night owl, so this wasn't much of a surprise. She liked to stay up, after Samuel had left for the day and her husband and daughter were sleeping, to read or otherwise enjoy her brief solitude.

Lissie passed by her father's room and was surprised to hear footsteps behind the closed door. It explained the cracked door to her mother's room. She must have left it open when she went to visit her father. This in and of itself was strange, though. Angelina Baker hadn't stepped foot into her father's room for months. Unless she'd been visiting at night all along? Lissie decided to give them their space, and she kept walking toward the bathroom. She got to her mom's room, glanced inside, and was shocked to discover her mom sitting in bed, reading a newspaper. She ran back to the door of her dad's room.

"Dad?" she said hopefully, turning the knob of the door, only to find it locked. She twisted it frantically. "Dad, is that you? Are you up?" Even as she said it, she knew it was impossible. Even if he'd regained enough of his mind to walk, would his body even be able to do it? Her mind shifted to the terrifying thought that someone else was in there with him. "Dad!"

"Lissie, what are you doing?" Angelina said as she emerged from her room, wrapping her flowing black robe around her.

"I heard footsteps!" Lissie was still twisting the knob and pulling on the door. "The door's locked."

"Of course, it's locked. I lock it every night." Her mom pushed her to the side and slid a key into the door's lock. As she opened the door, Lissie pushed past her into the room. It was dark and silent. Her father lay in the bed just as he had been when she'd checked on him earlier. His eyes were closed, and his chest rose and fell with a steady rhythm. Angelina gave Lissie a sharp look and pulled her back into the hallway. She closed and locked the door.

"Why do you lock the door?" Lissie asked.

"First of all, you will lower your voice," Angelina said in a whisper. "Secondly, you will adjust your tone. Now." Lissie nodded her head curtly. "Good. I lock it every night because despite a robust security system, we are a well-off family. And therefore, a likely target. Your father is helpless in there. It might be a minor extra bit of security, but it helps me sleep a little sounder at night."

"Oh. Okay." Lissie was starting to feel silly. And with the adrenaline rush passing, she could feel the pressure in her bladder once more. "I'm sorry. I didn't mean to make a scene or anything. It just sounded so much like… I guess it doesn't matter." The look on her mother's face softened.

"It's okay, honey. I know. I know you worry. But it's a very old and creaky house. Now why don't you try to get some sleep?"

"I will. I just need to go to the restroom. It's the reason I came down in the first place."

Lissie headed down the hallway. Her mother watched her every step of the way. She turned around and smiled weakly at the woman. These moments were always strange. A small reminder of the way things used to be. In amongst the years of battling each other, and then the strange cold war they were now locked in, there were still moments when she remembered what it was like to be a daughter with a mother who loved her. They never lasted long.

Angelina Baker stood in the hallway and watched her daughter go into the bathroom. She waited for the sound of the lock bolting in the bathroom door before she dared move. She softly put the key back into lock and turned the knob as quietly as she could. She stood at the doorway and whispered into the darkness.

"That was too close. Well, you must be more careful. She can't know. She's not ready. I'm… I'm not ready to tell her." With that, the woman closed the door and locked it. She returned to her room, her shoulders stooped and feeling so much more tired than before.

# 10
# *Findings*

Kyle woke up late, around ten in the morning. He'd enjoyed the night at Max and Heather's house. So much so that he'd fallen asleep on their couch. Heather drove him home around six, while Max stayed behind to watch Zee. Although truth to be told, Max was so dead tired he was basically only there to be an adult presence.

"Zee can pretty much take care of herself, to be honest. At least for fifteen minutes. I might trust her more than I do Max," Heather said as she let Kyle out of her silver SUV.

"How did Max manage to nab you?" Kyle asked. They both laughed at his little joke, but they both knew how. Beyond being a pretty gorgeous specimen of a human being, Max was funny with a good heart. It's why they both loved him, although Kyle hadn't admitted that to himself until long after he and Max drifted apart.

Kyle managed to climb onto the downstairs couch and crash

for another four hours. He wanted to sleep a little more, but the birds seemed aggressively chirpy this morning, and the sun was streaming in through the lace curtains on the windows. As farmers, Kyle's parents did not have a concept of blackout curtains. They were up either with or before the sun.

Kyle zombie-walked to the kitchen to make himself some coffee and peeked out of the windows to see if Patrick might be around. He wasn't, sadly. If he had anything to do at the farmhouse today, he'd probably already come and gone. With a little caffeine in him, Kyle felt more prepared to face the day. But his neck was still sore. He needed to sleep upstairs on a real bed with pillows. He thought if he got more done around the house, he'd be able to rid himself of the sense of unease that pulsed through him. Starting with the photos was a mistake. This time, he was going to tackle less emotionally fraught territory. He grabbed the three packages of Post-its he'd bought the previous day at the dollar store. One was colored green, another orange, and the last one yellow. He planned to color-code the furniture and larger stuff in the house either to keep (green), sell (orange) or trash (yellow.)

After five hours, the house was covered in a lot of orange, a little yellow, and precious little green. The truth was whatever connection he'd had with the contents of the house was severed in the last fifteen years. Most of it was more foggy memory than cherished memory. And little of the furniture or the décor was his style.

He'd finished tagging the downstairs and decided he should tackle the other boxes in the basement. He started pulling boxes of Christmas decorations, old tools, knick-knacks and forgotten framed pictures out onto the living room floor. He was nearly finished clearing out boxes when he ran across a huge box that both excited and infuriated him in equal measure. It was labeled with his name. He cut through the tape that sealed it and opened it. He took one look and closed the flaps of the box again. He balanced the box under his arm, grabbed the cooler by its strap with his other hand, and headed toward the front door. He managed to clumsily turn the knob with the hand carrying the cooler and was surprised to see Patrick out in the front hard.

He was bent over tending to one of the flower beds in front of the house. His jeans outlined his thick legs nicely. Kyle was momentarily surprised to see a bright purple underwear waistband visible above Patrick's jeans. But then he remembered that thanks to the internet even straight country boys could buy cute underwear these days. The man must have heard the door open because he stood up straight and looked back. He smiled at Kyle, and Kyle waved back. Patrick was shirtless—his t-shirt was stuffed in his waistband—and it was as glorious as Kyle imagined from the glimpses before. He was toned, but not chiseled. A little thick in the middle, but with some definition to his abs. Kyle tried not to stare too long and busied himself with getting the cooler and box situated.

"Want a Guinness? The ice in the cooler is mostly water now, but did its job," said Kyle.

"You don't have to ask me twice," said Patrick, as he bounded up the stairs. "I mean, it's a little early for me, but not that early." He sat down in the rocking chair next to Kyle and grabbed the bottle he was offered. The wet bottle dribbled drops of cold water down onto his pecs, which beaded up and slid downward toward his right nipple. Kyle cleared his throat.

"Yeah, same. Going through some old stuff. Thought a drink might make it go a little smoother," he said.

"Your old stuff?" Patrick was reading the name on the side of the box.

"Yeah. When I left home, my relationship with my parents was rocky. I didn't have a lot of time to grab anything. I left a lot behind. I thought my mom and dad pitched it all. But I guess they didn't."

"But they let you think they did?"

"Yeah. I guess so." Kyle opened the flap of the box again and took out a rolled-up poster of Kevin Sorbo. He unrolled it, showed it to Patrick, and they both laughed. "Guess I can throw this one out now."

"What happened? I mean, with you and your parents? If you don't mind me asking?" Patrick was rocking slowly in the chair now, slightly slumped in it and relaxed as he took a swig of Guinness. Kyle hated to admit it, but he probably would have told him anything he wanted to know, looking like that.

However, this was also the moment where Kyle started doing the mental math every gay person—anyone who might be able to 'pass' as something they are not—must do when meeting new people. Do you speak the truth, and risk alienating or pissing people off? Or did you lie by omission and hope that carried you through? The problem with the latter was it worked mostly with people you barely knew, or whose path you were crossing momentarily. Besides, Kyle had long ago decided the days of hiding in half-truths was over. He needed to keep that going, even while in Essen.

"When I was sixteen, I told them I was gay. It did not go well," said Kyle.

"Damn. That sucks man. That's exactly why I haven't told my parents yet." Patrick took another swig of his Guinness, closing his eyes, and pressing the bottle to his forehead, enjoying the cooling effect of it. Kyle was glad he did because that meant Patrick didn't see the surprise wash over his face. He managed to regain his composure by the time Patrick's eyes opened again.

"They wouldn't take it well either?"

"Oh hell no. Mom's constantly bugging me about when I'm going to get a wife and start making some grand-babies. As if that's easy while I'm living at home in the middle of nowhere," said Patrick.

"Why do you live at home still?" asked Kyle.

"My dad had an accident five years back. A tractor rolled over his legs and busted them up bad. I came back home after college to help do the work around the farm he couldn't anymore."

"Fuck. That's rough. I mean, I know times change, but I can't imagine Essen is exactly hopping as far as a gay scene goes." This made Patrick laugh his hearty, boyish laugh.

"You got that right. I get up to South Bend most weekends and hit the bars and clubs, and there's always the apps." He looked a little sheepish.

"Nothing wrong with that. I've been known to hop on them now and again," said Kyle.

"No guy for you?"

"No. Not anymore. I was with a guy for seven years. We got engaged and everything but… eh, shit happens."

"Pretty much. Anyway, let's see what's in your box," said Patrick. They both got off the rocking chairs and sat on the porch with the box in front of them. The tension Kyle felt when he'd thought Patrick was straight was released. He felt slightly uneasy when talking to straight guys he didn't know. There was the uncertainty of how they'd feel once they knew he was gay. He was wary about becoming too friendly in case the guy freaked out. Now he felt more at ease with Patrick, in one way. But it was replaced by a new, different tension. He couldn't help but steal glances at the man as his naked torso hunched over the box while he inspected its contents. His disarming grin flashing at the toys, posters, or video games he recognized, and his brow furrowing when he encountered something he wasn't familiar with.

"Who's this guy?" Patrick asked, pulling out a squat action figure with a clear body and pale, muscular arms and legs covered in purple tubing.

"Oh, this is Mutagen Man. He's from Ninja Turtles," Kyle said excitedly, genuinely happy to see the little chunk of plastic. "This was my favorite figure in the entire line."

"I watched a lot of TMNT as a kid, and I don't remember this guy at all."

"That's because you watched some reboot. This is one of the original turtle figures," Kyle explained. "You filled him up with water, and these organs float around in his body." To demonstrate, Kyle took the plug out of the figures back, submerged it in the cooler's water, and then retrieved him.

"That is so gross," Patrick said in appreciation. "No wonder you 90s kids are twisted."

They proceeded to go through the old comic books, movie magazines, CDs, and books the same way, and Kyle found going through it made him happy. He'd barely touched his bottle of Guinness. Whatever anger he felt at his parents for not telling him they kept his childhood possessions, and whatever confusion he still had that they'd bothered to keep them, all disappeared in the moment. They'd exhausted the contents of the box when Patrick stretched back onto the cold gray stone of the porch, giving his back a rest from being hunched over the box. He let his latest bottle of Guinness rest on his flat stomach, held in place by his left hand. Kyle joined him in stretching out, and they looked up at the white-painted wood beams under the porch's cover.

"This is a nice house. A shame for you to sell it," he said.

"I know. Hey, if your parents buy it from me, maybe they'll give this to you as a wedding present for you and your new wife. Be a great place to raise a few kids," Kyle joked. Patrick slapped him on the stomach.

"Not. Funny," he said. "Besides, it looks great from the outside, but who knows what mold-ridden mess it is inside."

"Wait, you haven't been inside?" asked Kyle, turning to prop his head up on his left hand. Patrick shook his head.

"Nope. When I was bringing that casserole in—that was the first time I'd ever been in the house at all."

"Oh. Well, I guess I can give you a tour," said Kyle, getting up and trying to ignore how sore he felt from a short time lying on the cold stone. He wasn't that much older than Patrick, he supposed. Maybe six or seven years max, but the other man obviously took better care of himself. He looked around at the darkening sky. "Looks like it's going to rain anyway. Better get my childhood memories inside."

Patrick helped him gather everything back into the box, and then grabbed the near-empty cooler and carried it inside while Kyle hefted the box.

"Very country chic," said Patrick.

"Well, very country," said Kyle.

"It's like a clone of my parents' place. It's eerie. I'm a little jealous of this TV though."

"Yeah, that might be coming with me." Kyle took him through the downstairs, explaining the scattered Post-it notes.

"You know, if you do decide to sell the farm, you could probably leave most of this here. My mom would love it. It's totally her style. Hell, maybe she'll finally make good on her threats and move in here by herself," said Patrick.

"Your folks don't get along?"

"Eh, I think it's typical marriage stuff. I don't know, my dad acts like he resents her sometimes. He never got used to having to rely on us. He doesn't act that way toward me, but I'm his son, not his wife."

"Well, that's the downstairs. Not a ton to see. Now for the upstairs," said Kyle. He hesitated at the bottom of the stairs, suddenly realizing a full tour of the house meant going into his parents' bedroom. He thought about trying to make up some excuse as to why they couldn't go in as he climbed the stairs, but Kyle felt embarrassed he hadn't already done it.

"There's the bathroom if you need to release any of the Guinness," Kyle offered.

"Better not break the seal yet," said Patrick as he sidled up next to Kyle. He still wasn't wearing a shirt, and the heat of his body near Kyle was exciting. Before Kyle let the thoughts in his head go too far, he broke away and angled toward his old bedroom.

"And here is my childhood bedroom. Although I guess it's been a guest bedroom nearly as long as it was mine by now," said Kyle as he stood at the doorway. But Patrick took a few steps inside and sat down on the bed. It creaked as the metal springs below the mattress strained under his weight.

"Is this the same bed you used?" he asked.

"I think so. Sure sounds like it."

"How did you jerk off? You'd make a racket."

"I jerked off in the bathroom. Which had its own problems. I was using up all the hot water," Kyle said. Patrick laughed.

"Oh, I'd hate that. I like to jerk off lying down. I want to relax. Plus, I like… eh, never mind," he said.

"You can't start a sentence like that and leave me hanging!" Kyle crossed his arms to show he was serious. Patrick got up off the bed, to a cacophony of metallic squeaking. As he passed by Kyle on the way out of the room, he finally finished his thought.

"Sometimes it's fun to… you know… catch it." Patrick's face reddened. Kyle's mouth dropped open in shock. Now, of course, this was not the most shocking thing he'd ever heard. Or seen, even. But there was something about hearing it out of Patrick's mouth that was shocking. He'd been thinking of him as the latest in a long line of straight, unobtainable men he'd fallen for. That was no longer necessarily the case. Also, Patrick was saying it in his old childhood bedroom.

"Well, good to know," Kyle commented. He looked down the hallway to the closed door of his parents' room. He took a deep breath in and then let it out. "As long as we're making confessions, I have a less sexy one to make."

"You're an ax murderer, and these are my final moments?"

"Not quite that unsexy. But close. This door is my parents' room. And I haven't been able to go into it yet," said Kyle.

"Why not?" asked Patrick, a hint of concern filtering into his voice.

"I'm not sure. It's dumb. Maybe going in there will make this all too real? And when it starts feeling real, it starts churning up all this shit in my head. Old resentment. Old anger. I'd thought I'd left all that behind me."

"That doesn't sound dumb to me."

"Well, that's not the dumb part. The dumb part is I keep having this weird sense of… I don't know. Dread? Foreboding?"

"Foreboding? You are a writer," Patrick said.

"Hey, when the word is the right word, it's the right word," said Kyle. He realized they were just standing in front of the closed door now.

"Well, look. I'm here. Maybe now's a good time to do it?" suggested Patrick.

Kyle couldn't argue with that, so he grabbed the doorknob, steeled himself, and purposefully averted his gaze away from the Jesus painting as he opened the door. Rain began to fall noisily on the roof and against the windows in waves. The effect was like the rising and falling of static. Kyle opened the door. As with the rest of the house, it was mostly unchanged. The bed was neatly made, with a blue bottom sheet and a white top sheet covered with a pattern of tiny blue flowers. At the foot of the bed was an old chest that held the comforter. There was no headboard, but above the bed was a long wooden gun rack with two mirrors at either side. Two rifles, facing different directions, were displayed on it. They had been in the family for decades and were no longer functional; one of the last vestiges of the Thomas clan of old. Kyle had no aunts or uncles and no brothers or sisters.

As his father had reminded him the last time they'd talked, Kyle was the last of the line. And now that line was going to die out because of Kyle. He didn't bother pointing out to his dad there were all kinds of ways he could continue the family line if he wanted to. Mostly because he knew his father wouldn't accept that, and also because (at the time) he didn't want to give his dad even a sliver of hope.

Kyle walked over to the Jesus painting that hung to the left of the bed, took it off the wall without looking at it, flipped it around, and sat it against the wall.

"Not a Jesus fan?" Patrick asked.

"Not really. I mean, I like his greatest hits," said Kyle with a shrug. Patrick, clearly curious, crept over to the painting and snuck a quick look.

"Hmmm. Yeah, not my favorite thing ever. Good call on turning that around."

"It's pretty creepy, right? The one time I tried to tell my mom that, she called me a heathen."

"This your dad's?" Patrick asked as he walked excitedly to the far-right corner of the bedroom. There was a little wooden desk with a small black typewriter on top of it. There was even a fresh white sheet of paper in it as if the typewriter was waiting for its owner to return any minute and continue the good work.

"Yep. That's the old Royal Quiet Deluxe Portable. Quiet is a relative term, by the way. Dad did most of his work in the winter, or after dinner and before mom went to bed," Kyle replied.

"All my dad ever did was veg out in front of the TV and smoke like a chimney," said Patrick, with a little awe in his voice. "I read five of your dad's books. I mean, technically I listened to them when I was in the tractor to pass the time. But I liked them."

"Well, you've got me beat. I only read three, and two of those was when I was a kid. You can probably guess one of them."

"I don't believe any of the bullshit people are saying," said Patrick as the rain outside began to beat more intensely against the windows, the wall, and the roof. "I mean, I'm no writer. But I know writers pull details from their lives and sort of…"

"Blend it," finished Kyle as he nodded his head. "That's the analogy I've heard. They stick their lives into a blender. Different artists use different speeds—even from project to project. The higher the speed, the less recognizable the individual pieces. The mystery, then, is what speed my dad used when he wrote Dunbar's Grove?"

"What do you think?"

"I think it was on high. I have to believe it was on high," Kyle said. He looked at Patrick, and the light coming in through the blinds seemed to highlight his eyes, which were staring out the window thoughtfully. The nape of his neck. His small, pink nipples on his smooth torso. The rain on the window caused circular patterns to break up the slats of light across the other man's body, and Kyle found his gaze drifting downward as he watched the light and shadow play across it. When he returned his gaze upward, he saw Patrick was staring at him.

Kyle was caught in that strange, magic moment when two people connected wordlessly. That beat of wondering if he was reading the signs right. The peculiar glimmer in the other person's eye that somehow said: "no, you're on the right track." The nearly imperceptible drift as both people drew closer. All of this was a rarity in Kyle's world. He could count on one hand the number of times it'd happened before. Usually, all of this was navigated and bargained out and situated beforehand. Bland messages were exchanged on apps, as both parties played courter and courted. And then the more vulgar messages began. Pics were exchanged. It was all exciting in its own way, but it didn't leave much room for mystery or uncertainty. And at this moment—this excruciatingly prolonged and beautiful moment— Kyle remembered how much he missed it. When his lips touched

Patrick's and found them somehow soft to the touch but with a firm, seeking intensity, any sense of self-awareness fled him.

He wasn't even sure who pushed who onto the bed. One moment they were standing, the next they were lying down. The bed was as creaky as his old one, and it caused Patrick to laugh a little in between kisses. Kyle found this adorable, and started kissing him harder, and all over. Patrick ripped at Kyle's clothes, trying to get him out of them. They reached for each other's hardness almost simultaneously, and Kyle gasped, not only at the thickness of what he was grasping but how good Patrick's hand felt on him. After that, Kyle was lost in the frantic, fumbling, and creaking intensity of it all.

Kyle had no clue how long he'd slept, but he awoke to Patrick's head resting on him. The other man was lazily running his hands through the hair on Kyle's chest. The rain was still going but was much softer now.

"Welcome back, sleepyhead," Patrick mumbled into Kyle's chest.

"How long was I out?" asked Kyle.

"No clue. I was afraid of waking you up if I tried to find my phone and check the time."

"Let's never look at the time. Let's just stay here in bed."

"Mmmm, that sounds nice." Patrick nuzzled his nose into Kyle's chest hair, which tickled. "But my parents are going to kill me already. I think I can say I was waiting for the rain to get done. But that'll only get me so far."

After ten minutes of saying how they needed to get out of bed, but did not want to get out of bed, Patrick finally made a move. He got up, his beautiful butt bouncing as he stood, and got his phone.

"Shit. It's almost seven! Time flies, I guess," he said as he gathered his clothes. Kyle got up and decided to sit at his father's desk. He could not deny that he felt a sort of perverse thrill having sex in his parents' bed and decided to push it a little further. He guided his fingers to the home keys and began to type, speaking the words aloud as he hit the keys.

"Hello dear homophobic parents, I wanted to let you know how much fun I had," he said, advancing the typewriter for a new line, "with the beautiful boy next door. I was pleased to find out that not only is he gay but he has a gloriously thick…"

"Go on, I'm liking this story," said Patrick. "Do you know where you threw my underwear? I can't seem to—oh, here they are." Patrick looked over at Kyle in concern. "Something wrong?"

"I'm not sure," said Kyle. He stared at the small typewriter window he'd been focusing on as he typed. When he last advanced it to start a new line, he'd noticed the top of some already typewritten words in the bottom of the window. He twisted the drum of the typewriter to advance the paper so that it was half out and easier to read. Patrick came up behind him and laid a hand on Kyle's shoulder.

Kyle stared down at the words. It was one small line, perfectly centered on the paper.

It's up to you now, son.

# 11

# *Mrs. Manchester*

atrick had made a quick exit,  as neither of them had been sure of what to say or do after the strange note found in the typewriter. It was, without a doubt, a mood killer. Kyle then spent the next three hours going over everything in his parents' bedroom. His father had a shelf next to his desk with copies of his past books, notebooks filled with story ideas, and some reference books. Kyle flipped through and skimmed them all, looking to see if his father had left him any other notes. He tried not to dwell on the insanity of it all.

The note left in the typewriter—discretely hidden from view— suggested his father hadn't trusted the security of his own home. It was a reckless chance he'd taken, assuming that Kyle would ever find it. For all he'd known, Kyle might have hired someone to go through the house before the sale. After all, Kyle had considered it. It was only the utter failure of his podcast, and the slow market for stories, that gave him the time to come back home. But his father had been desperate enough to take the chance. Days after Dunbar's Grove was published, Herbert Thomas took his own life. There was no ambiguity about this. There'd even been a suicide note, neatly typed on the same Royal typewriter that created his one-line message to his son from beyond the grave.

## It's up to you now, son.

Kyle realized his dad had to have typed this mysterious message after his suicide note. He tried to work this fact into the timeline of his dad's death as it appeared in the newspaper articles. First, he typed his suicide note. Then he typed the note for Kyle, rolled the drum of the typewriter downward, and left his house for the last time. He drove to the Kirby's farm, said he was going out of town a while, and asked them to look after his place. He gave them five hundred dollars to do it. He drove his BMW (one of the extravagances his father indulged in after the farm had turned around in the years after Kyle left) two hours to a little town called Silver Cove. It was night, and he parked his car on the road. He climbed over the grass-covered sand dunes and down to the shore of Lake Michigan. A couple making out on the deck of one of the many houses that dotted the beach in the area saw him do this. They saw him walk, fully clothed, into the lake. He dived in and never came back out. The couple called the police, but by the time they arrived, he'd already let the undertow take him. His body washed up a few days later, miles and miles away.

When Kyle told people that he couldn't believe his father had killed his mother and that Dunbar's Grove couldn't have been that autobiographical, it was with an unspoken caveat. He did not know his father. He wasn't sure he'd known him growing up, but he certainly did not know him fifteen years later. The proof of this was in the manner of his death. He could not have imagined Herbert Thomas taking his own life. It was this, and only this, that shook his faith in his father's innocence. He might have been a homophobe. He might have drunk too much on occasion. He might have been too quick with a switch and too slow with a hug. But those failings didn't make him a murderer.

Hoping to clear his head, Kyle decided to leave Essen for the night and head up to South Bend. He decided to treat himself to a good meal at a steak and seafood place called Monterey's. According to the online reviews, the restaurant was still a popular destination after all these years. He'd been there exactly once before, with his dad and mom. One of his mom's old colleagues from her university days was getting some award and invited the family to the ceremony and to dinner after. Before Kyle was born, his mom split her time between the farm and Notre Dame. She taught musical theory three days a week, and only stopped to take care of Kyle full time after he was born. It was only much later that Kyle realized what a sacrifice that was; after his mother was dead. Regret twisted in his stomach, so he pushed the thought away and focused on the memory of the way the lobster at Monterey's melted in his mouth.

The place had moved from its square gray brick building with its blue awnings and nautical theme to something much more refined and upscale, all windows, exposed duct-work, and bare bulbs with brightly glowing orange filaments. He enjoyed the meal immensely. The lobster couldn't quite compete with his childhood memory, but it was still delicate and buttery. He ate dinner quietly, enjoying the regular chatter as it washed over him like soothing white noise. He was back in the real world. He was back in the world that made sense, where innocuous comments from secretaries and Jesus paintings didn't spark deep-seated dread. Where parents didn't leave children secret and inscrutable notes. He was letting the last swirl of his far-too-expensive wine travel across his taste buds when a shrill, high-pitched laugh broke through the white noise and his hard-won sense of peace.

He did not have to turn to know who it was. But he did anyway because he couldn't fight the compulsion to. He caught a glimpse of her. Her hair was white, but still as curly and stringy. She might have been a little skinnier, but the skin on her face drooped unflatteringly around her mouth. Mrs. Alice Manchester was sitting with three other gray-haired women, and she seemed to be having a fantastic time. Despite himself, Kyle seethed. Not merely at the woman's presence, but at the fact that she'd ruined his attempt to get away from the ghosts of Essen. He got up slowly, took his wine glass in hand, and sat in the empty seat on the other side of the table.

"More wine, Sir? Would you like to see the dessert menu?" asked his waitress. She had a slight drawl that suggested she was originally from the southern part of the state.

"Yes. Both, I guess," he murmured, unable to take his eyes off Manchester.

The woman said something in reply, but Kyle didn't register it. Manchester seemed to be regaling her friends with some sort of tale. Her turtle mouth would suck the meat out of a crab leg in between telling her story, before widening into a butter-soaked grin that was often followed by a renewed round of laughter. His waitress refilled his wine glass and handed him the dessert menu. He took it at the exact moment Manchester saw him. He quickly opened the dessert menu and started browsing. Truthfully, he had no idea what was even on the dessert menu. He'd been too preoccupied with whether his old teacher had seen him or not. When the waitress returned, he selected the first dessert he saw on the page.

"That's delicious. And it'll pair well with your wine," said the waitress, who took the dessert menu from his hand. He nodded at her, and she departed. Kyle turned his head, deciding he'd dare one more peek at Manchester, only to discover that—to his horror—she was walking toward him. She'd removed the cloth napkin from around her neck and sauntered toward him with a wide grin on her face. Her dress was sparkling and golden, and it suited her figure well enough. It was a far cry from the dowdy rose-colored dresses she'd favored back in school. Unsure of how to react, Kyle's brain shifted into automatic social pleasantry mode. He got up from the table and shook her hand. It was strangely cold and spongy.

"Mrs. Manchester! I thought that was you," said Kyle, even as his face began to feel flush.

"Kyle Thomas, what a small world this is. And please, call me Alice. We're not in school anymore," Manchester said.

"I guess that's true, Alice." The name sounded like a forbidden swear word that he was trying on for the first time. He did not like the sound of it coming from his mouth at all.

"I thought I saw you over here, peeking over your dessert menu. You haven't changed much at all. A little taller. And you've lost weight."

"A little. You too, I see. You look great." Inside Kyle screamed. If only he hadn't ordered dessert. How could he get out of this conversation?

"Oh, thanks. Well, I've more time to look after myself now that I'm retired. I gave so much to the students, you know," said

Manchester. She stated it so matter-of-factly it made Kyle want to retch.

"Of course. Sorry I didn't come to say 'hi' right away. I didn't want to interrupt."

"A few of the girls from the club are having a little night out. Don't tell Chef Gregory, though. He'd be furious we were here instead of the club restaurant."

"Well, I'm not a club member and don't know the chef there so your secret's safe with me." For the first time, the sincerity in Kyle's voice was faltering. He couldn't help but think of Max. All these years later and the woman was still playing her old tricks, doing her part to keep people down even as she imagined herself as some hero.

"Of course. But you must come by sometime. I'm sure a successful writer like you has been to all sorts of beautiful places, but it is nice. You can be my guest," said Manchester.

"Well, I'm not in town long and have a lot of work to get done with the house, but I'll try," lied Kyle.

"Oh yes, your poor father," said Manchester. Kyle held onto the back of his chair to steady his nerves. Of all the tortures he was having to endure at this moment, he wasn't sure he could survive Alice Manchester's insincere sympathy.

"Yeah. So... not a lot of time, what with getting the farm ready for sale."

"Some families don't have any luck." Manchester shook her head sadly. Kyle, for his part, wondered what exactly she meant by this. The question was on the tip of his tongue when she started talking again. "Well, I shouldn't leave my company waiting for me, and it looks like your dessert has arrived." Indeed, the waitress brought a small chocolate cake, sizzling on a cast-iron pan. A scoop of ice cream was beside it, already half-melted from the heat.

"Of course, you have a good evening, uh, Alice," Kyle said, shaking her unpleasantly clammy hand once more. She smiled and nodded in return, and then turned back toward her table.

As he lifted his fork to take a bite of his dessert, he found his hand was shaking. He certainly didn't feel hungry. He destroyed the dessert more than he ate it. He wanted it to look a little eaten to avoid questions from the waitress about whether he'd liked it or not. Instead, he concentrated on drinking his second glass of wine. He barely tasted it, but it did help to stop his hands from shaking. He did not look toward Alice Manchester's table. But he did watch in his periphery as she and her friends got up and left the restaurant.

As he signed the receipt, filling in the tip box with an amount that would have bought a whole meal on a typical night out, Kyle decided he was thankful for his encounter with Alice Manchester. He understood now that there was no escape from Essen. There was no escape from the emotions it pulled out from him. There was no escape from the mystery of his father, the note he'd left, and Dunbar's Grove. He thought he'd escaped Essen fifteen years ago, but that'd been an illusion. He'd fooled himself for far too long thinking otherwise. He was determined now to put it all behind him. He was going to figure out what the hell his father wanted with him. He was going to sell the fucking farmhouse. He was going to figure out whether his dad killed his mom. Hell, he might even write an article about it. But there was no way he was going to let Essen hold onto him any longer.

# 12
# *Whispers in the Library*

Kyle wandered the Essen Public Library, and it instantly felt more like home than the old farmhouse. He had practically lived in the library when he was younger. His mom's best friend, Sally, lived a block from the library, and while the two of them visited, his mom let him walk there. He spent hours and hours there. The librarians knew him by name, and he knew their names as well. He was pleasantly surprised by how little was changed about the building. The VHS section was replaced by DVDs and Blu-rays. The card catalogs were gone and replaced by computers, but everything else was mostly in order. The children's and young reader's books were downstairs, and the books geared more toward adults were upstairs. The middle ground of young adult novels didn't exist when Kyle was a kid, and he passively wondered where they might be situated. But he had work to do.

He'd spent the first few hours of the morning on the farmhouse porch, attempting to read the book he'd brought with him. He'd been engrossed by the first few chapters. But now he couldn't concentrate. His mind was on the note he'd found in his dad's typewriter. It was also on Patrick. If he was honest with himself, he wasn't on the porch to soak up the sunshine. He kept hoping he'd see the man. And, yes, that was because he wanted to kiss him again. He wanted to feel what it was like to be with him again. But he also wanted to talk about the note with him, too.

By ten o'clock, it felt like Patrick probably wasn't going to make it over. Kyle hoped the note hadn't freaked him out. Or the sex. Patrick certainly didn't seem like that part of it was new to him. But he wasn't out to his parents and seemed to only let loose an hour away in South Bend. Likely doing it so close to home made him uncomfortable. In any case, Kyle decided that sitting around for Patrick was a waste of time. He'd been in Essen for days and not accomplished all that much. He remembered his promise to himself and decided the first place he should check was the library.

The problem was, he wasn't having much luck. After thirty minutes of searching for himself, he decided to get some help. He was surprised, however, when he saw Lissie sitting at the little circular librarian's desk.

"Oh! Hey, Lissie," Kyle said. "I didn't know you—" She cut him off.

"Max is a nice guy, but he can't pay me to work full time," she explained, anticipating his question.

"Understood. Actually, I'm glad to see you." Kyle looked

around and then leaned in conspiratorially. "Remember that topic you asked about? Whether I was looking into it? Well, now I am."

"I see," said Lissie. She looked up at him, unsmiling, and probed him with her eyes. She still had the contacts in that gave them an eerie, penetrating look. "Well, remember my advice. Did you need help?"

"That's the thing. I didn't think I would. Not like I'm not used to navigating a library. I looked up a book and a few articles on the topic, but I haven't had any luck locating them." Kyle handed the scribbled notes he'd taken while browsing the library's electronic catalog. Lissie said nothing but took the list and started typing on her computer. She clicked again and again, and right as Kyle didn't think he could take the silence anymore, her nose scrunched up in confusion.

"Most of these newspaper articles should be in the online database but aren't for some reason," Lissie said.

"Yeah, that was my problem too."

"We should have the originals on microfiche. I can look in the back for you. But this book—Midwest Mysteries & Other Phenomena by Silus Oak… we definitely should have that," she said as she got out of her chair and walked quickly away from the desk. Kyle was unsure of whether he was supposed to wait or follow her and finally decided on following her. She was fast, however, and Kyle was only able to find her because he had been to the very spot where she was now standing.

"I didn't think I'd lost all memory of the Dewey Decimal system," said Kyle as Lissie ran her fingers over the spines of the books that should have been on either side of Midwest Mysteries.

"It says we have it," said Lissie.

"I guess someone might have stolen it?" asked Kyle.

"Probably. But if they did, it wasn't that long ago. I checked that book out myself a few weeks ago. For, uh… the same reason as you wanted it, I guess." Lissie sounded slightly embarrassed at this, which surprised Kyle. She carried herself with such confidence that he wasn't sure the young woman would be capable of embarrassment.

"I guess I could order a copy online," he said.

"If you can find it. But I'm guessing you won't," said Lissie. "The book was self-published. We only have a copy of the book here because it was written by a local who just so happened to be the husband of the head librarian here. Do you remember her? Jeannie Oak?"

"Jeannie? Oh, yeah, sure. She was great." Kyle recalled her face instantly. Warm brown eyes. Dark red lipstick. Her brown hair pulled back into a loose bun. "I guess I never knew her last name."

"I remember she was giving out copies of it after Silus died. She apparently had boxes of them."

"Do you think she still has some?" asked Kyle.

"She died a couple years after her husband," Lissie said. Without saying another word, she shot off back toward the main librarian's desk. He followed her, but she disappeared through a thin door behind the counter. He assumed he wasn't allowed back there, so he decided to pretend to look at the shelf of recent arrivals to occupy his time. After twenty minutes of this, he'd thoroughly looked over all the books on the rack and was considering returning to the electronic catalog, when Lissie came back out. Her cheeks were red, and there were beads of sweat on her brow.

"They're gone," she said, whispering.

"The microfiche?" Kyle said. Lissie nodded her head. "Well, do you remember much from your reading of the book? Was there much about—"

"Look, Mr. Thomas… I'll see what notes I took. I think I even photocopied the relevant chapter. But let's talk about this somewhere else, okay?" Lissie's eyes darted from side to side. All of this took Kyle aback. He could think of few places safer than a library. This was the place he'd fled to as a kid after a hard day at school. This was the place that loved and cared about him. To see such raw panic on the young woman's face was disorienting.

"Okay. Look, I can try some other searches while I'm here. But… Lissie, why are you so afraid? What aren't you telling me?"

"I'll explain when we meet," Lissie whispered. "Maybe tomorrow at Max's insurance office? I'm done there at four. But remember what I said. Something's weird about all of this. Even before this. So be careful." With that, she walked away. He moved to follow her again, to try to get a few answers before tomorrow, when a different librarian came up to him. She was skinny, with silver-streaked black hair cut into a bob. Her chin was pointed and prominent. This, along with her thick black glasses gave her a slightly severe look.

"Can I help you with anything, Sir," she asked. Kyle thought she had a slightly unfriendly tone. He planned to object to this, when he realized that, from the outside, it probably looked as though he'd upset Lissie. He tried his most affable smile on the woman instead.

"No, thanks. The young woman already helped me. I think I'm going to do a little more searching. But I appreciate you asking," he said. The woman's features softened, and she smiled as well.

"Oh. Well, good. We always like to hear that. If you need anything else, we're here to help," she said. "I'm Yvonne, and I'd be happy to help you. I think the young woman you were talking to is due for a break. Come see me if you need anything else."

"Right. Will do, Yvonne. Thank you." Kyle turned from the woman and made a beeline toward the electronic catalog. The vague feeling of dread now transformed into a ringing in his head like a four-alarm fire-bell. It'd even soured the library now. He knew he was being ridiculous. All of this would have a perfectly reasonable explanation in the end. And this dread would be revealed to be nothing more than a mix of paranoia and old scars being torn open. He was confident in this, but he still had to solve the mystery. Or, more correctly, prove that it was no real mystery at all. He kept telling himself this, like a mantra, as he sat down to the computer and continued his search.

# 13
## *Codes by Firelight*

atrick was sitting on the back steps of the farmhouse when Kyle returned. The man hopped up immediately and flashed him a toothy smile as Kyle got out of his Prius.

"I don't know how you even fit in that thing," Patrick said.

"I'm an expert at squeezing into tight spaces," Kyle replied. Patrick's eyes grew wide with scandal for a second, he glanced around and then laughed.

"I guess I can testify to that." Patrick noticed the small stack of printed paper in Kyle's hand. "You doing some research?" Kyle jerked his head toward the door, indicating they should go inside. Patrick nodded and followed Kyle into the kitchen.

"So, are you —" started Patrick. But Kyle pinned him against the counter and kissed him hungrily. Patrick got the hint and started kissing back, his tongue searching Kyle's mouth. He slid his tongue over Kyle's, and they fumbled to take each other's clothes off. Kyle pulled on Patrick's shirt to pull it out from his tight jeans with such force that, once it finally gave, his hand flew to the side and knocked over an old jar filled with potpourri. The jar smashed as it fell to the floor, scattering its contents. The two men looked at it for a moment, and then laughed as the floral and sweet smell of dried seed pods and petals filled the room. Under the sweetness was something else. The dry and dusty scent of decay. But both were too preoccupied to notice it.

An hour later, they were both sitting naked on the old green couch in the living room.

"Sorry, I'm eventually going to be able to have a conversation again with you," said Kyle.

"Hey, you won't hear me complaining," said Patrick with a wink. "But you still haven't answered my question."

"Yeah. Sorry. I am looking into Dunbar's Grove. Or trying to. I've got nowhere to go with the note my dad left me. But I can't help but think the book is involved somehow in whatever this is. The weird thing is, all I found were some old interviews with my dad. He hadn't given one in five years. Or maybe people lost interest. And everything specifically about the grove—the place—was gone from the library. I even checked some of the online databases of the towns around here. And there are no signs of this book that was supposed to talk about it."

"That is creepy," said Patrick. They sat in silence then, for a little while longer. Kyle looked around the house. The photos were still on the floor where he'd left them the first night. The stack of half-used sticky notes sat next to the television.

"Is it possible I'm going insane? I'm freaking myself out?" asked Kyle. Patrick looked at him in concern.

"Hey. I was planning on going to South Bend tonight. You

can come with me. I can introduce you to my friends. We can blow off some steam. Maybe get a little high? Dance to some bad electronic music," he suggested.

"That sounds fun, but I'm not sure I'm in the mood," said Kyle, patting Patrick on the leg. "But you should go. I should probably get some more work done around here anyway."

"The longer you put it off, the longer you stick around." Patrick leaned over and pecked Kyle on the cheek. "Why not invite some people over and have some fun here? Have a bonfire and drink? The nights have been pretty cool. You could invite your friend Max. Invite Janie and her husband, too. It'll be fun."

"I don't know," Kyle said. He didn't want to say that, while that might seem like fun, that particular mix of people might prove more stressful than relaxing. But he was frustrated by the day's failed attempt at sleuthing. And if he kept pouting, he was probably going to end up alone and creeped out in his parents' old house again. And Patrick was looking up at him with his adorable eyes that were awfully hard to say no to. "Okay. Let's do it."

Lissie spent the rest of her shift (in between guests) searching eBay, checking different inter-library loan systems, and calling the few remaining bookstores in the area. No one had any copies of Midwest Mysteries. She knew more than a few people in town had the book considering the way Jeannie was giving them away, but asking around about it would invite more scrutiny. She hoped she was being paranoid. The disappearance of the book was unsettling. But for the newspaper files to go missing was positively eerie. She was tempted to pretend to be sick so she could go home and search her personal files for the photocopies she'd made. But Yvonne was being even pricklier than usual tonight for some reason. And Lissie didn't feel like poking that bear.

"Yvonne, I've got all the returns put back," she said as she wearily pushed the now-empty cart back toward the front desk. "Yvonne?" No answer came, but Lissie was sure she heard movement in the backroom. She abandoned the cart and stepped behind the front desk. She waited for more noise or movement. She mentally ticked off the checklist of tasks she'd done as she closed the library. She'd turned off all the main lights. She'd locked all the doors. Hadn't she? Yes, she was sure of it.  But if this was Yvonne, she'd have responded.

She heard nothing else from behind the door. She waited there, not daring to move or breathe, wishing the air conditioning would shut off for a moment so she could hear more clearly. She didn't hear anything coming from the other side of the door now.

"Fuck this," she whispered, annoyed with how scared she felt. She flung the door open.

There was nothing on the other side except the short hallway that connected to the cataloging room and archives. She shut the door again and expelled the breath she'd been holding. She was getting paranoid. She returned to the cart and pulled it back behind the desk. She crouched down and pushed aside a small curtain that concealed a cubby where the librarians stored their personal items while on shift. Lissie retrieved her wallet and noticed that Yvonne's large mauve purse was still there. Which meant she was still in the building somewhere. Probably downstairs tidying up the children's section a little more. She'd been known to go a little overboard with cleaning and sanitizing.

It was only as Lissie stood back up, the angle being just right, that she saw that Yvonne's purse was slightly unzipped. And inside she could see a tiny sliver of something aqua blue. It was only because the color was so distinctive that Lissie did something she would normally not have done. She bent down again, unzipped the purse, and retrieved the item inside. Midwest Mysteries, in all its hideously designed, self-published glory. There was no way she could ever forget the distinctive, eye-searing blue that Silus Oak had chosen for the book's cover. Combined with the crude drawings of Big Foot, a werewolf, and a lake monster on the front, it was easy to see why Jeannie Oak had to give so many copies away. Lissie felt slightly numb as she held it in her hands, flipped the book open to the first page, and confirmed that it was, indeed, the Essen Public Library's copy. She did not have long to consider the implications of all of this, however.

A large, strong hand suddenly clasped over her mouth. Lissie's eyes widened as an arm wrapped around her waist and pulled her backward. She held onto the book for a moment or two, before it fell from her hand. She kicked out her legs. She screamed into the hand that was covering the lower part of her face. But she could not stop herself from being dragged backward through the door. She grabbed onto the door frame with the tips of her fingers, a surge of adrenaline assisting. Hope rose within her that she could resist whoever was attacking her. She bit down hard into the flesh of the hand over her mouth. Her attacker did not howl in pain, but he—she was sure it was a he—did remove his hand. She screamed at the top of her lungs. She'd meant to call for Yvonne, or scream for help, but all that came out was a terrified roar. It didn't last long. She felt a quick, sharp sting in her neck and blackness overtook her.

A bonfire blazed in the backyard of the old Thomas farm. The group ended up being smaller than initially planned. Heather declined the invitation, and instead decided to spend the night in with Zee. Janie's husband sent his apologies (along with assurances he did want to catch up with Kyle soon) but said he'd had a long day at work. That way he could watch the kids and Janie could enjoy herself. Kyle wasn't too sure she would, though. She sat on the edge of the lawn chair and concentrated on the skewered hot dog she was roasting over the fire. Patrick, Kyle, and Max were bouncing along to the Bluetooth speaker through which Max was streaming his own personal playlist. It might have helped that the guys had all knocked back a few already, but Janie abstained.

"You okay over there Janie?" Max asked.

"Yeah, sorry. Trying to get this thing cooked," Janie said in reply.

"I'd say this is like old times, but there's no way in hell we'd be hanging out if that were the case," said Max.

"Why not?" asked Patrick right before biting into his own hot dog, sending a stream of ketchup and mustard gushing out the other end.

"Janie thought I was a bad influence," noted Max.

"To be fair, she was not wrong," said Kyle.

"Thank you. After all these years, it's nice for that to be recognized," said Janie.

"Hey, I was way better than those three dickheads he hung out with before I showed up. What were their names? Dick, Harry, and

Balls?" Max washed the last of his hot dog down with some beer and started loading up his skewer with marshmallows.

"Dustin, David, and Chad," Janie said, rolling her eyes.

"And Patrick wouldn't have been around. What with him being in… fifth or sixth grade at the time?" asked Max. Janie let out a snort, which she seemed more surprised by than any of the guys.

"And Heather would have been in seventh grade," countered Kyle.

"Gay guys don't blink an eye at age differences," said Patrick. "I mean, from my experience."

"No, that seems to be pretty true," agreed Kyle. "I mean, within a certain range. After a certain age."

"That's because you're both guys, and guys are creeps." Janie used her bun to slide her (now thoroughly charred) hot dog off the skewer.

"That sounds awfully homophobic," said Max, enjoying his own pot-stirring.

"Wrong. I like to consider it a statement made about the male of the species," said Janie. "I mean, I don't like to over-generalize, but most guys—left to their own devices—seem to lack boundaries. To put it nicely."

"Sounds refreshing to me," said Max.

"Hey, I did do my damnedest to make you see the light." Kyle wagged a hot dog at Max to emphasize his point.

"That's one of the reasons I didn't like you hanging out with him," said Janie. "I mean, this is back when I thought I still had a chance."

"You know, it's not like old times," Kyle said quickly, getting a little worried where the conversation was veering, "but man it feels good. I mean that. I'm glad to have the two people in Essen I would actually want to spend my time with beside me. And a new friend." Kyle turned to Patrick, who gave him a quick kiss.

"You guys are annoyingly adorable," Janie said.

"Thanks, I think," said Patrick. Suddenly his smile faded. "Oh, and if you guys don't mind, my parents don't know about me or all of this so—"

"Your secret's safe with me," Janie assured him. Max nodded his head in agreement, his mouth too full of melted marshmallow to do anything else. "I wish… never mind."

"What, Janie? Don't start holding back now," said Kyle.

"I was thinking how much I wish Henry were here. I didn't mean to bring the mood down."

"Nonsense," said Max, lifting his beer up. The others followed suit with their drinks. "For Henry." The other three echoed him, and they all took a drink.

"I hate to ask but… who's Henry?" asked Patrick.

"He was one of our friends from school," said Kyle. He didn't say anything about the fact that for a few years in middle school, Henry had gone from his best friend to the butt of his jokes. That was a little more truth than he cared to admit to Patrick this early on. But he did catch the look in Janie's eye as he spoke. It wasn't recrimination, exactly. More like profound sadness. "He died over in Iraq. His dad was always going on about how he was too soft. I think his dad was afraid Henry was queer. If he was, he never told me. Anyway, he decided to join the army and prove his dad wrong and…"

"He'd only been on active duty four months," said Janie. The words hung there between the four of them. Kyle could feel his buzz wearing off, and the general good spirit of the night was souring. He decided to take advantage of the lull in conversation to change the topic. It wasn't exactly a cheerier topic, but it was the one he'd been obsessing over the last couple days.

"I want to talk to you guys about something. It stays between the four of us. I mean, Patrick knows about it because he was here when it happened. But I'd love to get your thoughts on it," said Kyle. Both Max and Janie's interest was clearly piqued.

"Shoot," said Max. When Janie nodded in agreement, Kyle got up out of his chair.

"Great, I'll be right back. I'm going to run and get something," said Kyle. He practically ran up the stairs to his parents' room and removed the white sheet from the typewriter entirely.

"You know what this is about?" Kyle could hear Max asking as he returned with the page.

"Not sure it's my story to tell," said Patrick.

"Read this," said Kyle as he handed the sheet to Max. Max turned so that the firelight was falling on the paper.

"Hello dear homophobic parents, I—"

"Uh, you can skip down to the last line," Kyle said quickly. But Max gave Patrick a 'good for you' wink, which clearly indicated he had read everything.

"It's up to you now, son," Max read, the smirk on his face fading. "Your dad wrote this? To you?"

"Your guess is as good as mine," said Kyle. "I'm not aware of him having any other sons though." He filled Max and Janie in on the rest of the story. How he'd found the typewritten page, the mysterious disappearance of the book and articles in the library, and the rest. By the time he was done, Janie's eyes were wide. Max was sitting back in his lawn chair and he studied the crackling fire as it spat out a plume of glowing embers.

"You know, I think I have a copy of that book. I think Jeannie gave me one. I might have to dig around in the garage to find it, though," said Janie, who was now reading the typewritten note for herself.

"That'd be great. Lissie is supposed to give me the notes she took on it, but having the original might be a big help," said Kyle.

"My Lissie?" asked Max.

"Yeah. Apparently, her curiosity was piqued by my dad's book and the whole mystery."

"Well, hell. All of this shit is swirling right around me, and here I am clueless like an idiot," said Max.

"Hey, it is like old times," Janie said.

"Can you guys think of anything that might help?" asked Patrick, getting a little impatient.

"I can't think of anything off the top of my head, but I'll keep my eyes open," said Max.

"Wait, what's this?" asked Janie, who now had the bottom edge of the sheet right up to her eyeballs. She got her phone out, turned on the flashlight, and studied it even closer. "There are numbers on the bottom here. Well, the top half of some numbers. The three guys got up and huddled around her, and confirmed that there were, indeed, numbers on the bottom of the paper. The fact they were half-cut off made them a little hard to make out in some cases, but together they decided that they were two groupings of eight numbers each. Near the left edge of the paper was written:

20-8-5 7-18-15-22-5

And then on the right edge was written:

$$20\text{-}8\text{-}5\ 3\text{-}3\text{-}15\text{-}4\text{-}5$$

"It's some code, right?" asked Max. "The first grouping of both looks the same."

"Yeah, which is also weird. My dad hated codes. Especially in books. He said they were always so brain-dead simple and… fuck," said Kyle, as he grabbed his phone and opened the browser. "Give me the numbers." Janie read them out loud, and with a push of a button, Kyle had his answer.

"So, you knew the code?" asked Patrick, his eyes wide with excitement.

"It's pretty much the most basic code out there. You assign the number one to the letter A and then on down to the rest of the alphabet," said Kyle.

"Oh yeah, I remember that. I think it was pretty hot to send notes using that kind of code in third grade for about two weeks," said Janie.

"Until we realized that literally every human being in the world could figure out the 'code' and gave up on it," said Kyle.

"And? What the fuck does it say? Don't leave us hanging," urged Max. Kyle turned his screen so they could all see:

*20-8-5 7-18-15-22-5 = THE GROVE*
*20-8-5 3-3-15-4-5 = THE CCODE*

"What's the 'C Code'?" asked Patrick.

"I think that's supposed to be read 'the code.' I don't think dad was trying to make this hard for me," said Kyle.

"The extra letter is in there so they both have the same number of digits," Janie said quickly, catching on. "So that you knew they were equal. Dunbar's Grove is 'the code.'"

# The Long Path Through the Woods

An excerpt from
*Dunbar's Grove*
by Herbert Thomas

I did not see my way through the grove so much as felt it. The cold wind made it painful to open my tear-racked eyes, sweat was pouring down my forehead, and even in the midst of the trees of the grove, the rain was beating down heavily. I cradled Anne in my arms, trying to take extra care that her head and feet did not brush up against any errant limbs. I could not have stood any more damage to come to her once beautiful form. How heavy she felt now. I thought of all the times I'd held her to me or lifted her up in a hug. In life, she'd felt as light as air in my arms. In death, she felt like a lead weight. With each step in the mud and the muck of the trail, my feet seemed to sink further and further into the ground. If it swallowed me up then, I would not have protested.

The grove itself was so far from the sun-dappled paradise it used to be when Anne and I first met. In the forty years since, it'd grown rank with the disease of the world. I knew well enough to know now that the perfect serenity it held in the past was probably an illusion, and the spoil and rot that roiled beneath the surface had always been there. But there was a sort of holy reverence for the grove when I first met Anne on that checkered blanket, under the tree we all used to call The Grandfather. Now the graveyard in the woods was regularly desecrated. Limbs were torn from the trees, the bark of which held carvings of a much more crude and lascivious nature than the simple hearts and initials of my childhood. There was a sickness here, now. And I was a part of it.

My every ambition led me here. They manifested themselves in every root that sought to trip me up. My every naked want were the stones that stubbed my toes. My unrelenting need for a little more was the mud in which my boots were sinking. I did not fully understand why I was bringing Anne here. Fear was undoubtedly a part of it. But there was also a sense that this is where she belonged. The poetry of it did not escape me. This was the place I first laid eyes on her. This was the place she was truly born for me. And it was to this place that I ultimately sacrificed her. I did not want to bury her body in an unmarked grave. As tainted as the place seemed to me now, at least I could bury her in the graveyard in the grove. At least she wouldn't be alone. If these thoughts seem scattered or even mad to you, then you understand my mind as I took her to this place.

Finally, I reached the graveyard. I tried to find her a place of her own. But the graves were so destroyed and strewn all over. I had no way of knowing as my hands tore into wet dirt if they might find time-worn bones or the splinters of some long-degraded casket. More than once, I wondered if the thick strands of roots I pulled up and out of the hole I was desperately making were roots at all. By the time I was finished making a hole that seemed large enough to fit Anne's body, I was utterly covered in mud and filth. I slid her body into the hole, and to my horror, she did not sink into the mud and rainwater that already filled it. She floated there, as serenely as she did in the lake in the summer when the sun caressed her every curve. I pressed her body down with one hand and began sweeping the mud around the hole back into it, to cover her up. Slowly, enough of the rain-soaked earth was on top of her that it displaced the water and she stayed in the ground.

I found the mostly intact remains of a large headstone and dragged it with much effort over to the ground that swallowed her body. I hoped the weight of it might keep her down, even if the rains kept up. Hoped it would provide shelter from the rain so the mud wouldn't wash away. I don't know if that makes sense. But it did at the time. My throat was sore with choked sobs. I no longer even felt like a man as I dragged myself back through the path and out of the grove. The ground and I were one. I was a thing of mud and roots and scattered bits of bone. When I finally reached the car, I stripped off all my clothes and lay on the hood, letting the rain wash over me for some time before I got back into the car and drove home. But I wasn't entirely clean. I would never be entirely clean.

# 14

# *An Alternate Reading of the Situation*

Kyle woke with a start to the sound of nearby thunder. His copy of Dunbar's Grove, and his notebook, fell to the floor. He was still fully dressed, but at least his neck wasn't sore since he'd fallen asleep on his old childhood bed and not the couch. He'd had a horrible nightmare, as if the last passage he'd read from the book had come to life. Except his dad was the titular protagonist of Dunbar's Grove and his mom was his doomed wife, Anne. He wasn't sure how long he'd been up re-reading the book and taking notes. Max and Janie left thirty minutes after they'd discovered the other coded message his dad had left him. Patrick stayed a little longer, but he could tell Kyle was preoccupied, and he needed to get to bed for an early start the next morning. Kyle was a little sorry for that. He'd have liked to lay in bed with Patrick a while, to feel his heat next to him. But he was preoccupied. He wanted to get back to Dunbar's Grove. He wanted to see what his dad had hidden there for him.

Kyle looked at the notes he'd scribbled the night before. He didn't have a lot to go on. Nothing particularly new revealed itself to him. If Kyle was honest, he thought his dad's writing was a little overwrought. He did not exactly find it a page-turner. It'd been his dad's best-selling book, though. What did he know? Although he suspected the 'controversy' around it was one of the sales drivers. After his morning coffee, he decided to try to clear his head and get something done around the house. A few hours later, he'd tagged everything upstairs with Post-it notes, and even hauled the Jesus painting down from his parents' bedroom and placed it next to the large display cabinet full of dishes. He felt a little guilty throwing Jesus away, despite being a long way away from his religious years. Some new set of parents might want to hang it to torment their children for years to come.

After he'd showered, he found himself automatically getting into his car and driving into town. The rain was letting up some, and the sun was out again. His dad's book and his notebook were sitting in the passenger's seat. He pulled up to the AllCare insurance office and walked inside. Max came bolting out from his back office excitedly.

"Oh, it's you," he said, slowing and wiping his counterfeit grin off his face as he approached.

"What a warm welcome. Lissie off today?" asked Kyle. He'd hoped he might find Lissie here. They hadn't made any exact plans for her to give him the info, and it's not like they'd had a chance to exchange phone numbers.

"Yeah, she didn't show up for work today! Although I wasn't too sad, to be honest, because I wasn't sure if I could have paid her."

"She didn't seem like the type to skip out. I mean, from my

first impression."

"Eh. You can tell you've never been a manager. Anyway, sorry about the reception, man. Business has been slow as hell this week," said Max.

"No worries. I get it. Well, if you have a little time, want to help me out with something?"

"Well, if it's about some freaky messages and codes, I don't know if I'm the guy. I'm the only one of us who hasn't read the book yet." Despite his words, Max waved Kyle on back to his office.

"That's why I thought you might give me a fresh perspective," said Kyle as he sat in the same uncomfortable chair as before.

"Let me guess, Janie was too busy?" asked Max. Kyle immediately looked guilty.

"Well, uh, yeah she was busy at work."

"I'm at work," said Max, spreading his arms and looking from side to side as a reminder of where they were sitting.

"I said busy at work."

"Ouch. As I said, though, I'm not a big code guy," said Max.

"Well, I think that's okay. I don't think the book is literally a code. My dad hated codes in books. He didn't like mysteries either. Hell, he didn't even much care for Encyclopedia Brown books. He used to take mine after I was done to see if he could figure out the mystery within the first two pages."

"All right, what do you think he meant, then?"

"Well, that's where I thought I could use your help. As someone who hasn't read the book. I think the reason my dad told me that Dunbar's Grove was a code in the way he did—with a cheesy code system—was to remind me how much he hated that sort of thing. That way I'd know that wasn't what he was going to do in his book," said Kyle.

"That seems… complicated."

"Exactly. Dad was a lot of things, but one thing I did always admire was that he liked things to be straightforward. All of this—the note, the code, and the book—they don't feel like something he'd do normally. Then again, neither did him killing himself."

"Right. Okay, so can you give me the Cliff Notes version of your dad's book?"

"Basically, it's about a farmer named Dunbar. He's in an unnamed town that is pretty much Essen. It starts off with Dunbar meeting his future wife, Anne, in the titular grove," said Kyle. Max let out a small giggle, and Kyle rolled his eyes.

"Sorry, I forgot this was all very serious and creepy," said Max.

"Right, so the grove where he meets her is all sunshine and quaint scenes of boys and girls holding hands while having picnic lunches on checkered blankets. Real 50s Leave it to Beaver shit. The first half of the book is all about them meeting and becoming a couple and getting married, etc. It's pretty much classic Herbert Thomas from what little I read of his books as a teenager. I was more into Zahn's Star Wars novels at the time. Not an author who, as the blurb on the back of the book notes, 'captures with delicate intensity the daily lives of the American Midwest farmer with all its oft-ignored complexities.'"

"Yeah, I gotta say. Heather got me his last book… The Farmer's Wife? The Farmer's Niece? Something like that. I only got ten pages in," said Max.

"Halfway through, the book goes off the rails. Anne and Dunbar are fighting about his constant need to upgrade and improve the farm and maximize their profits. She's arguing that he's working everyone on the farm too hard. It might be worth noting here that the couple—who are undeniable parallels of my parents right down the descriptions of their house and their looks—are childless in the book. So, thanks for that, dad," said Kyle. Max didn't say anything, but he did throw Kyle a sympathetic look. "Anyway, they're arguing in the backyard. Dunbar gets mad, pushes Anne…and she splits her head open on the stairs leading up to the kitchen."

"Oh, shit," said Max, leaning forward a little in his chair.

"Exactly. He knows there's no way this will look like an accident, so he takes Anne's body to the grove and buries her in the mud in the graveyard. Somehow, I guess because he's well connected and loved in the town, Dunbar gets away with it. Everyone thinks his wife disappeared. The second half of the book is about how he unravels. The farm goes down the tubes. Dunbar starts to go mad with guilt. It ends with him returning to the grove. He lays down in the mud, and it swallows him up."

"That's… that's a lot, man."

"Tell me about it." Kyle looked at the copy of Dunbar's Grove. The cover was taken up mostly by the name of the book in large, bold letters on a black background. Within the letters was an artist's rendition of the grove itself, all massive shadowy trees. "There is a lot in the book that's autobiographical. The way he describes Dunbar and Anne's relationship at the start certainly feels a lot like how I remember them together. But beyond that… my mom only died five years ago, not twelve. And she didn't disappear. She died of a heart attack. I got her death certificate. Doctor Otto signed it. He's been our family doctor for forever. She was cremated as instructed in her will—which hadn't been changed in over a decade. And my dad… well… you know the story there," said Kyle.

"Yeah, I do." Max opened a drawer in his desk and produced a bottle of scotch and two tumblers. A quick pour later, Kyle took a tumbler gratefully and let the smooth burn of the scotch course down his throat.

"Even the first time I read it; I could tell the grove was some metaphor. I mean, that much is pretty obvious. It's this perfect thing that Dunbar is trying to recapture or remake. That's ultimately what leads to Anne's death. This search for a place that might not have ever existed except in his head. I've never heard any stories about the real grove in Essen that ever made it seem like some wholesome hang-out spot, though," said Kyle. "That's why I was hoping to get some info on the history of it. I hope Lissie has some luck with that book."

Max sat back in his plush chair. He was looking at Kyle thoughtfully. He finished off his tumbler of scotch and then poured himself another before he spoke again.

"Kyle, look. We're basically like brothers, right? I mean, I know we haven't talked in a lot of years. I got busy, you got busy. We had our own lives. It happens. If I'm honest, I wasn't sure what it'd be like when you got back in town. But the way we fell right back in… it convinced me. We're brothers. Because that's what brothers do. Hell, in another life—"

"Yeah. I feel it, too Max. Although you're worrying me a little with this touchy-feely preamble," said Kyle. Max smiled weakly. Max wasn't one to talk about feelings. He'd go out of his way to do anything but. Except one time before. Kyle and Max had gotten way too drunk. But instead of getting horny, Max got somber. He'd finally told Kyle about his sister, Serena. She was three years old when a drunk driver smashed into their family car. She'd died instantly. It was the reason his parents moved from Texas and came to Essen. A fresh start. Kyle held Max then and let him sob onto his shoulder.

"Well, then take what I'm about to say like it's from one brother to another. I know it's been rough for you since you've been back in town. You've had the creeps, right? I mean, for lack of a better word for it?"

"That's as good a word as any, sure."

"Well, do you think that all that might be affecting how you're taking all this in? I mean, maybe your dad did leave you that note. I'm guessing he probably did. But what if he wanted to make sure you knew that he wrote Dunbar's Grove for you?"

"I think that's pretty much established," said Kyle. He felt strangely defensive, and he wasn't sure why.

"No. I mean, you're thinking there's some dark secret you have to uncover here, right? I mean, we don't know what that might be, but that's the vibe you're giving off," said Max.

"It sounds a little cheesy when you say it like that. But I guess that's the general gist."

"What if your dad wrote this book because he regretted what he did? What if it's an apology to you? I mean, you said in the book he killed his wife after an argument twelve years ago. Well, fifteen years ago he kicked you out of the house. What if Anne isn't your mom but… it's you?" asked Max. Kyle felt like he'd been punched in the gut. He could hardly believe Max of all people was the one to deliver the blow. He did love Max like a brother. Max was his friend after he finally stopped hanging around with Dustin, David, and Chad. Henry wouldn't talk to him again at first. And Janie didn't much like him either. Max had been an unlikely friend; he was handsome, muscular, and good at sports. But they recognized the strangeness in each other. They understood that as they both made their way through the halls of Essen High, they were apart from their classmates, and not by their own choosing. But Max was never the most emotionally complex person. Kyle relied on Janie to be his support system for all of that. Yet, here he was, pointing out something Kyle hadn't even considered.

"Damn. Heather must have been a good influence on you," Kyle said.

"I'll tell her you said that. I think she might have a little crush on you," said Max with a wink. The jingle-jangle of the front door sounded.

"Hello? Anyone here?" asked an elderly voice from the front of the office.

"Shit. Oh man, I hate to—" began Max.

"You've already been a huge help. Go make some money. We'll catch up later," said Kyle, quickly getting up out of the seat and making his way to the front right behind Max.

"Well, Mrs. Broadwell, you're a sight for sore eyes," Max said happily to a small, hunched-over woman. Kyle nodded at the woman politely and then headed straight out the door.

He couldn't help but feel a little like a balloon with all the air let out of it. He sat in his car, looking at Dunbar's Grove and his notebook and felt like an idiot. The one thing he'd been resisting the whole trip was getting to know his parents. It's why he hadn't wanted to look at the photos again. It's why he'd resisted going into their bedroom. It's why he hadn't read any of his dad's books since he left home until Dunbar's Grove. But that's precisely what his father wanted him to do. His dad wanted to explain to him who his parents were. Except, since his dad wasn't the sort of person who liked to talk about his feelings (it was too sissy) he wrote an entire book as an allegory about his regret? It both made every bit of sense in the world and made little sense at all. Because it did seem a little too complicated for his dad's tastes. But Kyle had to admit the idea certainly appealed to him more than Dunbar's Grove being a murderer's confession.

# 15
# *All Smiles*

Kyle didn't feel like going back to the farm yet. And now he had a new angle to tackle with his research. He was back at the Essen Public Library. He watched the shadows of the trees sway lazily in the post-storm breeze over the brown brick of the building. All the menace was sucked out of it, now. The creeping dread in the back of his brain was gone. It'd been replaced by guilt and embarrassment. But he pushed on because that's what you do when you are an adult. And he was here to find out more about his parents.

"Hi Mr. Thomas," called a familiar voice the instant he walked into the building. He was shocked to see Lissie there at the main librarian's desk. She was smiling and waving at him.

"Hey, Lissie. I was at AllCare. Max said you were a no-show," Kyle said. Lissie rolled her eyes, which was way more in character than the smile she'd greeted him with.

"I told him I was changing up my hours this week because one of the other librarians was on vacation. He probably forgot," said Lissie. "Anyway, I have good news and bad news about the materials you wanted that had to do with The Grove." Kyle's eyes darted around. Lissie wasn't loud, exactly, but she was talking much more boldly about it all than she had been before.

"Oh. That's great. I might be on a different track, now. But I'd love to see what you have. Did you find the photocopies of the book?"

"That's the bad news. I'm afraid not." Lissie frowned as she pulled a folder of papers out from under the desk. "I must have thrown it out. I don't think there was much of interest in it. Silus Oak wasn't all that great about documenting sources, either. What little there was to it wasn't even that reliable. However, I did figure out where our missing articles disappeared to."

"Really?" Kyle took the folder from her and saw it had pages of print outs from the digitized archives.

"They're on the computer now, too. I talked to the tech guys who do our site, and I guess they changed the web hierarchy on the site, and half the articles in the database weren't tagged properly. You were just the first lucky customer to run across them," said Lissie.

"Huh. Well now I feel even more stupid for getting all worked up about it," said Kyle. "Any luck with the microfiche?"

"Eh. I was right there with you. Welcome to Essen. We've got to take our excitement where we can," said Lissie. "And I talked to the head librarian about the microfiche. She said some of it had been disposed of due to a miscommunication when everything was digitized. They had an outside company come in and do it. It's horrible to think that those are gone." A slightly imperious woman in her forties with freshly-bleached blonde hair and a white leather jacket came up beside Kyle.

"Miss, can you help me find the mysteries, please?" she asked, apparently not even noting Kyle's presence. Lissie glanced at Kyle, who nodded his head, so she knew it was fine with him if she helped the woman. As she did that, Kyle sat in one of the large chairs at the end of the aisle that held the history section of the library. He glanced through the articles in the folder hungrily. Even though he was looking at this little mystery from a different angle now, he did wonder if his dad might have researched The Grove too, and whether that might give any insight into the book. But the articles were largely a disappointment. Even the articles with the more eye-catching headlines ("Mysterious Disappearance at The Grove Concerns Sheriff") ended blandly. The mystery was solved. The people were found—often it was some teenager who was found the next day at a friend's house with a hangover. One of the articles was a review of Silus's Midwest Mysteries book. It was not particularly kind. In two neat paragraphs, it summed the book up and decided that "while the subject matter has definite potential, the lack of sources and meandering focus gives the effect of a book of fairy tales in need of a good editor."

Kyle closed the folder and glanced over and saw Lissie helping the woman in the white leather coat. She gave the woman a teeth-baring smile as she checked out a stack of three paperback mystery novels for her. The old tingle of dread started back up again. He told himself it was silly. He'd only met Lissie twice. He did not know her. But there was something about this smiling, talkative Lissie that felt unnatural. He flipped through the articles he'd been given again. They'd all been published in the now-defunct Essen Town Crier. He'd searched other sources, but it seemed like few people outside of Essen were concerned with The Grove.

However, he could see that the book review of Midwest Mysteries was picked up from the South Bend Tribune. A quick check on his phone confirmed that the Tribune was still in business, and even had an electronic archive. The review was far back enough that it hadn't been fully digitized—the text wasn't searchable. Instead, there were images of the pages. But Kyle knew the rough period the review must have been published in, and it didn't take him long to find it. The instant he saw it, his body felt like it'd been flooded with ice water. The printed review didn't have two paragraphs. There were three. And the excised portion wasn't from the end of the article but from the middle. Kyle glanced up and saw that Lissie was still at the front desk, looking at her computer. She lifted her head and caught Kyle's stare. She smiled at him, and Kyle was sure it looked unnatural now. He nodded his head back at her and returned it, but his mind whirled. It's possible the review was edited down for space when it was picked up by the Town Crier. But he had no way of confirming that now that the microfiche was gone. And the section that was omitted was precisely the sort of thing he'd been looking for.

While many of the so-called "mysteries" presented in the book are likely the result of some combination of a lack of electric light, homemade moonshine, and good old-fashioned ignorance, one section does stand out. Oak's description of the mysterious grove near town and his recounting of the many tales of disappearances in the area is particularly moody and evocative. It's a shame there's not more of that. Of course, it's as under-documented as every other section, though the author insists this is due to an extensive cover-up by the nearby community.

Kyle closed the folder, got slowly up from the chair, and walked as casually as he could toward the front door. He made sure not to make eye contact with Lissie. He sat in his car and gripped the steering wheel. For the first time, he was genuinely unsure of how to proceed. Two paths were now clear to him. The way that Max suggested was much clearer and made so much more sense. The other path, the far murkier one that led to nothing more than a vague sense of menace, was certainly more interesting. And this interest made him wary. As an investigative journalist, he tried to follow the story where it was leading him. He tried not to bring a lot of his own preconceptions or desires into it. But he was finding it impossible to do in this case. Still, he had to try. For now, he had to walk both paths. At least until one became clearer.

# 16
## *Connections*

Kyle wished he hadn't left the library so quickly. Despite the eeriness of the way Lissie was acting, and the possibility of the doctored articles, there was more research he could have done. Now it'd have to wait. He'd been expressly avoiding what he was now planning. But he didn't see how he could continue to avoid it, and he wanted to get there before it got dark. He needed to see The Grove for himself.

When he'd driven out to the Lake of the Grove, it'd been from the family farm with Max. This time, he was coming from town, and he was truly surprised by the number of developments that stretched out from the town center toward the lake and The Grove itself. It was like some well-to-do arm reaching out from Essen. They all had hilariously nonsensical names, too. Grafton Cliffs, Hanover Lake, Baker Falls, and so on. As if the glacier-scraped flat-lands of northern Indiana contained cliffs or waterfalls. He supposed Hanover Lake was the large retention pond next to the development, which was currently overrun by what looked like a thousand geese.

The other odd thing about it was how many houses there were. A few quick glances down the streets showed that the houses were not empty. Parents walked side by side while pushing strollers in front of them. A small gang of children on bikes roamed one of the streets. A teen and her dad played basketball in a driveway. It was as if half the town now lived in the enormous new houses that lined these new streets. Freedom Lane met Independence Boulevard. Honeysuckle Avenue crossed Wild Iris Lane. Fifteen minutes later, the new developments fell away, and Kyle rolled down his windows, cranking his stereo and letting the wind blow into his car in an attempt to soothe his nerves.

He made the turn onto the small wooden path that led into The Grove, and immediately had to slam on his brakes. A tall, chain-link fence blocked the way, with multiple signs warning that it was private property, trespassers would be prosecuted, and that the area was monitored. Kyle got out and tried to see how far the fence stretched. It appeared to surround the entirety of The Grove. He was sitting there, trying to make sense of this new development, when his phone rang. It was Janie.

"Hey Janie," he said, trying to sound calm.

"Kyle! Good, I got you. Are you okay?" she asked. Of course, she noticed he sounded strange. She always noticed.

"Did you know The Grove has a ten-foot-tall fence all around it now?"

"Yeah, I did. Wait, are you there?"

"Yes. I drove out. I thought—"

"Kyle, get in your car. Now," said Janie, with such steel in her voice, it didn't even occur to Kyle to protest. He got into his Prius, carefully backed up onto the main road, and headed toward the farmhouse.

"Okay, I'm in my car. What's wrong?" Kyle asked.

"I don't know, I think your paranoia is infecting me." Janie sounded a little exhausted and panicked. This frightened Kyle more than any of the other oddities of the last week. He'd thought of Janie as nearly unflappable. No matter what happened, she seemed to have a practical way to look at or deal with it.

"Tell me what's going on," Kyle urged.

"Well, we didn't have afternoon Kindergarten today. After I taught my last class, I left the kids at the sitter's and tried to find that book that Jeannie Oak's husband wrote. The one you mentioned."

"Did you find it?"

"Yes. I did. I was just reading through the section on The Grove. Kyle, there's a lot of creepy stuff in here. Some of it sounds like old ghost stories. But there was a note about… well, once I found out where you were… it's the coincidence of it…"

"Janie, please. Please just tell me," said Kyle, trying hard to summon all his patience.

"Silus Oak published this five years ago. He wrote 'Unfortunately, any answers about The Grove might remain forever out of our grasp now. The longtime owners of the property, the Minty Green Club, have decided to close it off to the public at the behest of the club's new president. Supposedly for safety reasons.'"

"Wait, the club owns the property?"

"Yes. I had no clue. It's right here in this book, but I can guarantee most people don't know that. I assumed it was part of the Baker's land since their farms are all around it," said Janie.

"Fuck. I guess I figured the same thing," said Kyle. He gripped his steering wheel tighter. He couldn't help but feel the other path was a little less murky now.

"It felt off. Especially since you couldn't find the book in the library. It's almost like… someone knew you might come looking for info. And for whatever reason, they didn't want you to find it?"

"Yeah. It feels a lot like that."

"There's one more thing about all of this. But, before I tell you, I want you to promise me you're going to try to keep calm about it," said Janie.

"Hey, I've managed to stay on the road so far," Kyle reassured her.

"Okay." Janie didn't sound entirely soothed by his response. "So, five years ago, Alice Manchester retired. It's when she took over the presidency of the Minty Green Club." Kyle did not respond right away. Without even realizing it, his foot pressed the gas pedal, and the car whined in response to the sudden acceleration.

"Janie, when do you pick up the kids from the sitter? Can you spare an hour? Meet at my house?" Kyle asked.

"Oh, man, Kyle, there's no way I can do it tonight. Sean's in South Bend for work. I have to pick the kids up in a half hour."

"I totally understand, Janie. Maybe tomorrow night then? I'll call Max and Patrick too and see if they can come. I've got a theory brewing. And I need a gut check on it. I need to know if it sounds totally insane."

"I'll be there. But I have to admit, all of this is making my own connection to sanity feel a little touch and go," said Janie. Kyle laughed, although it was mirthless.

"Well, at least you're in good company," Kyle said. He hung

up his phone and sped down the country road. The fog was lifting from the mysterious other path in his head. And he didn't at all like where it was leading.

# 17

# *No One Belongs Here Less Than You*

rs. Manchester's ultimate betrayal came at the end of the seventh-grade year, in a one-two punch that would send Kyle reeling and rethinking everything about the identity he'd crafted for himself. As an adult, he'd wonder at how deeply it affected him back then, and then when he returned to Essen again, he'd marvel at how deeply he still felt the sting of it all. After the incident with the blue polo, Kyle moved on. He still didn't understand why Mrs. Manchester had acted the way she did. But so tall was the pedestal on which he'd placed her, that he supposed it was some sort of character test.

And the character of her students was always on her mind. The speeches continued in class. She told them that they needed to take their responsibility as the caretakers of long-established morals and values seriously. At the same time, she urged them to question those that didn't work in today's society. This message spoke to Kyle on a personal level. Although it would be a little while longer before he fully understood why he felt different, the difference was still there. It set him apart from the rest of the world. Mrs. Manchester's uplifting speeches reminded him of the philosophical musings found in the pages of The Silver Surfer, who was one of his favorite superheroes.

He was still an alternate on the Academic Challengers team. There was a set number of team members in the competition. But he had high hopes for the next year since the eighth graders on the team would be moving onto high school. He still cheered the team on in his thirty-dollar polo. He joked and laughed with them as they sat around the little red candle-holders in the dark interior of Pizza Hut. For the first time in his life, he felt like he made sense. He felt like he had some clue of how he could fit into the world beyond the confines of his family's farm. There was a sense of relief in that he could not have explained to anyone at the time. He no longer felt like an imposter. He no longer felt like one of the shape-shifting Skrulls in the comic books, trying to pretend to be human.

And then, two weeks before the end of the school year, as he and his classmates struggled to keep focused on their work and not the upcoming summer break, Mrs. Manchester asked him to stay after class.

"Hi Kyle, thanks for waiting," she said.

"No problem. My mom's not picking me up until after our Challengers practice, so I've got time to kill," Kyle said. Mrs. Manchester's wide grin collapsed into its default pucker. This made Kyle instantly nervous.

"Well, I wanted to say how proud I've been of all the work you've put in this year. I know it's not been easy. But you managed to pull yourself out of the C you had mid-year to an A- now. That's an accomplishment," she said.

"Thanks. I… thanks," Kyle managed to utter.

"The thing is, Kyle: it gets harder in eighth grade Honors English. And the last thing I want to do is push you too hard and not have you set up for success in high school," Mrs. Manchester said.

"You don't have to worry about that. I've learned a ton—thanks to you, and the team. I know—"

"Kyle, wait. I've recommended that you not be placed in Honors English next year. It'll give you a chance to shore up some of the basics. That way, you'll go into your freshman year ready to tackle it."

"Oh. Okay." It was all Kyle could stammer out. The next moment, the woman was thrusting a blue sheet of paper into his hands.

"I thought you'd understand. Here's a copy of my recommendation for your parents to read. If they have any questions, they can ask me."

"Okay. I'll be sure to give it to them," said Kyle. There was a thick vein of people-pleasing at Kyle's core. His father, impossible to please, had unknowingly nurtured it his whole life. So as stunned as he was, and as angry as he was on some level, it would never have occurred to him to question Mrs. Manchester. He wouldn't have questioned any teacher, really. But especially not Mrs. Manchester. She'd called him the cream of the crop. She'd made him believe it. If she was now rescinding that, it was her right. He obediently folded the piece of paper and placed it within his backpack. The final 'practice' for the Academic Challengers team was more of a pep talk from Mrs. Manchester and a suggestion for how to study over the summer.

"But don't study too hard. Enjoy yourself. You've earned a

break," she said at the end.

But Kyle heard little of it. Leanne Brookes, a pale-faced girl with a tiny button nose and cheeks that always seemed too pink, approached Kyle after the meeting. She was one of the eighth graders who was leaving the team next year. She could be a little superior acting, but she had a kind heart. She asked if Kyle was okay, and it was all that it took to break through the wall of confusion that had formed in Kyle's mind since Mrs. Manchester dropped her bomb. But he smiled and said he was fine. It'd been a long day. He didn't start crying until he got into the car with his mom, and then it came out as messy blubbering. His mom was so concerned, wondering if someone had hurt him, that it added another layer of guilt to the proceedings. He found he couldn't talk, so he grabbed the blue piece of paper and handed it to her. She read it and frowned. She hugged him tighter.

"We'll talk to your dad about this," she assured him. This did not comfort Kyle, though. As he suspected, his dad didn't understand why he was so upset. He thought Kyle was being a baby about it. And Kyle thought he might have a point. He couldn't argue about Mrs. Manchester's reasoning. On the surface, it made perfect sense. She'd been compassionate about it when she told him and insisted it was for his own good. His mom was plainly furious with his father, but once Kyle accepted his father's point of view, that was the end of it.

It was only the next day while talking it over with Janie during their free period, that Kyle was able to explain why it'd hurt so bad.

"I guess it feels like it's been coming for a while. Ever since the thing with the polo. Even a little before that. I've had this feeling that she doesn't want me around for some reason. I think I didn't let myself see it. But now…"

"I know. Kyle, I'm not even on the team, and I see it. But you must see why that might be, right?" asked Janie. Her dark brown eyes were sparkling with concern. She held Kyle's hand, and he thought he loved her. He did love her. But not the way she loved him.

"Not really? I mean, I know my grades aren't as high as some of the others—"

"Oh, please. Cindy Baker talks a good game but believe me, she's not exactly part of the mental elite of Essen Middle School."

"What then?" A little of the compassion in Janie's eyes seem to flee and be replaced by impatience. It was only for a second, but Kyle certainly noticed.

"Manchester's hand-picked Academic Challengers team members all have last names like Baker, Miller, Brookes, and Shaw. What do they have in common? They're all white. They're all rich. And they've all been part of this town for a long, long time. Now you've only got two out of three of those things going for you. You don't have the money."

"Why would she care if my family had money?" asked Kyle. As hard a woman as Mrs. Manchester could be, she'd been a moral one. Almost to excess. It didn't fit into Kyle's conception of her at all.

"The same reason there's not going to be an Alvarez on the team either. They stick to their own kind," said Janie.

"But why have me on the team at all?" Kyle couldn't help but think the chip on Janie's shoulder was affecting her views on all of this. The last couple of years, she'd confided in Kyle her annoyance at the name 'Janie.' It'd seemed like a gift when she was trying to get rid of her horrible 'Yak Nita' nickname. But she'd begun to wonder if it was as bad, only in a different way.

"I don't know, Kyle. You know, I never got why you thought she was so great. Maybe she thought your parents did have money.

I mean, most people in town probably would think they did if they didn't know better. Most of the farmers around here are doing pretty well." Janie looked away from him. Kyle could tell she had something else she wanted to say.

"What else are you thinking?" he asked her.

"What she put you through with the polo was cruel. It was. And this thing with taking you out of Honors English also feels cruel." Janie turned to face him again and squeezed his hand a little harder. "I know you might not want to see it that way. But that's what I think. So, is it possible she liked having you around… like a mascot or something? It was another way to be cruel."

Kyle ripped his hand away from hers, and the look on Janie's face made it clear she knew she'd make a mistake. He got up without saying anything to her and stalked down the hallway. He ignored her as she called after him. He got to the end of the hall before he finally responded.

"I don't think we should talk for a while, Jacinta," he said. Kyle wasn't sure exactly why he'd used her given name. He was hurt, and he wanted to hurt her. And he knew, somehow, said by him in that exact way, that it would hurt her. It didn't matter that she liked her name, and actually wanted to go by it. Here was the boy she loved, saying it like a dirty word. He was so effective that a while turned out to be the last week of school and all of summer break. They made up a few months into eighth grade, but something was lost between them.

Over the summer, Kyle replayed the conversation in his head so many times. It was the mascot talk that did him in. It felt so demeaning. And for the first time, Kyle realized that he was worried about more than feeling like some non-human thing that couldn't navigate the world. He was scared that he was somehow subhuman.

He was lesser than, and always would be. The thought that Mrs. Manchester—someone he idolized despite her foibles—could have been so cruel seemed impossible. It was easier to think Janie was jealous or resentful. That was, until the start of the new school year.

Everything started well enough. Kyle loved the fall and the feeling of a new school year. New books, new pencils, new pens—all of it. It was a chance to start over. And he desperately wanted to start over. He'd yet to make up with Janie and decided to place her in the same category as Henry. She was someone he'd outgrown. He would no longer see David, Dustin, and Chad in English class. But they still had a few other classes together, and they'd still see each other at Academic Challengers. They were going to hold try-outs for anyone who wanted to join the team, and Kyle was ready for it. That, combined with his experience, meant he was a shoo-in. He'd not talked to the three guys much over the summer, but they'd gone to see the Super Mario Bros. movie (a mistake), and they all agreed with his chances.

Kyle was walking down the hall after school when he saw David approaching him. David had changed out of the shorts and t-shirt he'd been wearing when Kyle saw him before and was now wearing khakis, a white button-up shirt, a blue tie, and a dark blue overcoat. Kyle smirked at him.

"Where are you going Mr. Fancy?" he asked. David looked at him in utter confusion.

"Where are you going?" David asked.

"I asked first. But I'm going to walk to the library. My mom's picking me up there today after she gets back from shopping."

"No, I mean… aren't you coming to the banquet?"

"What banquet?" Kyle asked, suddenly feeling like he was in

a nightmare where you were shoved on a theater stage, having never been given a script to read.

"The Academic Challengers banquet. We're getting our prize money from last year," David said.

David had beautiful blue eyes, and they were crinkled in concern. His untamed blonde hair shot out in all directions from his head. Kyle didn't realize it at the time, but he definitely had a crush on him. He was the nicest of the Chad/Dustin/David trio. He'd make fun of people and shun them like all the rest of the group, but there were times when he and Kyle locked eyes and shared in a brief moment of guilt. He was also the only one of the three who would have ever shown anything like concern for him.

"Well, I'm only an alternate," Kyle suggested. It was the only thing that made sense to him. He wasn't going to get any of the prize money. That's why he wasn't invited.

"Bullshit. You're part of the team." Something about David's conviction broke through the wall of excuses he was making for Mrs. Manchester, even now. David was right, he was a part of the team. He'd been there every step of the way. He owned the damned thirty-dollar polo to prove it.

"When is it?"

"It's, uh, in ten minutes," said David, glancing down at his watch.

"But… I…" Kyle looked down at what he was wearing. Jean shorts, white tennis shoes, and a Dick Tracy T-shirt.

"You'll be fine. We're sitting at a table." With that, David kept walking. Kyle hesitated for a moment. He should not go. He should go to the library. But David wanted him to go. His other teammates probably wanted him, there too. Was it possible his invitation was lost or misplaced? Part of him wanted all of that to be true. But part of him was also pissed off. There was only one way to know the truth. He followed David out of the middle school and into the high school next door.

He regretted the decision the moment they entered the banquet. He didn't recognize the room. It was large enough to accommodate six large tables that sat ten people at each. There was a small stage behind them with a podium. He supposed it might have been made for events like this. The high school football team alone had won all kinds of awards over the years. The tablecloths were blue with silver runners—the school colors. At one table sat the Principal, Vice Principal, and some of the administrative staff from the elementary and middle school. They had their spouses with them. Some of the other tables held people that Kyle did not recognize, but most of them were filled with the parents of his teammates, and even some of their siblings. His mom and dad were not there, of course, because he hadn't been invited. This was made crystal clear by two observations.

First, all the rest of his teammates were seated with Mrs. Manchester at the lead table, but there was no spot for him. David pulled an unused chair from a different table and wedged it in for Kyle. But the look Mrs. Manchester had on her face as he entered sealed it. Her eyes narrowed, her face reddened, and her mouth puckered to a tiny dot.

Most of his teammates greeted him warmly and seemed genuinely excited to see him. Cindy Baker was the lone exception, and after a curt nod, did not look at him for the rest of the banquet. Kyle felt his face redden as the dinner service started. He wasn't invited. He probably didn't have a meal reserved for him. But they did serve him food—a dry pot roast he choked down with a side of mashed potatoes. He wondered if he was eating the meal intended for the person whose seat he'd taken. Mrs. Manchester did not look at him for the rest of the banquet, except in sideways glimpses. She was practically radiating disdain for him. But she smiled her broad smile as the Principal took to the stage to introduce her. She grinned as she talked about how proud she was of the team's accomplishments. And she gave each of the team members hugs as they trudged up to collect their checks to the wild applause of their family.

Kyle did not have a check to collect, so he stayed in his seat. He was grateful for this because everyone else was wearing suits and dresses. The most casual anyone got was skipping the suit jacket. There were no other Dick Tracy shirts to be found. And certainly, no jean shorts. Kyle did not even remember leaving the banquet. He thought he'd said goodbye to his friends and teammates. But mostly he remembered the intense urge to go. He needed to be out of the school. As he walked to the library, hoping his mom wasn't already there and furious he was missing, his shame and embarrassment from the banquet started to shift. It was like the heat of the emotions burned brighter and brighter until they blossomed into something else. It was pure, red rage and it was unlike anything Kyle had ever felt before. Although he continued along his usual, well-trod path to the library, Kyle did not remember the trip at all.

All he remembered was the domino of thoughts and emotions. Janie was right all along. He could not fathom why, but Alice Manchester was being cruel to him. Even if she did not keep him around like some sort of pet to be laughed at, she definitely did not see him as part of the team. And his friends? Dustin, Chad, and even David… were they any less cruel? Was he?

He thought of poor Henry. The look on his face the first time he realized that Kyle was turning on him and was making fun of him now. The realization that Kyle was using the information they'd shared as friends against him. Surely to Henry, that betrayal was as confusing as Mrs. Manchester's was to Kyle. This began a cycle of anger, hurt, and guilt that swept through Kyle with such ferocity he almost felt like he had a fever by the time his mom showed up. Again, she looked at him in concern. Again, she asked him if he was okay. But this time, Kyle Thomas did not cry. He was done with that. He was done with the Academic Challengers. He was done with Mrs. Manchester. He was done with using cruelty as a weapon to help him feel superior. More than all that, he was done with the Kyle Thomas he'd made over the last couple of years. Because he hated himself more than anyone else in that instant.

# 18
## *Catching Up*

Kyle pulled up to the farmhouse, utterly exhausted from the ups and downs of the day, as the summer sky retreated, fading from blue to navy and then finally to a shimmering band of crimson and gold in the West. Patrick was there, leaning up against the back of the house and looking at his phone until he heard Kyle pulling in. Patrick looked up, and his face lit up. Kyle couldn't have imagined a more pleasing sight to come back to.

"Hey there, thought I'd pay you back for all the Guinness you've been giving me," Patrick said as Kyle got out of the car. He pointedly left Dunbar's Grove and his notebook in the passenger's seat.

"Ah, but that wasn't out of kindness. I was trying to have my vay vich you," said Kyle, momentarily doing his best Dracula. Although it was nearer to The Count from Sesame Street.

"How did it go today?"

"To be honest? I don't even know, and frankly…" Kyle pushed Patrick against the house and pinned him there by putting his knees on either side of his body. He punctuated each pause after with a kiss. "I do not. Want to think. Or talk. About The Grove tonight."

"Sounds good to me," said Patrick, with a wild look in his eyes, trapped somewhere between fear (they were pretty exposed to the road) and the thrill of it all. He closed his eyes and started kissing Kyle back passionately. Patrick dropped the case of Guinness he was holding, and it clanked noisily onto the grass. His hands free, he groped Kyle's butt and then moved his hands up his side. Patrick hooked his elbows under Kyle's shoulders. The pressure of Patrick's biceps as they pressed into his arms caused a shiver of pleasure to travel up from Kyle's groin. Kyle gasped, and it was immediately smothered by another kiss.

Somehow, they made their way up the back stairs and into the kitchen. But they got no farther. Minutes later, Patrick was on his back on the small kitchen table with the metal edging. Kyle took Patrick's gym shorts and underwear off in one motion. And then Kyle was inside him, watching the pleasure he was causing wash over the young man's face. The power of the thrusts shook the little table with such force that, for a moment, Kyle worried it'd shake apart. Eventually, the table moved so far, it was battering against the kitchen wall. Patrick screamed in pleasure as Kyle climaxed nearly at the same time. Kyle bent over him, and kissed him deeply, tasting the beading sweat on his lips.

Kyle looked into Patrick's eyes and marveled at the threads of gold and green and blue within them. It frightened him, a little, how much he already cared about Patrick Kirby. He wasn't going to be in Essen forever. And it already hurt a little thinking about leaving him.

This was Kyle's issue though. He did not fall often, but when he fell, he was sure to fall hard.

Kyle straightened back up and started laughing. Patrick looked up at him in confusion. Kyle reached up into Patrick's hair and plucked away the yellow post-it note that was stuck to it.

"Was that to sell or to trash?" asked Patrick, looking at the bright yellow square.

"Trash. Pure trash." Kyle kissed him before he could respond, while at the same time fumbling for something on the ledge of the nearby key rack.

"Ouch," said Patrick. Kyle retrieved the pad of green post-it notes from the shelf. He took one off and affixed it to Patrick's smooth, broad chest.

"There, that's better."

"What does green mean?"

"Guess," said Kyle.

"Can I spend the night?" asked Patrick, still panting, with his chest heaving up and down in short staccato bursts.

"I'd like that," Kyle said. "Your parents?"

"I can tell them I'm staying at my friend Mike's. Won't be a problem."

"Good." Kyle kissed him again, enjoying the slippery slide of his skin on Patrick's.

Hours (and another round) later, Kyle sat back on the ugly green couch in his shorts, watching late-night television and drinking one of the Guinness that Patrick brought over. Patrick was lying across the rest of the couch, his long legs dangling over the side. His head was resting on Kyle's lap. His eyes were closed, and he was snoring softly. Kyle ran his hand through Patrick's hair, feeling the fine black strands slip through his fingers. Every time his mind would drift back to The Grove and the strange mystery of it all, he'd force himself back to Patrick. He forced himself back to enjoying every minute he could with him. Finally, his eyes heavy with the activity of the day, the sex, the alcohol, and a sense of ease, Kyle pulled the chain of the small lamp beside him and turned it off. He hit the power button on the TV's remote, bent his head to one side, and fell asleep with the warm weight of Patrick on him.

The next morning, Kyle made Patrick some eggs and bacon before he headed back to the Kirby farm for the morning's work. He liked the feeling of this. It'd been a long time since anyone decent had come into his life. He had his friends back in Peoria—the family he'd forged when he moved to Illinois with not much more than a backpack full of clothes, a laptop, and a willingness to do whatever work was around. And that was a lot. But there was nothing quite like the feeling of sharing your life, even for a little while, with someone else.

The fact that their pop culture references were a few years out of sync sometimes wasn't that big of a deal, especially with the constant recycling of franchises, characters, and IPs. Patrick didn't know about the original Masters of the Universe cartoon, for instance, but he saw the reboot when he was a kid. He at least still knew his Orko from an elbow. He was not as much of a geek as Kyle was, at his heart, but he enjoyed all of that in a casual way. Patrick was into football—specifically Notre Dame—which was almost a requirement living in the area if you were into football at all. Kyle was vaguely a fan, having gone to plenty of games because his mom was an alumnus and used to teach there.

What mattered to Kyle–and what scared the hell out of him—

was everything else. He felt as comfortable with Patrick as he felt with Max, without the years of friendship to back it up.

"What're you up to today?" Patrick asked, patting the top of Kyle's foot with the bottom of his.

"Back to reality, I'm afraid. Back to The Grove," he said. "Well, not literally. I don't feel like walking around a fence again."

"Sorry I didn't mention that. It's been like that so long, I didn't realize you might not know."

"It's fine. Janie and Max didn't either." Kyle took one last swig of his now-cold coffee and enjoyed the sharp and bitter taste of it. "Honestly, I think today I'm going to focus on trying to put my thoughts together for tonight."

"Ah, yes. The mysterious new theory you refuse to talk to me about," said Patrick.

"It's nothing personal. I need to map it out a little more. And it'll be nice to only explain it once. And… well… it was nice to have a night off."

"It was." Patrick leaned in for a kiss. Kyle met him halfway and laughed to himself when he tasted the distinct smokiness and saltiness of the bacon. "Damn. I better get going."

They prolonged Patrick's departure with more kissing and groping until finally, Kyle figured he should let him go. He watched Patrick as he walked around the house to the main road that led to his family's farm. Kyle walked out to his car and retrieved his father's book and his notebook. He felt lonely, and the night seemed far off. He decided to try to get some more work done in the house, and at the same time, he tried to put to words the vague notion that was swirling in his head since the previous night.

He'd sat down to start sorting through the family photos

(everything else that had happened over the last few days made his discomfort going through them before seem quaint) when an idea struck him. He texted Janie to see if Dustin, Chad, or David still lived in Essen. He knew he could have searched online but getting the scoop from Jamie seemed the easiest thing to do. She surprised him by calling him back, even though Kyle assumed the school day had already begun.

"I know you think I worry too much, but why do you want to see those guys?" she asked as soon as he picked up the phone.

"Good morning to you, Janie," said Kyle.

"I'm sitting in a room with a bunch of five-year-olds who are somehow magically being calm while they color. This will not last. Answer the question."

"Okay, okay. To be honest, I've been actively trying to avoid Dustin and Chad. But I thought David might be worth checking in with. I'm sure he's a member at the Minty Green, right? What if he's got some insight about the club? He wasn't like the other guys."

"I think he and his wife moved away a couple years ago," said Janie. "Not my social circle. But that's what I heard.  Don't know if he was a club member or not but if he was, that's even more reason not to talk to him. I don't know where your mind is heading with all of this. But I can tell you mine hasn't gone anywhere good. The strangeness around all of this keeps piling up."

"I'll be careful," said Kyle. "Oh, and Janie… thanks for worrying."

Kyle hung up his phone and started searching his Facebook app for David Shaw. He came up immediately. His face was fuller, and his hair was thinning up top. But he had the same smile and twinkle in his eyes. He was living in North Carolina, now. The biggest shock for Kyle was that he knew his wife. Cindy Baker-Shaw was linked to his account and didn't look that different from the last time Kyle had seen her. She was slender and tan, and her hair was blonde. He'd never seen Cindy and David exchange more than two words back in middle school, and he was pretty sure they never dated in high school. But Essen seemed to have a way of drawing people back to it. At least David and Cindy managed to pull away eventually. It took no time at all to find David's number since he had a law practice in Asheville. After a brief exchange with the receptionist, he was put through.

"Kyle Thomas?" asked David the moment he picked up the line.

"Yep. It's me. Hey, David," said Kyle.

"Wow. Oh man, talk about a flashback. It's good to hear from you, man. Really good."

"You too." Kyle felt a pang of guilt. When he'd quit the Academic Challengers, he'd quit his friendship with Dustin, Chad, and David too. It'd felt like the right thing to do at the time. Hell, he was practically vibrating with righteous fury. But he hadn't fully convinced himself David deserved being thrown out with all the rest. "I heard you and Cindy Baker got married?"

"Oh yeah. She's in the next room. I'm working from home today because the twins are sick as dogs and I didn't want to leave her alone with them," said David. Kyle heard a muffled voice say something on the other end, although it was mostly unintelligible.

"An old friend from school, hon," David said back, his voice much quieter since he had his phone angled away. "Sorry, Kyle. What made you call?" Kyle prepared himself to feel even more guilty, as he knew he'd have to lie.

"Nostalgia, I guess. You probably heard about my dad. I came back to the old farm, to sort through my parents' stuff and—"

"You're in Essen?" asked David. The tone of his voice changed completely. The warmth was drained from it, and now it was clipped and urgent.

"Yeah, for another week or so."

"Kyle. Listen to me. You need to go. Take what you want and go." Now David was whispering and unable to hide the panic in it. Kyle felt cold prickling as his flesh became covered with goosebumps.

"David, what's wrong?" asked Kyle. But before David could answer, the voice in the distance was muttering again.

"I told you, hon. An old friend from school," said David. There was a pause. "It's… it's Kyle. Kyle Thomas. You remember him." There was a strange squeak, then a shuffling sound, and then it was clear David no longer held the phone.

"Kyle, it's so good to hear from you," said Cindy Baker-Shaw. She sounded as genuine as her tans had been.

"Uh, hey Cindy."

"I heard you were back in town, Kyle. That's so great."

"You heard I was back?" Suddenly, Kyle wished he'd heeded Janie and not made the call.

"Well, of course, silly! Essen is still a small town. Local boy makes good, returns home triumphant, etc."

"Well not sure that's the case for me," said Kyle, looking around at his parents' sticky-note encrusted home. "I'm only here to sell the farm."

"But look at your accomplishments! All the stories you did. The piece for Forbes. The podcast. That's nothing to sneeze at," said Cindy. There was a distinct disconnect between the words Cindy was saying and the feeling behind them. It made her compliments seem like threats somehow.

"I didn't realize you, uh, kept up on me."

"Oh, of course. You were a Challenger, after all! Mrs. Manchester keeps tabs on her Challengers. You know how she is. We were supposed to go out into the world and change it, right?"

"Right." Kyle couldn't help the icy note creeping into his voice. "Although, I was an alternate."

"And look at all you've done! I mean, David's a lawyer, and I'm a psychiatrist. It certainly pays the bills. But you, Kyle. You can reach people," said Cindy.

"My podcast listener numbers might indicate otherwise." Kyle attempted a chuckle, but it came out more like a pinched coughing sound.

"Well, I know Mrs. Manchester would love to chat with you. She said she saw you the other night in South Bend. She was sad you didn't get to talk more."

"Yeah, me too. Hey, Cindy, it's been great talking to you. Can you put David back on?" asked Kyle. There was a pause. It was long enough that Kyle was about to repeat himself, afraid the connection had failed when Cindy replied.

"Oh, sorry. He went to go check on the twins. From the sound of it, I think it got a little messy. Tomorrow?"

"Sure, Cindy. It was… I'll try to call David tomorrow." Kyle hung up the phone before she could respond. He forgot about sorting the photos and got his notebook out. Something was horribly wrong in Essen. It might have been horribly wrong for a long, long time. He was sure all the pieces were right in front of him. If he could put them together.

# 19
## *Following the Money*

ater that night, Max and Janie sat on the couch in the living room. The coffee table was cleared off, and Kyle arranged the pieces of the puzzle he'd spent the day trying to figure out as well as he could on it. He was sitting on the floor on the opposite side of the coffee table, drinking his fourth cup of coffee of the day.

"Where's Patrick?" Janie asked.

"He got roped into having dinner with his parents. He said he'd be here; he might be a half hour late. And I know you guys have families to get back to, so I figured we'd start," said Kyle.

"Sounds good to me. I almost came over last night and made you spit it out. You've got me on my last nerve with all of this shit," said Max.

"I wanted to have a little time to sort this all out. All I'm going to ask is that you hear me out."

"Take it away," Max said, taking an extra-long chug of his Corona.

"Right. Well, I don't think it's a stretch to say Essen has a lot of money in it. It always has. I mean, Janie and I spent our whole lives being reminded of that because our families didn't have it. Max, I remember it was one of the first things you noticed when you moved here—how ridiculously nice the school was," said Kyle.

"My family used to call it RWP Land," Max said with a nod. "Rich white people land, if you didn't figure that out."

"But did you ever wonder… where does the money come from? I mean, I didn't think about it as a kid. You had the Bakers who own seventy-five percent of the farmland in the area. They're rolling in it. And you've got dentists and doctors and some lawyers in town. There have always been some local businesses, like the old vinyl siding factory or the popcorn factory, or the place that used to make the mints."

"Oh man, I miss the smell of the mint cooking when you were downtown," said Janie.

"Really? I thought it smelled like someone mixed mint and lawn clippings and stuck it in hot water," said Max, screwing up his face in disgust.

"But most of those businesses are gone now. The hobby shop is gone. The variety store is gone. In their place, we've got a lot of bigger companies coming in that're owned by out-of-towners. But the town looks richer than ever before. I was trying to figure out how many huge, new houses there are between the developments and the houses at the Lake of the Grove. I mean, the math is basic, but it seems like more than half the town lives in those huge houses."

"That seems about right," said Max with a shrug. "I mean,

as a franchise owner myself, it's not like I'm not making some decent cash."

"Yeah, but even you said you've hit a wall. Because you can't get clients from the Minty Green Club, right?"

"They tend to keep to their own."

"Don't a lot of people commute to South Bend?" asked Janie.

"I thought that was the case. But that doesn't explain something else I found online. The median income in Essen is pretty much right on par with every other town around it. And I can tell you most of Plymouth isn't living in two-story mini-mansions," said Kyle.

"Rich people lying about their incomes? I am not shocked," said Max.

"That's my point exactly. If you're commuting to South Bend, that company is reporting your income. If you've got your own business, then eventually the IRS is going to come calling. Unless you're up to something shady."

"You think your dad wrote Dunbar's Grove because Essen is some… tax fraud capital of the world?"

"Okay, so this is the part where I'm fuzzy. But the entry in Silus Oak's book mentioned disappearances. No one paid much attention to it, because his whole book is about hauntings, UFOs, and Bigfoot sightings in the Midwest. So, people put even less stock in his assertion that the community was part of a cover-up. But what if they are up to something in The Grove? Something illegal that requires silencing people who come to know a little too much. Maybe drugs or human trafficking or… something that generates a lot of money. Enough money for everyone to share… as long as they are in the Club," said Kyle.

"And you think the Club is involved because they own The

Grove?" asked Janie.

"Yes! And because most of the people in those huge houses are Club members." Kyle got up on his knees and started flipping through his dad's book.

"But… aren't they in the Club because they are rich? I mean, they can afford to be?" asked Max.

"That's what they want people to think. But what if it's the other way around. They are rich because they're in the Club. You said you thought you might have an in to the Club, right? What was that?" asked Kyle.

"Well, it wasn't a sure thing. I mean, I'd heard that the Club has certain income thresholds you have to meet. They aren't official, but they're there. And I was always a little below it. At least, that's what I was told in whispers whenever I'd applied. The man telling me was the one brother they have in the whole god-damned place. Gordy Smith. Do you know Gordy, Kyle? He might have moved here after your time. Anyway, after the third time of getting turned down, he told me in secret that—he couldn't be certain—but he was pretty sure the Club still added a 'color tax' to that threshold."

"Why would you even want to belong to a place like that?" Janie asked, her face snarled in disgust.

"Because some of us have to live in the real world, Janie. Some of us know that sometimes you've gotta play the game by their rules to get ahead. If I could get into the Club, I could probably double my profits. I want Zee to go to the best college. I want her to become whatever the hell she wants. And let me tell you, my current lifestyle involves a lot of credit cards and crossed fingers. So that's why, Janie, I was more than willing to suck up my pride and sit with those white fucks and make nice." Max took another deep swig of his Corona, found he'd totally drained it, and cracked open another one. Janie was silent.

"And the in?" asked Kyle. Max looked down at his feet.

"Gordy said if I got enough people on board to sponsor my application, that they might let me squeak by. I've been talking to the people I'm close enough to who go to the Club."

"That does seem to poke a hole in your theory, though, Kyle," said Janie.

"Well, I'm not even done explaining it yet. But I'd say you could argue that they're trying to see how morally flexible Max is. Maybe it's a test. Anyway, that's not my only thought about all of this." Kyle looked at his now thoroughly ear-marked and note-covered copy of Dunbar's Grove. "In the book, Dunbar is consumed by greed. By his need for more and more. It ends up costing him his wife. He ends up accidentally killing her and hiding her body twelve years before he kills himself. Well, my mom didn't die twelve years ago. But I was trying to figure out what did happen then."

"Well, my wedding for one," said Janie.

"Right. Which I came back into town for," said Kyle.

"And left immediately after. Didn't even come to the reception." Janie looked like she regretted it the moment she said it.

"Janie that—look, we'll discuss that later. My point is that while I did not talk to my dad or mom at the wedding, I did notice my mom was wearing a new dress, new diamond earrings, and a new diamond tennis bracelet."

"And your dad bought that BMW. I remember we talked about how crazy that was."

"Like they were waiting for me to leave home to get rich," said Kyle, nodding his head. "And you said he must have just bought it because you'd seen him driving around the old smoke-belching Oldsmobile the week before."

"I don't get where you're going," said Max.

"I'm saying, what if my parents joined the Club? What if they got roped into whatever illegal scheme they've got going on? My parents weren't my favorite people after they threw me out. I hated them for a long time. But they certainly thought of themselves as good, moral people. What if mom's heart attack was brought on from the stress of being mixed up in whatever the Club was doing? And my dad couldn't live with that?" Kyle exhaled. He got it all out. All the pieces he'd managed to put together. It fit. It all made sense.

"Well, if what you're saying is true—and I'm not saying I totally buy it—but assuming it is true… I guess that would explain why Lissie warned you about prying too far into it," said Max.

"What do you mean?" asked Kyle.

"Lissie's parents are Club members. It's possible she's overheard secrets over the years. Or they even warned her off," said Max.

"And now someone's gotten to her. She was practically like a different person with me. I'm convinced the articles she gave me were doctored, and she lied about not finding her notes on Oak's book," said Kyle.

"Kyle, if that's the case, how did they know you were talking to Lissie? I guess they could have seen you in the library?" questioned Janie. Kyle shook his head.

"I don't think so. We were being cautious," he said.

"Then, the only people who knew what Lissie said to you are in this room," said Janie, her eyes growing a little wide.

"And Patrick," added Max. His words landed heavy on Kyle's

chest. He understood the implication immediately. But every fiber of his being resisted it.

"What would Patrick have to do with any of this?" he asked.

"Kyle… Patrick's parents are both Club members. Hell, he might even be one," said Max.

"They have that kind of money? The Kirbys?"

"Yeah. They joined shortly after Pat Kirby had his accident. I know because after AllCare paid out on their insurance policy, they dumped me like yesterday's news. Went with Brett Wilson. Who happens to be a Club member," Max said bitterly.

"That would fit with your theory. They might have needed money after his dad's accident. If the Club did offer a solution of some kind, maybe they felt like they couldn't refuse," said Janie.

"I can tell you for sure their policy did not pay a ton," said Max. Kyle's mind was reeling. He'd felt such clarity after finally getting the jumble of facts he'd collected into something that seemed to make sense. But he'd had no idea this is where it'd all lead him. He could feel tears start to sting his eyes. He looked to Janie, and then at Max, and then back to Janie again, hoping one of them would see a hole in all of this. He needed one of them to find it because he didn't trust himself to be clear-headed about it. His brain felt fuzzy, and the knot in his stomach tightened. And then there was a knock at the back door.

"That has to be him," Max whispered.

Kyle got up from the floor and walked toward the kitchen. Janie and Max looked at each other warily for a moment, and then followed him. Kyle got to the back door, and Patrick waved at him. It was a goofy, over-animated wave. He was grinning from ear to ear and held up a round dish to the window. Kyle steeled himself and opened the door.

"Sorry I'm late," Patrick said, starting to angle his body to come in. But Kyle shifted and blocked his way, much to Patrick's confusion.

"No problem," said Kyle. "We were finishing up. Max and Janie have to get going. It's a school night for their kids." Kyle turned back toward his friends. They stared forward, wide-eyed for a moment. But they recovered quickly.

"Yeah, Heather wants me back as soon as possible. Zee's been a pain to get to bed lately," Max explained.

"Yes. I… also have to put my kids in bed," Janie said, bending over to grab her and Max's shoes.

"Wow, that was so fast. I'm sorry I missed it. I guess you can catch me up. I'm dying to hear what you've come up with," said Patrick. The yellow light over the sink seemed to highlight the warm green in his eyes. Kyle had to look away from him. He had no doubt Patrick was eager to hear everything Kyle had figured out.

"If you don't mind, I might take a rain-check? Max and Janie brought up some good points. I'm not so confident in what I came up with. I think I'll spend some time alone tonight straightening it out," said Kyle. The smile on Patrick's face withered immediately.

"Oh. Okay, yeah," he said. The look on the man's face—the momentary wince of hurt—looked real enough. But if Patrick was a spy or plant or something, he'd already shown himself to be an adept actor.

"Thanks. We'll catch up tomorrow." Even as Kyle said the words, he wasn't sure if it was true.

"Well, this pie is for you," said Patrick, nodding his head toward the round silver container in his hand. "They make it at this

Amish place my mom and dad go to. It's Strawberry-Rhubarb. It's one of my favorites so… I guess I thought you might like it." Kyle took the container from Patrick. Max and Janie had their shoes on, now, and they squeezed past Kyle. Janie hooked one of Patrick's arms in her elbow and led him down the stairs.

"Well, off we go then. Patrick, do you need a ride?" asked Janie.

"Nah, I'm used to the walk. See you all later," Patrick said, flashing them all a somewhat sad smile before he turned around and headed toward the road. Max and Janie were at their vehicles. Max clambered into his Jeep, gave them a quick wave, and sped off. Janie lingered at the door of her car for a moment. She took her cell phone in her hand and waved it at her ear, wordlessly indicating that Kyle should call her. He nodded his head, although he felt thoroughly emotionally exhausted.

# 20
## *I Should Have Known*

After everyone left, Kyle marched to the living room and started scooping the family photos back into their original box. He'd go through them later. Maybe in a month. Maybe in a year. Maybe they'd sit and molder until his landlord called in a cleaning crew to empty out his apartment, a day after finding his withered old corpse.

"They didn't find him for thirteen days," the children at the apartment complex would whisper.

"Poor lonely old man," one of the women might say. This future was more vivid and felt more real than the tear-blurred present as he grabbed for handfuls of photos, not caring what was bent or folded in the process, and tried to shove them back into the box. There seemed to be so many of them, though. Far more than could ever fit into the neat confines of the dusty green box. He remembered when he was a child, and his mom would sometimes get the box out, and they'd cuddle and look through the photos, and she'd remind him of who the unfamiliar people were—dead uncles, unknown second cousins, and grandparents who'd almost all died before he was even born. Except for his dad's father, who died after he'd left home. Then he remembered what his mom had said to him, the day he'd finally come out to them his Senior year of high school. His dad was done raging, and was downstairs, slamming a Coors or two down his throat. His mom's eyes were red with tears, and she grabbed his hand.

"It just seems like such a lonely life," she said, before patting his hand, and leaving the room.

And somehow that tore through him more than anything his dad, in his anger, said. And it was a lonely life, sometimes. Kyle knew that everyone's lives were lonely sometimes. Even people like his parents, who stayed in the town they grew up in, surrounded by the same friends they'd had since they were kids, going to the same church they'd always gone to, and marrying the first person they ever dated. They were lonely too. Kyle recognized it in the way his mom would sit on the old green couch, doing her needlework and looking out the window toward the road that seemed to stretch into infinity once the fields were culled. He saw it on his dad's face when he was typing. He'd sneak upstairs and peek into his parents' bedroom and watch him. That was when his father looked the most haunted. His writing was the only place his dad actually allowed himself to think or feel much of anything. He let his characters feel for him.

Yes, it could be a lonely life. But it could be a full, joyous life too. Not only when he had someone to make bacon and eggs for in the morning either. He loved his job. He loved the family he'd made, who was there whenever he needed them. He liked living in a city that was large enough to have a lot going on, but not so large that traffic was oppressive. He tried to remind himself that Essen was nothing but a short pit-stop for him. He was going back to his life. A full life he'd made for himself, far away from all these old insecurities and fears. It didn't help.

His phone rang.

"Hey, Janie. Sorry, I didn't call. I thought you'd need longer to get home," he said as he answered.

"It's fine. How are you? I've got some time before Sean is back with the kids," she said.

"Sorry to rush you guys away. I panicked."

"It's fine, I get it. You didn't answer my question."

"Honestly? I don't know how I am. I'm angry. I'm hurt. I feel like an idiot."

"Why's that?" asked Janie. "I mean, the last part. I get the rest."

"Because I should have known. Some impossibly hot twenty-five-year-old who just so happens to be helping take care of my family's farm is also gay and into me. I've watched too much porn." Kyle sighed.

"If it makes you feel better, I was fooled too. I don't find it as hard to believe someone would be into you. Even reasonably attractive twenty-somethings." There were almost equal amounts of affection and annoyance in her voice.

"Oh, come on. Even you have to admit Patrick is basically like a model but walking around in real life."

"If you like that sort of thing. Which I know you do," said Janie. Kyle laid back on the couch, wanting to focus on the conversation.

"This fucking sucks."

"I know."

"Well, wait until tomorrow. I can't wait to tell him to take his pies, his aw-shucks smiles, and his little bubble butt back to Alice Manchester and tell her to fuck off," said Kyle, the hurt suddenly curdling into righteous anger.

"Kyle you can't do that," Janie said calmly. He was about to protest, but she kept talking. "For one thing, we don't even know if all of this is true. All of this is odd. And it's not adding up. But right now, all we've got is a theory."

"So I'm supposed to pretend everything is okay? Pretend everything is normal?" asked Kyle. He thought of kissing Patrick again, knowing he'd been toying with him for some… land grab? To hide the Club's secrets? Whatever the reason, the thought of touching him or being touched by him sickened Kyle.

"You need to find a way. There's something else I don't think you've thought of. If you're right, then the Club has altered files on the public library's computer, sent a spy to get close to you, and in the past, might have been responsible for the disappearance of people. Whatever they want with you, or whatever threat they think you pose to them… if you let them know that you're onto them…"

"You're right. Of course, you're right." Kyle slammed his fist against the side of the couch in frustration. "I need a break. When we were talking before, about the BMW my dad bought—it reminded me I still have to travel up to the Holland police impound to get it back. It's still up there from when my dad… when he drove to Silver Cove."

"Do you think he might have left some clue in it?" asked Janie.

"I don't know. Maybe. If he did, it wasn't obvious. The police searched it as part of their investigation into his death. But it's a good reason to get out of town and away from Patrick. Hell, I might even leave tonight. I'm sure he'll be around first thing tomorrow morning," said Kyle.

"Maybe that is a good idea. I'll keep nosing around here and see what I can find. Discreetly, of course," Janie said, anticipating the warning forming on Kyle's lips. "I left that Midwest Mysteries book there. You can look at that too."

"Okay, that sounds good. Thanks, Janie. Again. As always."

"Be safe if you drive up tonight, okay?" With that, the call was over. Kyle sat up from the couch. He only took a moment to make his decision. He grabbed his backpack, stuffed a couple days' worth of clothes into it along with his toiletries, and everything related to his investigation into The Grove. He knew full well the Kirby's had the keys to the house, and he didn't want to lose any of the pieces of the puzzle he'd collected so far. He got into his Prius and traveled down the drive slowly to the main road. He turned left, even though it would have been a more direct route toward Route 12 and up to Silver Cove if he'd gone the other way. He didn't want to pass by the Kirby farm.

# 21
# *Maps in Michigan*

The hotel choices in Holland, Michigan were not that inspiring, at least not near the police impound. Kyle planned to get his dad's car out, sell it to a nearby used car place for whatever he could get, and be done with it. First, of course, he'd drive it back to the rusted, crumbling ruin of a motel he'd checked into and give it a thorough looking over.

As he suspected, he was going to have to make the walk as no rides came up on the apps. Holland was nine times larger than Essen but walking down the streets that would take him to the impound, Kyle had a hard time telling. He was either far from the central part of town, or it was a diffused sprawl. However, Holland had a couple things going for it. There was the Dutch bakery he made an impromptu stop at for breakfast, with its thin Lacey pancakes, lingonberry syrup, and the adorable waiter with a thick chest and muscular arms. Then there was the fact it was a good two hours away from Essen, The

Grove, Alice Manchester, and Patrick Kirby. Being away from all of that lightened his mood considerably, even if the questions of what exactly was going on in Essen still haunted him.

Kyle had never needed to get a car out of police custody before and feared a bureaucratic nightmare. To his surprise, it was all pretty straightforward. A look at his driver's license, some forms signed, and he was driving his dad's silver BMW Series 3 down the road. The state of the car inside was a shock. He remembered the relentlessly polished family Oldsmobile with its fruity chemical scent of cleaner. His dad kept his car immaculate. They did not eat in the car. If the family got drive-through from the local Dairy Queen, they waited until they got home to eat it. If he dribbled ice cream onto the leather seat trying to sneak a bite of his Blizzard before it melted into soup, he'd get a thorough scolding.

When the dry, choking smell of cigarette smoke hit him in the face as he opened the door to the BMW, he couldn't believe it. The ashtray was overflowing with cigarette butts. There was a Burger King cup that was also full of butts. They'd clearly gotten wet at some point, the bottom of the cup had given way, and then the whole thing dried again into a sticky, ashy, congealed mess that made Kyle want to gag. He'd never been a smoker. He hated the smell. He hated the yellow tinge the smoke gave everything. His dad smoked when he was younger but gave it up when Kyle was ten. He still remembered his mom cleaning the lacy curtains from the living room, though. She'd dip the ocher-tinged curtains into the water, wring it so that brownish-yellow juice spurted out from them, dunk them into the now-murky water, and then continue the process again. That memory alone was enough to make sure Kyle never wanted to touch the things.

Instead of going straight back to his motel, he decided to find a car wash. There was no way he could sell it to a dealer looking like this, and he figured it was as good a way of giving the car a thorough once-over as any. He pulled up into the Happy Showers car-wash with its fake palm trees and daffodils with smiling faces in them and decided to embrace the drudgery of what lay ahead. The sun was shining hot now—impossibly bright in the deep sapphire blue of the sky. It was nearly cloudless, with a few feathery white wisps near the horizon line. He did a quick rummage through the car to start with. The back seat was pretty much clear, which was a blessing because, in addition to the mess of cigarette butts, the passenger side foot-well was stuffed with fast food bags. Kyle was amazed at how the scent of grease traps still clung to them a month after his father had abandoned his car. He worked his way through each of them, to be sure there wasn't some valuable scrap of paper thrown into them. There were greasy wrappers, salt-encrusted fry boxes, and (in a departure) one leftover salad container with some liquefied lettuce and molding ranch dressing.

All of this spoke to the fact that his dad had not been in the best place mentally. But he was on his way to commit suicide. That shouldn't have exactly been a shocker, Kyle supposed. Except, it was. Even if his dad was expressing his own mental decline through the protagonist in Dunbar's Grove, he still had a hard time imagining his dad breaking down in this way. His dad was an unfeeling, implacable, and unyielding wall when he was a kid. Experience had taught him that nothing was that permanent or that solid. So why did this view of his dad seem so unchangeable?

Kyle searched the glove compartment next. This was filled with ketchup packets, a tire pressure gauge, an old atlas, a bunch of napkins, some receipts for repair work on the car (all at least five years old), and an out-of-date coupon book for the local Dairy Queen. In the trunk, there wasn't anything but an emergency road kit. He lifted the panel that exposed the compartment for the spare tire, but there wasn't even a spare tire in there. Nothing but a pair of jumper cables and a jack. He looked under the seats in the front of the car. He even opened the hood. If his dad had tried to leave any more clues for him, he'd hidden them too well. Kyle wasn't that surprised. His dad had written a whole book as a clue for him. Kyle supposed scraps of paper in his car were unnecessary. The trip up here was mostly an excuse not to talk to Patrick right away. By the time he was finished, the noon sun was shining overhead, and it was starting to become unbearably hot.

After a little research, Kyle drove to Berringer Auto Sales, which had the best reviews online. He was offered a thousand dollars and accepted it immediately. He was about to hand over the keys when he realized he'd forgotten to empty out the crap in the dash after looking through it. He apologized, and then ran back out to the car, grabbed everything that was inside except the tire pressure gauge, and then handed the man the keys. The man offered Kyle a ride back to his motel, since they didn't have a shuttle service.

They made a small attempt at conversation, but quickly realized they didn't have a lot of common ground. Kyle looked down at the mish-mash of crap from his dad's car that was still in his arms. Kyle wished he'd remembered it was in there so he could have thrown it all away when he was cleaning the car.

"Oh, man, you're staying at this place?" the car salesman asked with a sharp laugh. "Hope you didn't get bed bugs in my car." He was being agreeable enough, but Kyle was hardly in the mood for dumb banter.

"Yeah, let's hope," was all he could manage. He let himself out of the car as soon as the man stopped his Mustang. With a little wave, the car salesman was gone. Kyle saw a round, wire-mesh trashcan near the office entrance of the motel. He walked the short distance to it and lazily threw the contents of the glove box in. Except, the atlas did not go in. The wind caught it and caused it to flap open and flutter to the ground. Kyle cursed to himself and bent over to pick it up. He didn't understand what he was seeing at first, as he looked at the map that the atlas opened up to. He picked it up and realized the thin spine of the book was broken in at this spot. A burst of laughter took his attention away from the map, as a girl with an army green tank top, pink bra, and one full sleeve of tattoos up her left arm wobbled up alongside a rail-thin boy clad all in black. The boy's eyes were tinged red. They were both equally drunk and high. That much was obvious.

"What ya lookin' at, fuck face?" asked the boy. Kyle was sure he could have snapped the little guy in two. But he had been staring at him. Even though he was too pale and had dark brown circles under his eyes, he had a pleasingly elfin quality to him as well. Kyle held his hands up in a passive sort of gesture.

"That's what we thought, face fuck," said the girl with an angry snarl.

Both the boy and the girl started giggling at her mix-up, passed him by, and made their way to their hotel room. They forgot about Kyle instantly as they fumbled with their key between wet, sloppy kisses. The keys were the old-fashioned kind affixed to a large key-chain instead of the more standard key card. And it was causing them issues. Kyle decided, as harmless as these two were, that he should get inside before studying the map further. Because the next people to come along might not be so benign. Kyle closed the orange motel door behind him, set the latch in place, and locked the deadbolt and the regular lock. Kyle was about to fall into the rickety old bed when he remembered Berringer's comment. He paused for a second, but the old blue chair next to the white plank that was supposed to be a desk had rough and minimal cushioning. That's why, in the end, he figured he'd take his chances since he'd already slept in the bed the night before.

He snapped on both small lamps that were attached to the wall on either side of the bed. The low wattage of the bulbs and the orange, ribbed cylinders of glass that acted as shades gave the light a murky quality. But it was enough to see the map in. The atlas was opened to a two-page spread of the Midwest region of the United States. It was a map like any other you'd expect—although it looked twenty years old. Pale pastel colors separated state from state. Roads were indicated by thick blue and black lines. There was a legend. There was a compass. The rest, all added by hand, was insanity. His dad—or someone— had taken one of those red felt-tip pens (the kind teachers use to markup papers) and scribbled all over the map. At least, that's what it looked like at first. However, the longer Kyle stared at it, the more he realized there was some sort of order to it.

There was a large red dot in northern Indiana, drawn in continuous red circles for so long the pen soaked through and punctured the map. Essen was too small to be indicated on this map, but Kyle could tell it was more or less where Essen was. A network of red lines emanated from Essen and merged with other drawn-in dots across the map. Most of the dots must have represented small towns like Essen, as they were not marked on the original map. But some of them were on cities that were on the original document, like Madison, Des Moines, and Youngstown. The lines were not straight, but curved and wild. Sometimes multiple lines were leading from one dot to another. Sometimes the lines did not lead to another dot but branched off and then thinned. Other branches curved off the arcs of the main lines, and then branched into themselves and then branched again and again. The end result was a maddening scribble that seemed impossible to follow.

As if all of this didn't seem psychotic enough, next to each dot was a symbol. Kyle did not recognize them. Unlike the sketched feel of the red lines, these were done in blue felt-tip, and there was a precision to their forms that Kyle would not have associated with his father. That was assuming his father had been the one to draw the map. But someone else drawing it was one variable too many to consider now. For the moment, he had to assume it had been his father. That left the question, then, of what were the symbols? They were formed of dots, half-moons, slashes, triangles, and arcs in various configurations. Kyle tried to quickly Google the symbols, even taking a photo and trying an image search, but not only were there so many results to comb through that it was worthless, but his phone was also having trouble keeping a connection. When Kyle asked the front clerk if they had WI-fi, the beady-eyed man snorted and said: "Sure, if some idiot nearby is stupid enough not to have a password on theirs." So that was that. He noticed it was late enough that Janie should be home and have the kids somewhat settled. He felt bad about bothering her again, but he knew she'd want an update anyway. It only rang once before she picked up.

"K-Kyle?" Janie asked, although she must have seen his name come up. She sounded strange.

"Yeah, it's me, Janie. Are you okay?" he asked her. She started sobbing. It was unrestrained, wet sobbing. Kyle's heart leaped into his throat.

"That fucking bitch," Janie suddenly screamed between sobs. "That fucking slimy bitch!"

# 22
## *Symbols, Symbols Everywhere*

acinta Alvarez using the word 'bitch' was out of character. Her use of the word 'fuck' was almost impossible to believe. It was not that Janie was a saint. But she was very, very Christian. Her father and mother had both been raised Catholic, hated it, and only returned to church when they both found Josiah Milton's Higher Faith mega-church. That's where her parents met, while they both were volunteering for the soup kitchen the church held every Saturday. Janie had gone there since she was a baby. She'd been baptized there, and even though it was an hour drive to South Bend, the family drove there for Wednesday and Sunday services, and they still helped out with the soup kitchen and other events when they could. Janie was the one who invited Kyle to Higher Faith, and he enjoyed it immensely. For a while.

She was the best sort of Christian. She took her faith incredibly seriously. But she was not pushy about it. Even when she disapproved of something (like Kyle's friends), she would explain why she felt the way she did, so she did not come off as judgmental. She didn't proclaim that people were going to hell. She did not wish this on them. And, she did not swear. Once, in shop class, she cut the tip of her pinky off, and still only managed to react with a tame (although emphatic) "balls!" She had her faith, she lived by her faith, and she definitely welcomed and encouraged any interest in her faith. But she did not use it to feel superior, and she didn't wield it like a cudgel to beat down others. She was the reason Kyle gave church another chance. His parents were Baptists, and Kyle was not a fan of religion, and it all started with that damned creepy Jesus painting.

Baptists believed God, Jesus and the Holy Spirit were all the same thing, and that Jesus was the head of the church. On a fundamental level, Kyle was creeped out about it. He'd had more than one nightmare of Jesus with his white skin and dead eyes visiting him in the night. By twelve, he'd finally convinced his parents to let him stay home, mostly by being a total brat. The fact that Higher Faith ended up a den of hypocrisy and judgment for Kyle was not Janie's fault. He certainly didn't blame her for it.

So, when she screamed a profanity into the phone, it was a huge deal, and it stunned Kyle into silence for a moment. Eventually, as she was still sobbing and not offering up any other information—screamed or otherwise—he found his voice again.

"Janie. Who are you talking about? What happened? You're freaking me out."

"Alice Manchester. I'm sure she's behind this. That bloated pucker-faced—"

"What did she do, Janie?"

"I was fired, Kyle. Fired from the school," Janie managed to choke out. She sniffled, and then Kyle heard the muffled sound of her blowing her nose.

"Oh, Janie, I'm so sorry. For what?" asked Kyle.

"That's the worst thing. A parent—James Leaper—told the principal that his son Stevie said that… that I touched him, Kyle. Stevie Leaper said I touched him! Me! I threw up when I got home just thinking about it." Janie was breathing heavily and still sniffling, and Kyle was so frustrated, he wish he could join her. But he needed to be strong for Janie. Like Janie was always strong for him. He ignored the heavy weight of guilt in his chest and willed himself to be calm and collected.

"Janie, they can't do that to you. They can't have any proof, of course. You can—"

"I'm finished in Essen, Kyle. You know that. I could try to get a lawyer. But what would that do? Sheriff Gadsby, Judge York—even my current lawyer— they're all members of the Minty Green Club. If this is all about some insane money-making scheme the Club members are profiting from, then I'm screwed. And even if it's not, and I prove I'm innocent… I'm still screwed. No one is going to want me teaching their kids now," said Janie. Her anger seemed to be canceling out her sadness, for a moment. The sniffling stopped, and her voice sounded harder. Kyle wished she didn't sound so defeated.

"But won't you have to prove you're innocent anyway? Aren't the boy's parents' pressing charges or something?" asked Kyle. Janie laughed bitterly.

"That's how I know this has to be a part of all of this business with your dad's book. They must have found out I was trying to help you. They said they wouldn't press charges if I was fired. That was enough for them. Principal Wallace looked sympathetic, but she knew as well as I did that I was finished no matter what."

"Fucking Patrick Kirby. He must have been the one who told Manchester about you helping me. I'm so sorry Janie. I'm so sorry I dragged you and your family into this."

"No. Don't you dare Kyle Thomas," Janie spat out, her voice trembling with rage. "This is not on you. You couldn't have stopped me from helping you, for one thing. And this is Manchester's doing. I'm sure of it."

"Does Max know? If they went after you—"

"I got off the phone with him a second ago. He sounded worried. But he thanked me for the heads up," said Janie.

"What a fucking mess. The worst part is, I don't even know what to do next," said Kyle.

"You nail her ass to the wall, Kyle. You nail all their asses. We must figure out how the Club is making its money. We need to figure out what's going on in The Grove. You need to write an exposé on all of it," she said.

"Right. You're right," agreed Kyle. There was no arguing the point. Kyle felt so helpless on the phone, while still being two hours away from his crying friend. He found it impossible not to blame himself. Kyle hated feeling so helpless. "I wish I could figure out where these symbols fit in."

"Symbols? Did you say something about symbols?" asked Janie.

Kyle filled her in on the map he'd found in the atlas. Janie was her usual calm self again, her mind occupied by something other than her current predicament.

"I tried looking them up on the net, but talk about a needle in a haystack," said Kyle.

"Kyle, have you taken a look at the Midwest Mysteries book yet?" asked Janie.

"No. It was late when I got in, and I pretty much got out of bed and headed out this morning. Why?"

"Flip through it quick. Look at the chapter title pages," said Janie. Kyle groped for the paperback book and did as she asked. He found chapter three's title page first. The text started halfway down the page. At the top of the page was written 'Chapter 3.' Centered below this was a symbol. Kyle quickly marked the page and flipped to chapter four. There was another symbol. He did this with four more chapters before he began comparing the symbols to the ones on the map. But he already knew they matched.

"The symbols in the book are the ones on the map," said Kyle.

"I noticed them when I was reading the book. They struck me as weird at the time, but not much weirder than the rest of the book," said Janie.

"That's not the only odd part. Janie, the stories in Midwest Mysteries… each chapter is a different story in a different Midwest town. I'd need to check it against a more detailed map online but… I think the symbols all correspond," said Kyle.

"Correspond? I don't understand what you mean."

"I mean, that chapter three in the Mysteries book is about Des Moines. The symbol in the book is the same symbol that's on the map in the Atlas," said Kyle.

"Do you think your dad read the book? And then wrote it on the map?" asked Janie.

"Or he didn't even make this map. Maybe he got it from Silus Oak? What if it's drug routes or slave trade routes or something. Whatever the case, this map feels important."

"Kyle. Kyle, I think Sean is home. I still haven't… I have to go," stammered Janie.

Kyle said goodbye, but Janie had already hung up. Kyle's head hurt, and he desperately wanted a drink. But he decided it was time to lay off that for a while. Certainly, until all this was done. His thoughts were cloudy enough from everything being thrown at him right now. If he could keep his mind clear, all of the insanity of the last week might resolve into something he could wrap his head around. No matter how much he learned, and no matter how far along the path toward an answer he got, he still felt like he was stumbling in the fog.

His phone buzzed, and it made him jump. Patrick's name came up on the incoming call screen. Kyle rejected it, put it on airplane mode, and shoved everything off the bed. He turned the TV on and started pounding the channel buttons, hoping to find something mindless.

# 23

## *Plums on Ice*

An hour later, Kyle was heading down a familiar road. He'd quickly realized that he was not able to shut his mind off. He needed to be active. He needed to do something. He needed to think. And none of that was going to happen in the motel room. When he left the motel, he wasn't even consciously sure of where he was going, but as soon as Kyle made the first turn onto the highway, he understood where he had to go. His car entered Silver Cove a few minutes after seven at night. A blue sign with white trim, attached to wide, rope-wrapped poles meant to simulate the end of a dock welcomed him. One of the poles was topped by a fake seagull, whose gray and yellow paint was flaking badly. As if there weren't enough gulls around as it was.

Kyle drove past the fruit stand that had been there since he was a boy but was sad to note that the produce didn't seem to be kept on ice anymore. One of his fondest memories as a child was coming back from a long day under the hot sun at the beach, stopping at the stand, and getting a bag of ice-cold plums. They were, of course, not allowed to eat them in the Oldsmobile, so he'd join his mom and dad (and occasionally Janie) on a little picnic bench nearby and bite into the deliciously cold and sweet fruits. Juice would run down all their faces, but his mom was prepared with a stack of leftover Dairy Queen napkins from the dash. Kyle had done his best to recreate the joy of that moment. Grocery store plums were useless. They would either be too hard like a nectarine, too sour or bitter, or have barely any taste at all. Sometimes at the farmer's market, he'd find some good plums, but even when he chilled them at home, it wasn't quite the same. It wasn't only the plums themselves. It was the exhausted and hot feeling combined with the cold plums.

He laughed to himself. Dunbar had his grove—his perfect place he could never recreate. Kyle had his plums.

As he drove into town, down the sloping street covered with shops, he was amazed at how much it'd changed, and how little it had changed at the same time. In the distance, he could tell that quite a few more buildings dotted the shore ahead—condos, apartments, and hotels—than before. But the quaint little town with its surf shop, upscale women's boutiques, cafés, restaurants, and souvenir stores was pretty much the same. He wasn't sure if the shops had changed much, because his family didn't have a lot of money at the time, so they never stopped in. Lunch was prepared at home, and consisted of hot-dogs cooked and put in buns and wrapped in plastic. A bag of chips and some cans of soda in the cooler completed the meal. Their only indulgence was the plums, and those were insanely cheap back then.

He reached the small parking lot near the public beach. They only charged until the park officially closed at eight. The lot was usually packed full of cars, especially on a Friday night. But since Kyle arrived at the lot during this in-between time—as the sun worshipers and families were starting to leave, and the nightlife seekers waited for the free parking—he found a spot quickly. He didn't mind paying a few dollars to get in. He grabbed his backpack and walked to the edge of the paved lot. He took off his shoes and socks and stepped onto the sand. It still retained some of the heat of the day, but in a pleasant way. He enjoyed the feel of the fine grains of sand sliding between his toes. It was impossible to stop the flood of memories here. But that was okay because that's part of why he'd come here in the first place. Some of his happiest childhood memories were here. And he felt it was somehow essential to connect with those again.

He walked along the sand to the grass-covered dunes. There were wooden structures built upon the dunes—platforms, and stairs to make it easier to cross and for sightseeing. He made his way to the highest platform and sat down on one of the benches there. The sun was starting to move closer to the horizon, and it looked like it was going to be a spectacular sunset. He did not plan the timing of his arrival. He didn't know where he was going when he left Holland, after all, but it worked out perfectly. A young couple—both lean and beautiful with smooth skin the color of hazelnuts—walked past him, hand in hand and shoulder to shoulder, and they smiled at him politely. He nodded back at them, and the woman pulled on the man's hand as she walked down the stairs from the platform. The man looked like he was going to protest (as they'd clearly meant to watch the sunset from here too), but the woman yanked a little harder. Kyle couldn't help but feel like the woman could tell he wanted to be alone. Or, she wanted somewhere where she and her beau could be alone. In any case, Kyle appreciated it.

Kyle took the backpack off his shoulders and dug out his father's typewritten note.

## It's up to you now, son.

The paper was wrinkled now at the edges from all the handling it'd received over the last few days. It was this piece of paper that'd driven Kyle here. That, and the condition of his father's BMW. He knew that the man was not the unchanging, immovable object he'd remembered from his childhood. Kyle supposed he'd known that on some level as soon as he found out his dad committed suicide. He'd not believed it, at first. But the more he came to understand his dad's mental state leading up to his death, the more Kyle realized that his dad had changed in some fundamental way during the fifteen years they were out of touch. He'd come to the beach, where the memories of his parents felt the safest, because he needed to try to understand them in a way he hadn't before. He hadn't wanted to know them after they kicked him out. He'd put up a wall when that happened. His mom had made a few efforts to reach out to him the first couple years he'd left home, and Kyle had ignored them.

There was his life before, and there was his life after. That was part of the reason he didn't keep in touch with Janie or Max after he left Essen. He'd tried at first, but he had his own (new) life to lead. And that was what he wanted to concentrate on.

Now he had to remember. His dad had chosen this place to die. He'd chosen the slowly rippling waters in front of him, shimmering and reflecting the golden-red orb above them, as his final resting place.

His body didn't stay in the lake, of course. Unlike Dunbar, who had lain down in the mud in the middle of his grove and was swallowed whole at the end of the story, his father was spat back out again onto the shore. Kyle remembered the fish carcasses that would sometimes litter the beach after a storm, and shivered. How he hated them. How they ruined his perfect memory of Silver Cove. But his father wasn't left to be picked apart and rot in the sun. They'd found him, cremated him like his mother, and scattered him onto the fields of the farm that had been in his family for a hundred years.

He'd stepped on one of the fish carcasses when he was five, and he'd cried. Its remains were like sickly white and red jelly on his feet. His dad yelled at him for crying. Said it was only some fish guts and to go wash it off in the lake. Then he remembered the time his mom forgot to pack the ketchup and mustard, and his dad complained about choking down the dry hot dogs so much that his dad and mom started arguing. And there was the time Kyle had gotten so sun-burnt it hurt to sleep, and his mom was furious with him for not putting on any sunscreen when earlier she'd handed him the bottle and insisted he cover himself head to toe. It felt like she was being unnecessarily rough with him as she smoothed aloe onto his back and scolded him. These memories came flooding back, and even the safety of Silver Cove was poisoned with them.

It was at that moment that it came to him. The something he'd driven here to discover. He was still thinking like a child. Getting mad because every single memory of this beach wasn't a happy one was a childish thing to do. There was no perfect thing. Wasn't that what Dunbar discovered by the novel's end? His parents had not been perfect. They were human beings, shaped by their reaction to the world, and the prejudices and compassion they'd learned over their lives. They'd been cruel to him, their own son. But they were not cruel people. Not at their core. This truth made their rejection of him all the more hurtful and unfathomable. But it was still true. There was no perfect bite of plum to be had. Ever since he'd come to Essen, he'd been haunted by all his old childish fears and doubts and reacted (or not reacted) to what was going on around him as a child might.

But he wasn't a child. He was an investigative reporter. He'd exposed a child sex ring in Philadelphia. He'd discovered the ties between Senator Rothchild and a white supremacist group. He'd even made a podcast on a ten-year-old cold case of a young woman who was murdered while on vacation in Santa Barbara. That podcast led to a new break in the case. Barely anyone listened to it, sure, but he helped the police catch the killer. Whatever was happening in Essen with the Minty Green Club and The Grove, he'd been handed the baton. Maybe it'd started with Silus Oak. He was trying to tell everyone something with Midwest Mysteries, but barely anyone bought it, let alone read it. A frustration that Kyle was acutely sympathetic with. His dad had a much larger audience, though. Whether he was spurred on by Oak's book or came to the info as a Club member, Dunbar's Grove had been his attempt to reveal something. His dad, in desperation, entrusted this story to him.

Kyle had no idea how much his dad followed his career, but it must have been enough to think Kyle could figure it out. And now, Kyle was determined to follow through. Not for his dad, but for Janie and everyone else the Club had terrorized or even erased all these years. He needed to get over himself to do it. He needed to do his job.

# 24
# *Wild Buck's*

"Thank you both for coming," said Kyle, as he settled onto the hard, wooden bench at the booth.

"What?" asked Max and Janie simultaneously.

"I wanted to thank you both for coming!" This time Kyle said it much louder, trying not to be drowned out by the country music that was blaring out of the speakers.

"Well, I might not have if I realized where you were asking us to come to," said Max, darting his eyes around quickly and taking in the sea of slightly haggard white faces populating the bar at lunchtime on a Saturday. Thirty percent of the population of South Bend was black, and a hundred percent of them were far away from Wild Buck's Saloon.

"Sorry, this used to be a gay bar. I wanted somewhere we wouldn't have to worry about running into Manchester or any of the other Club members," said Kyle.

"Well, mission accomplished, I think," said Janie.

"You'd think they'd have had the decency to change the name," muttered Kyle.

"I can't take this shouting over the music. Do they have a patio or something?" Janie didn't wait for a response but grabbed her drink and started toward the back of the bar.

There was no patio, only a smoker's area loosely defined by some plastic mesh. However, they did find one empty booth next to a dartboard towards the back where the music was less oppressively loud.

"That's better, I can finally hear myself think," said Max. "For a moment back there, it was so loud I started to think I had a dog named Waylon and a drive that needed pavin'."

"What's up, Kyle? Did you figure out the symbols?" asked Janie.

"Symbols?" wondered Max. Kyle quickly got Max up to speed, apologizing for not keeping him in the loop.

"As for whether I figured them out. No. Like everything else, we've got a lot of questions and not a lot of facts or answers. That's why I wanted to meet you two here. Away from prying eyes. When I came to town, the last thing I was looking for was a story. Now I think I've got one whether I like it or not. If there's a chance of any of us getting out from under the Minty Green Club's thumb, we're going to have to figure out and expose… whatever it is they're doing," said Kyle.

"Hell, yes," said Janie. There was a fire in her eyes that Kyle recognized, but hadn't seen in a long time. It was reserved for people who really pissed her off. It was not a stare you wanted to be on the receiving end of. Kyle knew that from experience.

"First things first, though, Janie. I know you're not going to like it, but I need you to step back. No more meetings with us. Not in Essen. I think we should break off contact, at least until this is done."

"No way," Janie said, as though the matter was settled.

"Janie, I don't want you or our family hurt any more than they have been. I mean, how are you doing? How is Sean taking it?" asked Kyle.

"It sucks but I'm dealing with it. He's furious at the school. But we're figuring it all out. Looking for a new place, maybe even here in South Bend. But I'm already knee deep in this. I doubt me standing on the sidelines now is going to help any of that." Janie punctuated her sentence by slamming down the empty glass that'd held her vodka and cranberry.

"Janie, you're the one who pointed out to me that all of this might be the Club treating us with kid gloves. If they find out that I'm investigating them… this could get way more dangerous," said Kyle.

"So, what you're saying is this isn't some sexist 'protect the woman' crap? Then why aren't you telling Max to sit this one out?" Janie asked.

"I mean, I do have a kid and wife too," Max pointed out, before quickly adding, "not that you could keep me from helping you even if you wanted me to."

"I do want you to stay away. But first, I need to get some answers, and I think you can help. Normally, I'd start an investigation by looking at the paper trail. But we already know that the Club is connected enough to make paper trails disappear. They can alter news stories in the library! I'm not sure how much of that I can trust. Not to mention they seem to have eyes on us at all times."

"What's step two in the investigator handbook, then?" asked

Janie.

"Boots on the ground. I need to get into The Grove. Max, I was thinking since you lived in the area, you could—"

"Way ahead of you, man," said Max, pulling out his phone. "Or did you think I spent the last couple days with my finger in my ass?"

"What have you been up to?" Janie asked, suddenly concerned.

"I've been carefully doing a little reconnaissance. Like you said, Kyle. I live in the area. Heather, Zee and I go for walks all the time. I happened to suggest walking around The Grove," said Max.

"Max, that…" Kyle was about to scold him for being reckless but then realized this was pretty much what he was going to suggest Max do anyway. "What did you find?"

"Might be a jackpot." Max turned his phone around and flicked through a couple pictures.

"What are we looking at?" asked Janie. Max looked at the pictures, realizing for the first time how inscrutable they were without context.

"It's part of the fence around The Grove. My guess some dumb kid was taking the curve in LaGrange Road a little too quick in his daddy's convertible. There were tire tracks leading right to it," said Max.

Kyle took the phone from him, huddled up with Janie, and looked more closely at the picture, pinching his fingers to zoom in. Part of the bottom of the fence buckled inward. It was covered with streaks of red where it'd dug into the car's paint job.

"It's hard to tell, but it doesn't look like it's pushed that far up," said Janie. Kyle nodded. He'd seen that too. The fence was no joke, with girthy poles and a thick gauge of woven metal for the main walls of it. It reminded Kyle of the fence around Haverdale Prison back home.

"It's not that high. We'll have to push it up some. Possibly even dig a little into the ground to get in. But it's a chance. I took these shots yesterday. Told Heather I was going to report it to maintenance. I didn't, of course, but I doubt that they'll wait long before they fix it," said Max.

"Agreed. I'm not sure I can do that alone. Max if you can come with me and help get me in, I can take the rest from there. And then you go home, and try to forget about all of this," urged Kyle.

"No way in hell am I going to let you go into that place by yourself. You have no idea what you're walking into. You need someone to watch your back. Period," Max said.

"And I guess I'll make some muffins for you boys so you can have a snack after all that hard work," Janie said with no small amount of sarcasm.

"Janie, for whatever reason, they haven't gone after Max yet. Maybe because it's harder for them to go after his job. Or they hoped going after you would scare you both off. If I could do this without Max, I'd do it. It'd just put my mind at ease if one person I cared about in Essen was safe during all of this, okay?" asked Kyle, meeting Janie's steely gaze with one of his own. With this, Janie seemed to relent.

"Fine. Okay. But you text me the minute you're back home. Both of you," said Janie.

"We should do it tomorrow night," said Max. "If you're ready for it, Kyle. Most of the Lake is at Sunday night services at Faith & Triumph. It won't be too busy. Heather's taking Zee to her mom's place for the night too."

"Faith & Triumph?" asked Kyle.

"It's a church out by Minty Green," said Janie with disgust. "I think most of the Club goes there. I don't think they officially have said you can't go there if you're not in the Club, but one-time, Higher Faith tried to arrange a sort of fellowship field trip there. It's a pretty regular thing they do, sending people to different churches to see what the experience is like. Faith & Triumph is the only church that ever turned them down."

"Well, that might be good for us. The more Club members who are there, the less chance we have of running into them in The Grove. Fuck. Okay," said Kyle, downing his drink with one last swallow. "Let's do this."

From the front of the bar, the blaring pop-country was replaced with something far sadder. It was more like the country music Kyle remembered from his childhood when he'd ride with his mom in the Oldsmobile. She'd crank it up loud and sing along. Although he didn't recognize this one.

*Bury me deep / under the earth and stone*
*When the trumpets call / I'll find my way home*

# 25
# *Chicken & Guinness*

Kyle finally arrived back home around eight at night. He left most of the supplies he'd bought in the car since he planned to do his final packing at Max's. He also didn't want any prying eyes to see him take it inside. Ten minutes later, Patrick Kirby knocked on his door.

"Hey, Patrick," Kyle said as warmly as he could manage.

"Kyle! I've been worried sick! Where have you been? I tried calling and texting you," said Patrick. Kyle looked down at him; he was still standing at the bottom of the stairs that led up to the back door.

"Sorry. Come on in, I'll try to explain."

"Do I smell fried chicken?" Patrick asked as he walked in, sniffing the air. Kyle smiled and waved him on into the dining room. A bucket of fried chicken, a tub of mashed potatoes, a container of green beans, a tub of coleslaw, and a box of biscuits were sitting there

205

next to two paper plates and two newly-opened bottles of Guinness.

"A peace offering," said Kyle. Patrick rubbed his hands together hungrily, walked over to the table, picked up the bucket of chicken, and looked at the logo on the side of it.

"Champion Chicken! You remembered," he said. Patrick had told Kyle it was his favorite fast food. It was also a pain in the ass because the nearest one was in South Bend.

It nearly made Kyle ill to be in the room with the man, now that he knew he was working with Alice Manchester and the Minty Green Club. But Janie was right. They needed the Club to think they hadn't caught onto Patrick. It was even more important now that their guard wasn't up since they had a plan to infiltrate The Grove. Patrick sat down, got out two drumsticks and one breast, scooped out three large spoonfuls of mashed potatoes, and buttered his biscuits before digging in. Kyle watched him and realized he'd have thought all of this was adorable a few days ago. He pushed the sadness that welled up in him down again and tried to look apologetic.

"I had to go up to Michigan and get my dad's car out of the police impound," Kyle said finally. "And I needed to clear my head."

Patrick stopped mid-bite into the side of one of the chicken legs. He took the drumstick out of his mouth and frowned."About what? Did you find out something about all of this? The note your dad left? His book?"

"No, that's the problem. I haven't found out anything."

"So that's why you didn't answer the phone?" asked Patrick.

"That was the other thing I was thinking about. The part you're not going to like," said Kyle. Patrick put the chicken back down on his plate, took a swig of Guinness, and wiped his hands on his pant legs.

"Okay, lay it on me," he said.

"I'm leaving Essen. I mean, I always was. But I'm planning on leaving soon. Maybe even in a couple days," explained Kyle, observing the other man's reaction. He looked a little shocked and then sad. But Kyle thought he saw something else in his eyes. His eyes looked more yellow than green to Kyle now, like diseased piss. The thoughtfulness he'd seen before seemed more like calculation now. It was funny how easy it was to fool oneself. He didn't think Patrick was nearly as good an actor as he had previously given him credit for.

"Oh. I guess I thought you might stick around a little longer," Patrick said.

"I thought about it. But, to be honest, I'm not getting anywhere here. You should have seen my dad's car. I am starting to wonder if he was just a sick, confused man. And I do have a life to get back to."

"In Peoria."

"Right. And you and I… we've been getting close. A little too close too fast. I don't want to hurt you, and I don't want to get hurt. That's why I think it's better that we cool things off and be friends," said Kyle.

Patrick's eyes misted up. Kyle wondered what his technique was to start the waterworks. Was he thinking of his mother dying? His hand was in a fist. Was he digging his nails into his palms? Had he been trained by the Club for this sort of infiltration? Or was he naturally good at faking emotions to get what he wanted? He certainly wouldn't be the first guy Kyle had met with that particular talent.

"Okay. I don't like it. But I can accept it. Maybe it's even the smart thing to do," Patrick said quietly.

Because of course he did, Kyle thought. This was working out perfectly for Patrick. He was getting rid of Kyle. The Club had finally scared Kyle away. And Patrick wouldn't have to pretend to be into him. Wouldn't have to open himself up to him. Kyle thought about getting one last go at him before he cut off the relationship sexually. But he felt a revenge fuck would probably do as much damage to him as it would Patrick (once he and his collaborators were exposed) and, to be honest, Kyle wasn't sure he had it in him. Kyle forced all these thoughts away, reached out his hand, and squeezed Patrick's.

"It's entirely possible I'm being an idiot. But you're not so far away. We can keep in touch. Let this progress a little more naturally," Kyle said, taking a scoop of mashed potatoes into his mouth. But he couldn't even register the taste of them. All he could think about was the next night. He was more determined now more than ever to find something in The Grove. The Club had to be hiding something. And he was going to damn well find out what it was.

# 26
# *The Lady Dancing*

"Bottoms up," said Max Williams as he and Kyle downed the second shot of whiskey he'd put before them.

"Okay, enough liquid courage," Kyle said through a wince as the warm burn traveled down his throat. "I need to be able to hold my camera straight."

"We're going to do this?" Max glanced over at the blue LED numbers shining brightly from the clock on the stainless-steel oven in his kitchen. It was nearly time to head out.

The vast majority of the inhabitants of the Lake of the Grove, as well as Minty Green Club members from around Essen, we're heading to the Faith & Triumph Fellowship church right now. A little after the eight o'clock service began, Max would be leading Kyle to The Grove.

"You don't have to come with me," Kyle said. "Help me get through the fence, and then come back here. I mean it."

"Don't tempt me," Max said grumpily. "I'd never forgive myself. Ride or die, man. Ride or die."

Kyle turned away from him and focused his attention to the central island in the kitchen. He began to pack up his bag, taking one last look to make sure he had everything he needed. Kyle had done a little shopping the previous day in South Bend after leaving the meeting with Janie and Max. He had a water bottle, a few protein bars (in case he got lost or couldn't get out right away,) a small hunting knife that he hoped he'd only to use on any dense vegetation, and a new video camera. He'd considered using his phone, but the camera on that was pretty much useless in low light. He wasn't sure what he might have to capture as evidence in The Grove. He wanted to be ready for anything. Anything he was afraid of losing—like the map— was left at home, though he had plenty of pictures on his phone to reference as needed.

"It's not too late for you to turn around, too," said Max. He looked sideways at Kyle, knowing the suggestion wasn't going to sit well.

"I can't do that," said Kyle.

"Yeah, yeah. I know." Max took a small flashlight from a drawer in the kitchen and handed it to Kyle. "I get it. You need to do this. You probably should do it."

Kyle didn't respond at first, because he'd been readying himself for an extended argument. He was grateful that Max relented so quickly. He wasn't sure he had the mental space or patience to have the debate. His every thought was focused on the task they were about to undertake. At eight o'clock sharp, an alarm buzzed on Kyle's phone.

"It's time to go," said Kyle.

Max nodded his head, and they crept to the sliding glass door at the rear of his house that overlooked the lake. The lake itself was motionless and reflected the inky, starless sky above them. More clouds moved in. They were dark and gray and looked ready to burst, but they hadn't yet. They did bring a chill breeze with them, however. It was gentle, though, and barely seemed to disturb the surface of the lake. Max led the way, with Kyle creeping slowly behind him. They kept to the lakeside, as there was little in the form of light back there. No one wanted bright lights shining across the lake and into the back windows of their house. So other than the occasional dull blue dock light, Max and Kyle could move in shadow. The humidity in the air made the grass wet and cold, and Kyle could feel the top of his socks and the bottom of his jeans get damp as they made their way through some of the taller grasses that dotted the lake-shore.

They walked with purpose, but not too quickly. Even though most of the Lake attended the Sunday night church service religiously, that didn't mean everyone was there. They tried to be as quiet as possible. Kyle concentrated on the wet rustle of the grass against his shoes and the gentle lapping of the lake against the docks and soft mud of the shore. Max lived on the side of the lake farthest from The Grove, but they were already halfway there when Kyle heard music from across the lake. It was distorted and strange—both tinny and echoing. It featured a high male voice (or a low female voice) with a heavily stylized falsetto singing over a piano. The full effect was positively eerie, and Kyle couldn't help but stare across the lake and try to figure out where it was coming from. He started making out some of the lyrics.

*Hey brother / oh sister / won't you tell me / 'bout your mister.*

Kyle narrowed the source of the music to a two-story house of a modern, squared design with large windows that looked out on the lake. He peered into the blackness of the windows and thought he could see a figure walking by in the dark, half-hidden by the mirrored image of the house's surroundings. Suddenly, the lights downstairs blazed on, and it shocked Kyle so much he nearly lost his footing. The singer was doing some sort of freestyle vocal noodling now, and as it echoed and reverberated across the lake, Kyle was astonished to see a ghostly white figure dancing in the window. She drifted across the floor with such grace she looked like she was floating, her long white hair flowing as if it were underwater as she spun around and side to side. Her arms were raised up as if dancing with an invisible suitor.

"What are you doing?" Max said in a hoarse stage-whisper.

Kyle broke his gaze from the figure in the window, his heart pounding now. He was surprised to see Max was the length of two backyards away from him and making his way back. His eyes were wide with disbelief.

"I heard the music. And then in the window—" Kyle began.

"You saw Mary Winston practicing her dancing and decided to play Peeping Tom?"

"What?" Kyle asked, looking once more again across the water and into the window. He saw her more clearly now. The music changed to something more contemporary. It might have been a Mariah Carey song. The woman was dressed all in white. What he'd thought was her ghostly white hair was a veil that flowed down her back and partially obscured her face.

"She's getting married next week. I guess she's practicing her moves for the reception," Max said. "I thought getting to The Grove was, I don't know… urgent?"

Kyle nodded his head and wordlessly urged Max onward. Kyle did not know why he'd become entranced with the dancing figure. He didn't understand why he'd even entertained that she might have been some sort of specter. It was precisely the sort of childish nonsense that was getting in the way of him thinking clearly the whole trip. But there was something about this place. He could feel it in his bones.

When he was in Holland and then Silver Cove, it'd been easy to see that his fear and feeling of nameless, creeping dread were silly artifacts of his youth. Like the face in the tree that stood to the right of the farmhouse when he was young. He hated that tree. When he was around four or five, he used to dash past the window that offered a clear view of it because he was sure he'd seen a face there. For months he avoided looking at the tree and closed the curtains when he thought he could get away with it. Finally, one day his dad figured out he was scared, despite his efforts not to show it. Even at that young of an age, he knew his dad had no time for that kind of sissy thinking.

He'd waited until night and told Kyle they were going to look at the tree. Kyle shook with sheer terror at the prospect. He screamed as his dad tried to drag him out of the house. He kicked as his dad picked him up in his strong arms. Then his dad gave him three hard swats on his behind. He stopped kicking and held back his tears for fear they'd earn him more slaps. His dad sat him in front of the tree and made him stare at it.

"There's nothing there, Kyle. Grow a pair and look at it," Herbert Thomas growled. "Now."

Kyle knew that tone. He understood that there was no more arguing or bargaining when his dad sounded like that. He told himself that there was nothing there. His father wasn't scared. He wouldn't be either. He opened his eyes. But the face was still there. It was sleeping, to be sure. But he could see it so clearly. The sleepy round knots for eyes. The jagged break in the bark was its yawning mouth full of sharp pointed teeth. It was asleep because they'd gone to look at it. But it would be angry now. It'd watch Kyle so much more closely. Kyle knew it with full certainty.

Eventually, the tree had gotten some sort of rot. When Kyle was ten, his dad cut it down. Even six years after being forced to confront it, Kyle was relieved. He'd learned to live with the face in the tree. But he never liked looking at it. When he entered the living room, he walked straight forward and didn't look to his right. But he could feel it staring at him. He understood that the face could not be real. But that didn't seem to make it any less frightening or feel any less real. He realized now that the creeping fear he'd been feeling ever since he'd arrived in Essen—from Lissie's warning to the fully lit farmhouse at night, to the Jesus painting and now Mary Winston's ghostly dance—had been a warning.

He didn't understand how. But he knew there was something real here to fear. And that fear was growing exponentially the further he walked toward The Grove. Kyle did not believe in the metaphysical. He wasn't opposed to it as a concept, but he'd never seen any practical use for it in his everyday life. A disproportionate amount of gay men were into tarot cards, astrology, chakras, and the like. Kyle had gone from being a believer to a total non-believer to a more casual feeling that if it made an individual happy, they should be welcome to their belief. He was starting to reconsider the arrogance of his thinking. His sense that he was somehow above all of that. Because a thought popped into his mind. He wondered if whatever the Club was up to in The Grove—whatever evil they may have done—might have seeped out into the rest of Essen. The thought was ridiculous, with no basis in any sort of reality Kyle knew. But edging along the lake in the darkness toward The Grove, it felt real and it felt right.

Max turned around and looked at him. He was clearly concerned, and Kyle thought he had the right to be. But there was no way in hell he was going to share all of this with him right now.

# 27
# *Churchgoing*

anie pushed her green beans around on her plate. She'd over-salted them for her tastes. She'd forgotten about the bacon she'd added while cooking them, which meant not much more salt was even needed. But her husband and kids all seemed to be enjoying them, at least.

"Chunhua, tell mommy she has to eat her vegetables, too," Sean Hackett said to their oldest daughter with a smile. Chunhua turned her head, clearly delighted with her task, and started to repeat her father dutifully. Janie cut her off.

"Chunhua, tell your daddy that mommy isn't in the mood," she said through a forced grin and gritted teeth.

Chunhua's eyes grew wide, and she smiled mischievously. She was young enough to think of mommy and daddy getting testy with each other as a fun novelty and nothing more. She also knew that relaying this message to her father would not be necessary. Sean already had his hands up in surrender. The twins, Oni and Lanre, were not even a year old yet, so the squabbles of their parents held no particular fascination. Instead, they were more concerned with mashing their fingers into the green beans, and then shaking them vigorously and watching the pieces fly across their highchairs.

"Sorry," Janie said quietly. "My mind's preoccupied."

"I could tell," said Sean. He glanced down at Chunhua's plate, which was empty. "Honey, why don't you go wash up and brush your teeth."

The seven-year-old looked at him grumpily, fully aware she was being sent away while the grown-ups talked. But she complied after she saw her father meant business.

"Good girl," Janie said, giving her a quick kiss on the forehead as she passed by. Sean waited for Chunhua to leave and then reached out and gave his wife's hand a gentle squeeze.

"I'm guessing this has something to do with Kyle Thomas," he said. Janie exhaled.

"Yeah. I'm worried about him," she said.

"He's a big boy, Janie."

"I know that. He's… on assignment. It might be dangerous."

"From the scraps of his work you've collected over the years, it seems like he gets into possibly dangerous situations regularly," noted Sean. "And you never even knew about it. Until after the fact."

"Yes, well this time I do know about it beforehand," said Janie. She gave up on her food, sat her fork down, and threw the blue cloth napkin—a wedding gift from her parents—onto the plate. "I can't turn it off. Not even after twelve years."

"Can't turn what off?" Sean said this in a way that made it clear he knew the answer. He wanted to hear Janie say it.

"I can't turn off caring about him," she said.

"You can't turn off loving him."

"It's not like that."

"It is a little bit, though, honey," Sean asserted. His tone was even, with all the emotional baggage of someone reciting the state capitals. Janie knew he'd had a long time to mull this all over. They'd never talked about it. Kyle was gone, so there was nothing to talk about. But she knew it was lurking there, in the back of his mind. As it was lurking in the back of hers. "And he loves you."

"As a friend, yes," said Janie.

"Janie, you seem to forget I was there at the wedding, too. When you invited him to be a maid of honor—or man of honor, I guess—he was up there with the wedding party and smiling. But his heart was breaking. Believe me. I've seen that look before. In the mirror."

"He's gay, Sean. Full on. Believe me, if there were some inkling of something else there, I'd know," said Janie. She laughed at this, but it sounded forced and fake.

"I believe you. I also know that he loves you, and you love him. The two things aren't mutually exclusive," said Sean. Janie opened her mouth to protest some more, but Sean cut her off with a wave of his hand. "I'm saying all of this not because I'm jealous or feel threatened because he's back. I'm saying this because I want you to know I understand. Okay?"

Before Janie could respond, Chunhua called from the bathroom.

"Daddy, the toilet's not going down!" she cried, a mild note of disgust in her voice.

"Chunhua, you didn't put anything down there again, did

you?" asked Sean as he got up from the chair. He gave his wife a "what're you going to do?" shrug and headed for the bathroom.

Janie looked at her watch. It was past eight. Max and Kyle were making their way to The Grove by now. And here she was, expected to twiddle her thumbs. She hated it. She'd felt so helpless since she'd lost her job. A lot of her friends and colleagues didn't believe the accusations. But not all of them immediately sided with her. On some level, she thought that was probably a good thing. When children came forward, they needed to be heard and believed. It was only that, in this case, it wasn't true. But there was no un-cracking this particular egg. So now all she and Sean could do was move forward, taking Chunhua, Oni, and Lanre with them. Kyle talked to her once, before the wedding, about the people he'd found in Peoria—about his "found family." She'd liked that concept. She thought of Sean and the kids as her "forged family." Assembled from all over the globe to be here and right now. She knew they'd make it through this. But it made the loss of her job, and the possible loss of the respect and trust of her friends, no less hurtful.

The truth was, she was still enraged. She wanted revenge on Alice Manchester, and her concern for Kyle was as much about her needing him to succeed as much as it was a concern for his safety. And not being able to help was driving her mad.

Sean came back to the dining room, and it was the instant that he sat down that Janie had an idea.

"That girl. She swears it just happened, but I was sure there was more toilet paper on the roll when I washed my hands before dinner," Sean said. He returned to his dinner, taking a chunk of the pot roast onto his fork and then scooping it into his mouth.

"Honey, I think I might go to the church. To pray for Kyle. I am worried about this assignment he's on," she said.

"The church? Higher Faith? You're going to drive an hour to pray?" There were equal amounts of confusion and suspicion in his voice. "God can hear your prayers wherever you are. You know that."

"It's less about God, and it's more about me," said Janie. "I think I would find it calming."

"Does Higher Faith even let people in at this hour? It's not like one of those Catholic churches in the movies."

"Yes, they have the small chapel on the East side of the complex for that very thing." Janie made sure her tone suggested she was a little scandalized that Sean didn't know this. As she hoped, he looked abashed at not having known about the chapel. Janie knew her husband well. He had a strong belief in God, but the church was more a social club for him than anything. He put his own napkin on his plate and shook his head a little wearily.

"I mean… if it'll make you feel more at peace… I can get the kids to bed," he said.

"Thank you!" Janie said, springing up from her chair. She wrapped her arms around Sean's head and squeezed him tight. She pulled back, looked into his blue-gray eyes, and then kissed him deeply. She could hear Oni giggling, and she smiled.

"All right let's start the washing-up process," Sean said, scooping the still-giggling Oni into his arms. Janie watched him for a moment, as Sean took Oni into the kitchen. She walked to the little table next to their front door and retrieved her keys. She felt awful lying to her husband. She'd try to make it up to him at some point. She'd been honest about one thing, though. She was going to a church. But not the one he assumed.

# 28
# *Infiltration*

ax and Kyle finally made it to the edge of the tree line that created a natural perimeter around the Lake of the Grove. Now they had to cross LaGrange Road, and they'd be at The Grove itself. Thankfully the moon was obscured by clouds, so there wasn't a lot of natural light to expose them as they crossed the road. But it was the most open and vulnerable they'd be the entire journey. Max crossed first since he knew exactly where the break in the fence was. He looked in both directions, making sure there wasn't a sudden burst of light as a car came speeding around the curve. This was a regular occurrence and was the reason they had an opportunity to get into The Grove at all.

Satisfied nothing was coming, Max shuffled in a crouching position across the road. Despite the danger and seriousness of everything, Kyle wanted to laugh. Max looked back at him and waved him forward. Kyle took one look himself either way and then walked briskly across the road without crouching.

"Haven't you ever heard about keeping low to the ground?" hissed Max.

"I don't think crouching down by four inches is going to make a lot of difference," Kyle said. Max rolled his eyes and turned from him, still shuffling through the wet grass. Kyle could make out the faint glimmer of the fence here and there, but otherwise, the night seemed almost impossibly black and murky. Kyle walked slowly behind Max, suddenly aware of how exposed they were to the road. There was no way they could use flashlights while they tried to get through the fence. Anyone coming around the curve would see them instantly. His thoughts were cut off by a loud metallic jangle ahead of him.

"Fucking fuck!" whispered Max.

"What are you doing?" asked Kyle.

"Sorry, it's dark here under the trees. I ran right into the fence. But I found the hole."

"I bet you say that to all the boys you bring out here." Kyle could not see, but he could practically feel, the eye roll now being directed at him. Kyle reached out his hands, and it was freakishly dark. He felt the fence, and then felt the indent where it had been bowed in by the impact of the car crash. He exhaled in relief.

"We're not in yet," said Max.

"I know. There was part of me that was scared we'd get all the way here, and they'd have already fixed it," said Kyle.

"Jesus, well glad you didn't share that. I'm stressed enough as it is," said Max.

Kyle took off his backpack, got on his belly, and made an experimental attempt to slide across the wet grass and under the battered fence. He didn't get far before the sharp bottom ends of the fence dug into his shirt and scratched his back.

"Well, we knew it wasn't going to be that easy," Kyle said. He felt for his backpack, found it, and fished out the work gloves he'd packed. All of this would have been so much easier if they could only use a flashlight. He put the gloves on, grabbed the bottom of the fence, and tried to shove it upward. It gave a little with a metallic groan. Kyle pushed up with all his strength, but the fence was not giving that much. He pushed it up an inch or so, and then released it. A metallic twang shook and reverberated through the fence as it bounced back into place.

"I guess we'll need to dig some? To make the opening a little wider?" asked Max.

"I don't think we have the time," said Kyle. He knew it'd take some time to get to The Grove, but it was already nearing half past the hour. The more time it took to get in, the less time they'd have in The Grove before they might have visitors. "I think if we hold the fence up for each other, we can squeeze through. The indented section is fairly wide. Just not that tall. It snaps back into place, but it has a decent amount of give when you're applying pressure. You go first." Kyle slid over to give Max room to slide in next to him. Then Kyle pushed the fence up with all his might. Again, the metal groaned in protest, but it did give. Max started to inch his way forward.

"I need to switch to a light beer," Max said. He grunted in pain as Kyle heard the fence rip through the front of his shirt.

"You okay?" asked Kyle.

"Yeah, a few scratches. Nothing I can't handle." Max continued to wiggle under the fence for what seemed like eons. But finally, he was free. A burst of air jetted out of his mouth, and Kyle realized he must have been holding his stomach in. After giving himself a moment to catch his breath, Max reached down and pulled up on the bent fencing as hard as he could. Kyle moved to inch forward when he heard the steady thrum of tires on the road. A splash of white light—only interrupted by the diamond-shaped shadow pattern from the fence—fell onto Max's shocked face.

"Car!" Max said hoarsely, although Kyle was way ahead of him.

Kyle had the vague sense the fence wasn't yet high enough, but he knew there was no time to worry about that. He braced himself, got some leverage with his legs, and slid under the fence in one quick motion. Unfortunately, the fence was still too low, and three of the bottom ends of the fence ripped through cloth and skin as he made his way under. He only allowed himself a small grunt of pain as he lifted himself up. The full beam of the car's headlights fell upon them, but they were sheltered by the darkness of the trees and the fence now. However, as the car's lights flashed over them, Kyle saw three streaks of crimson on his chest. He touched it experimentally, and his hand came away covered in something sticky and warm.

"I'm so sorry, Kyle. I didn't get it up high enough," said Max when he saw the wounds.

"It's fine. Deep scratches is all, I think," said Kyle. "The important thing is we're in, Max. We're in The Grove."

# *The Grove: Essen, Indiana*

An excerpt from
*Midwest Mysteries & Other Phenomena*
by Silas Oak

And now for the mystery that sparked my interest in all things weird and strange to be found in the Midwest. A quick search on the internet (which my wife helped with, love you Jeannie) will show no mention of The Grove. But to me, it holds much more fascination than any of the other tales in this book. I'll admit, I'm probably partial to it because it's in my backyard. But this was definitely where this journey started for me. It's the heart of the web from which all the rest of these stories were spun.

The Grove, as it has been called for as long as anyone can remember, is (as you might guess from the name) a cluster of trees that covers 10 acres to the southwest of Essen, Indiana. If you were to go visit it (more on that later), you'd see that it's near a small lake. Because people back in the day didn't see much need to be clever, they called it The Lake of the Grove. It's surrounded by the same trees that make up The Grove—the mighty white oak. White oaks are large trees, and these are no exception. They can live hundreds of years, and some of the fallen oaks in the area have been dated at well over three hundred. Indiana, like much of the Midwest, used to be home to vast forests that went on and on. This is the land the Potawatomi called home when ninety-percent of the state was covered in trees. The land stayed that way, even until 1816 when Indiana became a state.

In the early 1900s, the mass deforestation of the land began. This is also when the story of The Grove (as we know it today) began. Essen officially became a town in 1853. Its name was chosen by the large population of German immigrants in the area. There was much debate over whether it should be Essen or New Essen, but it was ultimately decided the latter was a little too awkward on the tongue. Two families bought a great deal of land in the area at this time—the Bakers (derived from the German "Beck") and the Langs. The Bakers would eventually win the bid to dominate land ownership in the area, but it is the Langs who most shaped the fate of The Grove. August and Gabriele Lang moved to the area from New England, where their parents were successful shipping magnates. The brother and sister duo were eager to escape their parents' shadow (using their parent's money of course) and settled in Indiana. They bought hundreds of acres of land to the south of Essen. Gabriele was the main driver of their business ventures, however. She was the one who led the charge to cut down the trees and make a move toward farmland. It was a strategy the Bakers were having a great deal of success with. August, however, was occupied by other pursuits.

August had been a member of a secret society called The Priory Club. If you've not heard of them, you're not alone. As far as I can tell, they're an entirely American invention—a sort of rural, new-world answer to the Masons with no connections to any similarly-named

European organizations. Unlike the Masons, whose history is still well kept within their halls across the nation, the history of the Priory Club is scattered at best. By the early 1930s, there was not much left of them. What we do know is that August decided to open a chapter in Essen, hoping to make it a destination spot for men across the area. The Essen Priory Club was a beautiful two-story house that sat on land adjacent to The Grove (to its West) and The Lake of the Grove (to its South.) August wanted privacy for his fellow society members, so he ordered that the land around the Club was not to be developed. There should always be a wall of white oak around the Club. By 1899, the Priory Club was infamous for its debauchery.

Then the disappearances began. A story printed in the Essen Town Crier, dated September 3, 1899, briefly notes "several women of dubious character" were reported missing in the area. It then quickly gets to the actual subject of the story, which was the disappearance of Ms. Josephine Loretta Baker. Ms. Baker was different from the other disappearances in that her family had money and was one of the most prominent families in the area. Her father was also engaged in a bitter battle with the Langs over property lines. As you might imagine, when Ms. Baker's best friend, Hettie Jones, said that she'd last seen her heading to the Priory Club, life became tense for August Lang. That is, until Josephine Baker returned to her family a few days later, wandering out from under the twisting branches of the white oaks that surrounded the Priory. Her dress and face were dirty, and her hair was matted and wet. But she could not remember where she had been. She experienced occasional bouts of forgetfulness long after her disappearance. August Lang considered the matter closed, guessing Josephine had merely gotten turned around and was suffering from some womanly stress after the ordeal. The man she was supposed to meet there, Zachary Herbert, long maintained that she never made their planned, secret meeting.

However, all of this did not sit well with Gabriele Lang, and a rift began to form between brother and sister. The details after this are sketchy, but more young women disappeared from Essen in the area of The Grove. None were ever of the same social standing as Josephine Baker, and it seems that August Lang was able to pay off the local authorities because no more charges were ever brought against him or the Priory Club. However, the story of the Essen Priory Club came to an end in 1924 when the building burned to the ground, taking August Lang and two of his associates with him. No cause for the fire was ever discovered, but there was plenty of talk.

The rumor was that Gabriele Lang smiled as her brother's coffin was lowered into the earth. Those who saw it said the smile was not one of happiness, but of satisfaction. The remains of the Priory Club were taken away or buried, and the land upon which it sat was turned into farmland. However, stories of ghostly voices coming from the area became popular and continue to this day. There was a rumor that August Lang still held parties for the dead at the old site of the Priory Club.

Gabriele Lang, realizing the business worth of having a popular destination for people in the area, decided to start a club of her own. This club, however, would be a little more inclusive. Men and women were encouraged to join. It was not a secret society, but a golf and social club. She named it the Minty Green Club, after one of the major crops that was grown on her land. When I say inclusive, however, that does not include any people of color. The new club was built to the Southwest of town this time, to further distance it from the old Priory Club. The strange decision made at his time, however, was that The Grove, and the nearby lake, were virtually abandoned. It was no surprise they left the lake as it was, but The Grove was ten acres of potential farmland. The fact it was left standing and not cleared is intriguing. Locals still frequented the two spots, with the Lake of the Grove becoming popular with families, and The Grove taking on a more spiritual air as it became home to a graveyard.

As far as I can tell, the Minty Green Club has owned the property ever since. Gabriele Lang died ten years after the fire that claimed her brother's life. She had no heirs, and her estate was left to the Club.  By the late 60s, the graves in The Grove were vandalized so regularly, families stopped burying their dead there. The Lake of the Grove was similarly mistreated. With no one making a claim on the land, squatters began taking over. When I was a kid, you didn't go to either unless you were up to no good. And I can tell you, no one in town that I knew had a clue that the Minty Green Club were the owners. If they did, I'd suspect someone from law enforcement would have made them clean up their property or secure it. Then again, it's a little unclear how much power the law held in The Grove and at the Lake.

You see, the stories of disappearances didn't stop after the old Priory Club burned down. They seemed to increase. I wish I could tell you how many disappearances there actually were. I probably spent more time researching this than any other part of this book, and although I could find plenty of people sharing stories of friends or relatives who went missing in the area, I couldn't find much in the way of official police records about it. The relatives were told the cases were hopeless. The cases were closed. And then the cases themselves disappeared off the books. This is part of what intrigues me so much about The Grove. Unlike the ghosts of Alton or the skin-walkers in

Des Moines, the nature of the mystery is something of a mystery itself. People feel uneasy in The Grove. There are disappearances. And then, there are the reappearances.

Josephine Baker was not the only person to disappear and then mysteriously return days later. They would also have no memory of what happened to them. A scientist friend of mine has speculated there might be some sort of strange gravity or electric field at work in The Grove that throws people's internal processes off balance. Another, less scientific friend speculated it was aliens. Like all the other mysteries here, I can only speculate. I've been to The Grove many times in my life. I've felt the eerie pulse of it, even when I've been driving by. I studied the shattered and weathered gravestones. I also watched it every night for three weeks straight, wondering if I might see strange lights in the sky or unidentified figures going in or out of it. I saw nothing.

Unfortunately, any answers about The Grove might remain forever out of our grasp now. The longtime owners of the property, the Minty Green Club, have decided to close it off to the public at the behest of the club's new president. Supposedly for safety reasons. It's hard to deny this is probably for the best. The recent redevelopment of the Lake of the Grove into an up-scale neighborhood might have something to do with it. I only hope fencing it off might stop the string of mysterious disappearances associated with the place. May no other family be left awake at night, wondering where their father, mother, son, or daughter was stolen away to.

# 29
# *Faith & Triumph*

anie pulled into the parking lot of the Faith & Triumph Fellowship and was unsure of whether she could even find a spot, let alone one out of the way so she could go relatively unnoticed. The church was only a mile away from the Minty Green Club itself, which was relatively isolated and on the way out of town. There were no side streets to park in discreetly. The lot was full of SUVs, mini-vans, and a few sedans. All of them were luxury cars, or at a minimum, a fully trimmed-out middle-tier brand. They all looked freshly washed, and Janie realized her dusty little powder-blue Honda was going to stand out no matter what she did. Finally, she found a spot on the shadowed East side of the church.

Warm orange light shone through the multi-colored facets of the stained-glass windows. She could not deny the beauty of the church. It had been a Methodist church when it was first built. It was decently-sized but not huge. The humble building was a far cry from the Higher Faith church Janie attended. They did not like to call it a mega-church. But it looked more like a convention center than a church at first glance, with its arena-like central congregation hall, multiple-levels of meeting rooms, on-site school, coffee shop, 24-hour chapel, and even a theater to show inspiring films. This church was much more of the classic model, with white walls, a pointed roof tiled in brownish red, and an elegant white steeple with a bell. Janie rolled down her window, and she could hear the muffled voice of the preacher inside, his voice rising and lowering in undulating rhythms. She could not make out the words, but she could hear the response of the congregation as it clapped or called out amen. Suddenly, a choir began to sing something slow and melodic, and Janie could hear the congregation sing along. She thought she recognized the song, but she realized that from this far away, many of the church songs she knew would probably sound like each other.

For a moment, she found it strangely comforting to be sitting out in her car and listening to a service that sounded so much like the ones she was used to, if more traditional. There could be unity in belief. She almost felt bad for spying on them. As soon as she thought this, however, she remembered that there were people inside this church—forty or fifty judging by the number of cars in the lot—who were all a part of whatever was going on in The Grove. They'd gotten her fired. Whatever they'd done had driven Kyle's father to suicide. They might have even driven Herbert Thomas to madness before that. Assuming, of course, their current theory was correct.

She knew all too well the hypocrisy of churchgoers. It was unavoidable, since what was a church but a group of human beings? She'd been the one who'd spoken up about the youth pastor who'd made the crude gay jokes that drove Kyle away. "How can we be good Christians," she'd asked the pastor's wife, "if we make anyone feel lesser than?" The youth pastor was fired, and the church made its message of inclusivity clear. But it was already too late for Kyle. He was done with the church, and Janie could hardly blame him, although she did argue with him a few times about not giving it another try. That was just one example of dozens in all the years she'd attended Higher Faith. But the thought of people in those pews singing songs praising Jesus, and then doing whatever they did at The Grove was sickening. They were destroying lives for the sake of worldly things.

Janie's anger at the thought of this gave her a renewed sense of purpose and even perked her up some. She sat up straighter in the driver's seat of her Honda and watched. It wasn't much, but at least she could text Max and Kyle when the church let out. At least she felt like she was doing something.

# 30
# *Into the Grove*

Kyle kept his flashlight pointed to the ground. It was still a risk using it, but the foliage was thick above them. The already dark night became so devoid of light underneath the canopy of trees that it was difficult to see their own hands, let alone navigate the grounds of The Grove, which was littered with roots, fallen branches, brambles, and tall grasses. The amount of growth felt unnatural to Kyle, although he was hardly an expert. He'd walked through plenty of woods and forests, though, and he hadn't remembered one in the area that felt this thickly populated with vegetation.

"Should have brought a machete," Max said, echoing his thoughts.

"Or a bulldozer," Kyle said quietly. The reality of searching through ten acres of wooded land in a limited amount of time was starting to sink in. He knew it'd be difficult, but now, the task seemed impossible.

"What exactly are we looking for?" asked Max.

"I don't know. That's the problem. Some more security? A hidden tunnel entrance or something like that."

"Did you say a hidden tunnel entrance?"

"Does that sound so insane at this point?" asked Kyle, a little more sharply than intended. But he felt like they were long past the point of disbelief now. "Let's start by heading toward the graveyard at the center."

"Okay. I guess that makes as much sense as anything," said Max. Kyle hoped so. The cemetery was the focal point of his dad's book. In Dunbar's Grove, the protagonist visited the graveyard three times. At the start when he met his wife Anne, when she died, and then finally at the book's climax. Kyle had only properly visited The Grove once. When he was sixteen, he heard some guys at school talk about how the place was being overrun with "queers" getting off in the woods. Despite the fact the guys also talked about finding these "queers" and beating their asses, Kyle was intrigued. Smartphones and apps were years off still, and he didn't know anyone else in Essen who was gay. Or, to be more precise, there were no other gay guys that he knew of. He borrowed the family Oldsmobile, saying he was going to the movies with Janie to watch Independence Day. Instead, he'd come out to The Grove. In those days, people parked their cars along LaGrange road and walked in.

It was an easy hike through one of the many trails that were worn into the place. Kyle was clueless when it came to cruising, so he walked around the path for a while, and then off the trail for as far as he dared to go, hoping something might happen. What exactly that something was, he couldn't have said. But he was sure he'd know it when he saw it. A knowing look. A dick hanging out of an open fly. Nothing ended up happening though. He saw a group of stoners from school huddled around a bong. That was it. He got bored, and since he was supposed to be at a movie, he drove to the library and stayed there until it closed, looking through copies of GQ and feeling horny and lame.

After another five minutes, Kyle and Max found one of the old trails. It was overgrown, but a far cry from the denseness they were slogging through. Having a path to follow also meant they were able to put their flashlights away. Occasionally, Kyle would turn his phone on to use its light to double-check they were still on the trail, but they were making good time now.

"I think the trail is turning," Max whispered.

Kyle took out his phone to use the light again, and sure enough, the trail began to curve around the black mass of three trees that grew so close together, they'd become intertwined. Kyle kept his phone pointed down and followed the curve of the trail until it straightened out. He hit the button to lock his phone and was surprised to see the trail was still somewhat illuminated even after his cellphone was dark. But this light wasn't the harsh blue-white of the phone's screen. It was warm and orange. Kyle lifted his head up and was shocked to see flickering orange shimmers of light poking through the vertical shafts of the trees and scattering in constantly shuffling patterns through the leaves. Kyle could smell the distinct smoky sweetness of wood burning. He saw the rays of light as they highlighted occasional swirls of smoke floating through the branches.

"What the hell is this? Are they having a bonfire?" Kyle asked.

"Maybe that's whatever we're looking for?" suggested Max, shrugging his shoulders.

Kyle stayed crouched there, wondering what to do next. He listened intently and was sure he heard voices in the distance. There was always a chance that the Club would leave some guards behind, of course. But the fire worried him. Guards wouldn't make a fire and announce themselves, would they? But there was nothing else they could do. They had to go check it out. They were almost to the graveyard. Either this would be something of interest or something to avoid. They needed to know what it was in any case.

# 31

## *Here's the Church and Here's the Steeple Open it Up...*

anie rested her head against the frame of her car window. It'd been nearly a half hour since she arrived. She hadn't thought about how dull her little stake-out might be. The air was getting colder, presaging the storm that was coming. She could smell it on the air, and the clouds had been ominous and full-looking most of the afternoon. She still listened to the congregation, waiting for any sign that the service might be over. The group began to sing another song, and out of boredom, Janie decided to guess which one it was. She tried to filter out the sound of the blowing wind and listened to the duh-duh dum duh duh-dum of the music. She recognized it. It was That Old Rugged Cross. But there was something odd about this. She thought back to the first song she'd heard when she'd pulled up. The other one she couldn't nail down. Hadn't that been That Old Rugged Cross? No, she'd said it herself; so many of these church songs sounded similar. They were often made to be sung easily, so they weren't necessarily the most complex of arrangements.

She surprised herself when she unbuckled her seat-belt and opened her door. She walked slowly toward the church. The song finished, and there was a chorus of hallelujahs once it was done. The pastor started speaking as he had been before. She still couldn't make out the words, but she could more clearly hear the responses of the congregation. A woman with a high, staccato laugh (that reminded Janie of dolphin chattering) let out a guffaw. The woman must have been easily amused because Janie remembered hearing her laughing it up earlier too. Janie looked at the stained-glass windows. They were purely abstract rather than pictorial. She watched them as the pastor continued his sermon, and there was something about them that did not seem quite right.

It bothered her enough that she walked all the way up to the window and tried to peer in. But it was impossible. The glass was so textured and warped that the inside of the church was an inscrutable pattern of light and shadow. Janie pressed her ear to the window, and for the first time, she could hear the preacher clearly. His voice was deep and resonant and pleasant.

"—to thank you all again for coming. As we begin tonight's sermon, I want to talk to you about something I've been contemplating for many days now. You might think that preachers—"

Janie pulled her ear away. Were they just starting? She knew her pastor could ramble on a while before getting down to the meat of the sermon, and indeed their praise and worship team could get a little caught up in their performance, but this seemed a bit ridiculous. The hairs on the back of Janie's neck stood on end. She knew she should go back to her car. But something compelled her toward the door of the sanctuary. She reached the brownish-red door and gave the latched handle an experimental press and tug. The metal of the latch clicked softly, and as she pulled the door open; it did not creak. Emboldened, she slipped into the church, immediately turning around to guide the door closed slowly. It did so with a nearly silent clunk. Janie turned around. She was so stunned by what she saw that her mind rejected it at first.

The church was empty. No, that wasn't entirely true. It wasn't completely empty. But before she could take that in, she looked to her right at the stained-glass windows. She realized the something that her mind couldn't make sense of. The thing that felt off about it. There were no shadows cast on the glass from the congregation. She turned her head slowly, taking in the empty pews, and saw the first of two people in the church. It was a boy—or a slight man—sitting next to an ancient reel-to-reel recorder. His brown hair was shaped into a bowl cut. He had a pale, gaunt face with a mouth that hung open. His hand, with its long and knobby fingers, hovered near the chunky plastic buttons on the reel-to-reel. He stared out, slack-jawed, toward the stained-glass windows. But then his gray eyes slowly turned toward Janie, and she took a step back and quickly looked away towards the other occupant of the church.

He was a preacher, in black pants, a black button-up shirt and suit jacket, and a white collar. He was standing at the pulpit. His arms were rigid and grasping either side of it. He was thin, with a long face to match his long limbs, and had a shock of silver-white hair that stood so tall, it added to the long appearance of his body. His mouth and his eyes were closed. The preacher and the congregation, forever captured on the reels in the recorder, kept on sermonizing, and shouting amen, and singing songs. Now Janie could see the tape in the reels were set up in a loop. This was all wrong. She took a step backward, and the preacher's eyes suddenly flew open. His eyes were the same gray as the man/boy working the reel-to-reel. His mouth slowly contorted into a smile, as if it were the first time he'd ever tried it.

"Sister Jacinta Isabella Alvarez-Hackett," the preacher said. His voice was somewhat nasal and phlegmy. His was definitely not the sonorous voice on the reel. "This is a genuine surprise. Which is something that happens so rarely. But not an unpleasant one."

"I don't… I don't belong here," Janie said, not knowing why she'd even said it. But she felt it on some primordial, instinctual level. She was still backing up toward the door.

"You're most welcome to join us," said the preacher. His eyes crinkled, but there was nothing warm or merry about them.

Janie could take no more. She turned and ran the short distance to the door, flung it open, and ran to her car. Her heart beat like a drum in her chest. She fumbled the keys into the steering wheel and latched her seat-belt, all while keeping her eyes on the reddish-brown door. She didn't know what she expected. But she wouldn't have been surprised to see the preacher and the man/boy lurch out of it, coming to take her back inside.

With this thought, Janie slammed the gas pedal. Loose chunks of parking lot rattled against her Honda's undercarriage as she bolted forward. She didn't turn hard enough, and the Honda scraped against the backs of three SUVs, all parked in a row, sending a small shower of sparks into the air. The car alarms of two of them sounded off, protesting the new powder-blue gash carved into their rears. Janie willed herself to calm down and tried to breathe naturally as she careened down the back-roads. With one shaky hand, she attempted to call Kyle, and then Max. They were going to have their phones on silent, of course. Hopefully they were on their way back to Max's house. She had to find out. She had to be sure.

# 32
# *The Gathering*

"Maybe it's some kids, who came in the same way we did," Kyle whispered as he and Max both inched toward the light. He was crouching right alongside Max now, but Max didn't respond. This frightened Kyle more than any of the other weirdness of the night. Kyle could see a look of intense concentration on Max's face. His eyes were wide open and searching. Kyle held out his hand to stop Max from moving any closer. The smoke was getting thicker, and they could hear the voices in the distance a little more clearly. There were more than one or two of them, to be sure. One voice—a woman's voice by the sound of it—was louder than the rest. The others were murmurs.

"Are you okay?" Kyle asked. Max turned to him with a stricken look.

"Sorry. Yeah, I'm good. Creeped out, but good," Max said.

Kyle felt like Max wasn't telling him something. He worried

that Max was starting to lose his nerve. Not that Kyle would have blamed him. But he could become a liability if he did. Kyle took the new video camera he'd purchased out of his backpack. His cellphone vibrated in his pocket, as it had almost continuously the last five minutes. But he couldn't worry about it now.

"Do you want to hang back?" asked Kyle in a whisper. "I want to get in closer with the camera."

"I said I had your back," Max said. He sounded a little defensive. "I've got your back."

Kyle nodded, and they both pressed onward. As they got closer and the trees thinned, they saw that the light was coming not from a bonfire, but a circle of torches. They could only see a few of them through the trees, still, but there was so much light, Kyle supposed they must have encircled the entire perimeter of the old graveyard. They could hear the people beyond clearly now.

"—and so, we welcome another into our fold. She gives of herself so that we all might thrive. Join me in blessing her," said the woman's voice.

"May her blessing return a thousand-fold," came a chorus of voices in response.

Kyle froze in his tracks and looked at Max. There were many more voices than he'd expected. He had no clue how many, but it sounded more like twenty people than four or five.

"I bless you, too, my brothers and sisters. For you are the chosen few. It is through you that we reshape reality. Through you that we correct a wayward world. It's through you that we remain strong," said the woman's voice.

Kyle felt like someone had poured ice water down his back. He knew that voice. Of course, he knew that voice. Although the context was bizarre, even her words were much the same.

"It's Manchester," Kyle whispered. "What the hell have we stumbled onto?" He searched Max's face, but it was blank. Kyle could see in the glow of the torchlight that he was sweating profusely. He was clearly as rattled as Kyle was.

Kyle came into The Grove with ideas of finding a secret entrance to a tunnel or underground storage bunker or something. Not this. Kyle didn't say anything else to Max and decided to let him be. He moved forward, crossing to the edge of the tree line so he could get a good look at what was going on in the old graveyard. His hands trembled as he pointed his video camera forward and he took in what waited for him within.

The torches were set all around the graveyard, their flames whipping back and forth in the wind and billowing smoke. Kyle could see now that each one bore one of the symbols that had been drawn on the map. The cemetery was packed with people in long, hooded robes of blue and silver. There were at least forty of them. Broken chunks of gravestones littered the ground and cast dancing shadows around them. In the center of the graveyard stood a large monolithic tombstone of black marble. The top of it, which had been tapered into a pyramid, had broken off long ago and lay to one side of it. The flat surface that remained was turned into a sort of makeshift altar, with a midnight blue cloth draped over it. A silver cup sat on top of it, as well as blue candles flickering in two silver holders. At the altar, cloaked in the same dark blue and silver-trimmed robes as the others, although with the addition of some sort of silver scarf draped on her shoulders, was Alice Manchester. She held a long silver dagger in her hand.

Kyle felt Max sidle up next to him but couldn't break his gaze away. He dearly wanted Max to crack a joke. Because there had to be one in all of this. Kyle himself felt caught between a laugh and a scream. There was something ridiculous about it all. The country cult, meeting in a graveyard. He expected the scene to cut back to Elvira for some witty remark. But standing in front of the scene, now—even with his old English teacher leading the proceedings—Kyle felt the humor drain away. His dad had been a part of all of this? His mom? What had Manchester been talking about? A sacrifice of some sort?

"I have some exciting news," said Manchester. There was a murmur in the crowd. Some of the hooded figures turned to each other, and Kyle saw they were wearing perfectly smooth chromed masks that reflected the firelight. There weren't even eye holes. "Because this night has not reached its end yet."

The assembled flock all roared in approval. In unison, they looked downward, somewhere below the altar where Manchester stood. But Kyle couldn't see what they were staring at. Kyle looked over at Max, but he still seemed frozen by fear.

"I'm going to try to get a closer look," said Kyle. "I'll be right back."

Leaving Max behind, he walked carefully, applying as little pressure as possible at first as he made each step, making sure there wasn't some errant root or twig that might snap under his weight. He crept along the perimeter of the tree line until the robed figures (who were all eerily silent and still and staring downward) thinned and he got a side view of Manchester at the altar. At the base of the altar were two rectangular patches of earth that looked freshly tilled. Or like newly dug graves. Kyle shivered as he brought the video camera up and tried to zoom in on them.

"What are they waiting for?" Kyle whispered to himself.

"They're waiting for you," said Max, his voice directly in Kyle's ear. Kyle jumped and was about to give his friend a dirty look when he felt a slight sting in his neck. He lifted his hand to swat at the insect, but it hit some sort of object. Something plastic. Being held in a hand. Max's hand. His vision began to swim and darken at the edges. Right before the blackness claimed him, he saw Alice Manchester turn her head in his direction. The top of her face was hidden by shadow. But her mouth was twisted into her horribly wide grin.

# 33
# The Knock, Knock, Knock
# of the Dock

The tires of Janie's Honda squealed as she drove up Max Williams driveway, not hitting the brakes until she was right on it. She was in full panic mode. She'd not been able to get a hold of Kyle or Max. The lights were all dark in the Williams's household, which most likely meant that Max and Kyle hadn't made it back yet. She put both hands on the top of the steering wheel and leaned her forehead forward until it rested on it as well. Janie tried to breathe in and exhale slowly to calm her nerves. She needed to think clearly. She should probably call Sean before she did anything else. He'd be annoyed she'd lied to him, but it was better he knew where she was. Unless that might put him or the kids in danger too? The preacher at the church saw her with those gray eyes of his. He'd known her name, although Janie had never seen him around town.

"Right. Get it together, Janie," she said to herself. "Dear God.

Please give me strength. Help me find Kyle. Help me find Max. Let them be okay. God, please let them be okay."

She would have to head for The Grove herself. She wasn't sure exactly where the damaged part of the fence was, but Max said a car coming around LaGrange Road had damaged it so that narrowed down where it could be. But before she did that, she figured she might as well make a quick check of the house, in case Kyle and Max were there, but hurt and unable to call for help. The thought knotted her stomach, but it also helped her gather her courage. They might need help. She turned off her car, unbuckled the seat-belt, and stepped out of the vehicle.

The night was so silent and still. Even the wind seemed to have died down. She thought she could hear music—distant and distorted—but that was it. As she walked up the drive, security lights suddenly glared on, and she had to use her hand to protect her eyes from them. They did illuminate the front of the house, though, and she could see clearly there was no one there. So that meant all she had to do was check the back. She kept close to the wall of the house, hoping it'd help obscure her from any prying eyes. There was a large deck at the back of Max's home that led to a dock, which floated lazily in the lake, making soft knocking sounds as it bobbed from right to left. There seemed to be no security lights back here, which meant she didn't have to worry about anyone across the lake spotting her creeping around Max's backyard, but also meant most of it was cast in deep shadows.

She could see the outlines of a large umbrella that was left open. There were deck chairs, a grill, and some large flowerpots with flowers spilling out of them. Janie couldn't decide if she should call out for Max and Kyle or not. She decided to only after she'd made sure she was alone. She walked across the deck slowly. It creaked from her weight as the rain-swelled boards rubbed against each other. That's when she saw something on the dock. She could barely make it out, but it was a lumpy, irregular form. Instantly, her mind filled in what she did not know with the most horrific details. It was Kyle or Max. They were hurt. They'd climbed onto the dock but not made it any farther. She walked more quickly to the dock; the knock-knock-knocking of it against the deck seemed to increase as a cold wind burst across the lake and toward her. She did not want to see what was on the dock. She had to see what was on the dock.

Finally, she was nearly on the narrow projection of wood, but could not force herself to go any further. She got onto her knees, got her phone out, engaged its flashlight, and pointed it at the dock. To her relief, she saw that it was a tarp or a grill cover that had blown off. She exhaled, suddenly feeling a little ridiculous. That's when she heard the dock creak again. The same as when she'd walked out on it. But she wasn't moving now. She was still on her knees. The creaking got closer and closer, increasing in speed. She gripped her keys in her hand, letting the pointed ends of them poke between her fingers, as she'd been taught in a self-defense class at Higher Faith. She spun around, but he was already there. He clamped a hand on her shoulder with such force, she winced. She couldn't see his features. Only a glimmer of light, reflected from his eyes, glittering out from his shadowed face. But she recognized him immediately.

It was Patrick Kirby.

# 34
## *Dreams in the Dark*

Mrs. Manchester's classroom in Essen Middle School was bathed in the golden early light of morning. Kyle had arrived before all the other students, as she'd requested. Flat morning light shone through the windows. Motes of dust and fine grains of chalk moved lazily through them. It smelled newly cleaned, with the astringent tang of bleach and ammonia filling the air. Mrs. Manchester was at the board, apparently not having heard him come in, and was scratching something out with her white chalk on the dark green board. Kyle stood there for some time, his English book and a copy of The Iliad in his hands. Mrs. Manchester methodically worked from left to right, her hand moving ceaselessly as the chalk scratch-clacked across the board.

"Mrs. Manchester," he finally said, "I'm here. Like you asked."

She did not turn her head. She did not stop writing. "Yes, Kyle. Thank you. Did you do your assigned reading?" she asked.

"Yes. I finished it last night."

"That's good," she said, still scratching at the board. "I was disappointed in your last paper. That's why I called you here."

"Oh. I'm… I'm sorry. I did try my best."

"No, you didn't. If you'd tried your best, you'd have turned in an adequate paper about the Trojan Horse's role in the fall of Troy," said Mrs. Manchester, who was now back on the left side of the chalkboard. Kyle couldn't help but notice the woman looked bigger, somehow. She was a thick woman in general, but she seemed wider somehow now. Wider than she'd been the day before, anyway. That's when her words fully hit him.

"The Iliad doesn't talk about the Trojan Horse," he said, his voice cracking.

"Are you doubting me, Kyle? I suppose you're the one with the education degree from Dartmouth?" the woman asked, as she finally turned her head to watch him. "Although that seems unlikely since your family couldn't afford it. Perhaps a community college. Or you could go work on your family's farm."

Kyle was taken aback at the harshness of her tone.

"But it doesn't make any sense to do a report on the Trojan Horse when we're reading The Iliad," Kyle insisted, trying to grasp what was happening. Suddenly Mrs. Manchester spun her now considerable bulk entirely to face him. Her face was getting red, and her mouth twisted into the familiar, awful little pucker. Kyle knew the look all too well.

"There are a great many things you don't know or understand, Kyle Thomas. About the world. About yourself. But that's why I'm here, Kyle. I'm here to teach you. I'm here to educate you," Mrs. Manchester said, now towering directly over him, her face filling up his entire field of vision. Her breath smelled strange—sweet and earthy at the same time.

"I want to learn," he said, pleading with her. "I'm trying to understand."

"Then you'll like today's lesson. It's all on the chalkboard, Kyle. All you ever need to know." Mrs. Manchester was breathing heavily now in wheezing gulps.

Kyle was afraid to look away from her for some reason, as he suddenly felt that he could not trust her. But he needed to see the chalkboard. He needed to know what the day's lesson was. He wanted her to be proud of him. He wanted to show her that her faith in him was not wasted. He angled his head to the left so he could stare past her round face and head as she exhaled her hot, earthy gasps onto him. He saw the chalkboard was filled with writing. The same sentence over and over again.

*Kyle is a poor dirty queer. Kyle is a poor dirty queer. Kyle is a poor dirty queer. Kyle is a poor dirty queer. Kyle is a poor dirty queer. Kyle is a poor dirty queer. Kyle is a poor dirty queer. Kyle is a poor dirty queer. Kyle is a poor dirty queer. Kyle is a poor dirty queer. Kyle is a poor dirty queer. Kyle is a poor dirty queer. Kyle is a poor dirty queer. Kyle is a poor dirty queer. Kyle is a poor dirty queer.*

Kyle screamed. Mrs. Manchester screamed. But her mouth wasn't open. Not yet. Her tiny, puckered lips spread into that same wide, horrible grin he knew so well. And then her lips parted, and her jaw opened impossibly wide. Her teeth were jagged gravestones. Her throat was black as night. The ridges of her esophagus broke apart and became the rigid shafts of trees.

Kyle was still screaming when he came to and found himself

staring up at a pitch-black sky. Orange light danced around at its edges, like the ring around a solar eclipse. Kyle took a quick intake of air and felt smoke fill his lungs, which caused him to cough and choke. Yellow flashes shimmered at the edge of his vision.

"Well, it seems our guest has decided not to sleep through the whole ceremony," said Alice Manchester, though Kyle could not see her. Ripples of laughter sounded off all around Kyle. And then Manchester's face was filling his vision, as it had been in his nightmare. But her face was thinned and more heavily lined, framed by the curved angles of a midnight blue hood instead of her stringy brown mop hair.

"I did tell him not to use the full syringe unless there was a struggle," said a man to Kyle's right. His voice sounded vaguely familiar.

"I have no doubt in your abilities, Doctor Otto," said Manchester.

Doctor Gregory Otto was here too. He'd been his family's physician Kyle's entire life. He had Highlights magazine in his waiting room and gave away Blow-Pop suckers. Not the cheap little ones other doctors gave away. Kyle remembered where he was the same moment that he realized his feet and hands were bound with zip-ties. He struggled against them, but the sharp sides of the plastic strips dug into his skin painfully. He was in The Grove. Everything was going all Rosemary's Baby. He'd been… he'd been knocked out. Rage surged through him, and Kyle turned himself onto his side. His face landed in loose dirt. He was on one of the rectangular patches of earth he'd seen before. He craned his neck to the left until he found him.

Max Williams stood next to Manchester, a look of concern on his face.

"You fucking bastard!" Kyle cried, his voice sounding screechier and more raw than he would have liked. But he wanted Max to feel every ounce of venom.

"Kyle, I—"

"Now, that's no way to talk to your friend, Kyle," said Manchester, who was (fittingly) still looking down upon him. "He's given you a precious gift. Hopefully this time, it's one you'll appreciate."

"I'd like my 'friend' to explain himself," Kyle said. There were plenty of other things to worry about, of course, but this was the thing that felt the rawest at the moment. Max looked at Manchester. She nodded, and he came forward slowly, bent down on one knee, and looked Kyle in the eyes.

"You've got this all wrong, Kyle. I'm sorry I couldn't tell you. But what you stumbled on here... it's big. It's important, Kyle. They wanted... they wanted a more permanent solution to your investigations. I got them to agree to this. They said it should work. That'd you'd understand once it was all over," Max said. His eyes were tearing up. It was the first time he'd seen Max like this since he'd told Kyle about his sister Serena. The moment their friendship became a brotherhood. The flash of memory only seemed to ignite the rage roiling within Kyle more.

"He's right, Kyle. He's saved your life," said Manchester.

"What is all of this?" Kyle tried to control his rage. Tried to quiet the tremors of it that were racking through his body.

"It's a ritual. This is how you join the Club. But it's way more than a golf club, as you were starting to figure out," said Max.

"Wait. This is how you're getting into the Club? By giving me up to them?"

"Yes. But this isn't everything. This is in addition to the regular ritual. I wasn't lying when I said people like me—outsiders—have to do a little extra to get in," said Max. He looked desperate to make Kyle understand. "Just a little of your life force. Nothing serious. A year or two's worth."

"Life force?" The words felt like a foreign language in his mouth. He understood them. He understood the concept. But to be saying them out loud, in the real world… he couldn't wrap his head around it.

"It's totally safe. Heather's already gone through it. I wouldn't send Heather through it if it weren't safe, Kyle."

"Heather's here?" Kyle twisted away from Max and then strained to see to his right. He searched around for her but could not find her. "She's joining too?"

"You won't see her Kyle, if that's what you're trying to do. She's already gone below," said Manchester smoothly. "And while Mrs. Williams, much like yourself, did not come of her own volition, I can guarantee you, she'll be thrilled that her husband has been so brave and decisive."

Kyle looked at Max in utter disgust, which caused Max to wince visibly. He hadn't known Heather long. He'd only seen Max with her once. But he knew they loved each other. He knew Max loved her more than life itself. And he'd even betrayed her?

"What is all of this for? What do you get out of it?" asked Kyle. Manchester was the one that responded.

"Access, of course. And our benefactor provides for Club members. It's one of the perks of being a member."

"It's just a little life force, Kyle. A sacrifice to their benefactor. To Wah'halesh." Max said this in the same tone one might explain the basics of swinging a golf club. He saw the confusion on Kyle's face.

"This was an ancient Indian burial ground. One of their deities—Wah'halesh—sleeps below. The Club worked out a deal with it, though. We feed it a little life force, and it can… change things in the world. It's why everyone in town is so wealthy."

Kyle looked at Max and then looked at Manchester. And then around at the hooded and masked figures all around him. And then he laughed. He laughed so hard that his side started to ache. Manchester shot him a look of warning, but Kyle could not and would not heed it.

"You idiot! This isn't an ancient Indian burial ground! It's a moderately old cemetery for white people," Kyle spat out with as much ferocity as he could muster. Max looked at Manchester, a hint of doubt creeping onto his face. "What the hell happened to your dignity? Or your loyalty!" This had been the wrong thing to say. Max's face twisted in fury, his usually good-natured, jovial self utterly dissolved as he thrust himself on top of Kyle and started shaking his shoulders.

"Don't you dare even try that!" Max roared. "Loyalty? You're going to talk to me about loyalty? To the guy you left behind—abandoned—and never bothered to call? Who was stuck here while you went and made a new life? Your 'best friend'? Or were you just using me like everyone else? The guys on the team who thought I was just some big dumb ape to scare the white boys on the other team? Or the girls who wanted a night with me to just check off a box?"

"Max, I—"

"You knew I wasn't like you!" The anger flooded away from Max, and tears started to sting his eyes as he slumped off Kyle and onto the ground next to him. "I couldn't just pick up and leave. But I would have gone with you. I would have gone with you."

"Max…" Kyle began, but he found he didn't have any words

in his defense.

"All the shit I took for being your friend. On top of all the shit they gave me anyway. And you just left without a word." Max got up off the ground, dusted himself off, and wiped the tears from his eyes. "You left me here to make a life for myself. And now you're going to judge me for it? No. No way."

Manchester knelt beside Kyle, grabbed the sides of his mouth with surprising force, and pried it open. Kyle winced in pain, but all his efforts to fight against her grip were meaningless. With her other hand, Manchester stuffed a blue cloth into his mouth. Judging from the pungent taste of soil and wax on it, Kyle assumed it was the cloth from the makeshift altar.

"I think that's enough talk. Don't worry, Brother Williams. When all of this is done, your 'friend' will understand," assured Manchester. She was staring down at Kyle, a glimmer of menace in her eyes.

"It'll be okay, Kyle. You know I was scared too," said a voice that sounded familiar but hard to place, the drugs he'd been pumped with still addling Kyle's mind. One of the robed figures approached a little nearer. Lissie removed her silver mask and lowered her hood. She smiled at Kyle with glittering blue eyes. The eerie contacts were gone, but somehow, the eyes that confronted Kyle now were far more unsettling. There was a blankness to them, just like the last time Kyle had seen her.

"You too?" Kyle asked, although the words were mostly muffled by the cloth in his mouth.

Still, Lissie seemed to understand. She laughed and rolled her eyes. She pointed to two of the other robed cultists behind her."I've been given a gift, Kyle. Honestly, everything is so much clearer now. I want you to have that, too. That's my mom and dad over there. Dad, would you mind?"

The shorter of the two robed figures nodded and removed his mask and hood as well. His skin was ashen, and his gray eyes had dark circles under them. Kyle shook his head in confusion. What had they done to him?

"I wanted you to see him, Kyle. Dad fought against the process, and it went wrong. He never fully got back to himself. So much so that my mom had to hide him away," Lissie said, a placid smile never leaving her lips. Kyle started to scream, to plead wordlessly with Lissie. Didn't she know this was horrific? Didn't she know this was all wrong?

"I wanted you to know, so you won't fight. You belong here, Kyle. Just like I do. You deserve to be just as happy as the rest of us. You always did."

Tears stung Kyle's eyes. He hadn't known Lissie long. But he mourned the fact that she seemed utterly gone from the eyes of the woman in front of him. He was no nearer to understanding what exactly was going on in Essen. But he was sure whatever line Manchester was feeding Max and the others wasn't true at all. He tried to force the cloth out of his mouth with his tongue, but it was too well lodged in. And then there was a more pressing issue to deal with. He could feel the dirt around him begin to shift. It was slow at first, the gentle rustle of grains of it against his skin. But then there was an odd sensation all along Kyle's back. It made him jump a little, the small, distinct dots of pressure all along it.

The pressure became more insistent, and all at once, Kyle had the horrific mental image of a hundred fingers poking at him. But then they began to do more than poke. They twisted at the light jacket he was wearing. And then they began to tug. The movement of the dirt around him became more pronounced. Kyle realized that he was sinking—no, being pulled—into the soil. He panicked, twisting his body against his slow descent, trying to get away from the insistent pressure of all those fingers. He screamed into the cloth stuffed into his mouth. He looked at Max with pleading, terror-filled eyes. The thrashing only seemed to increase the rate of his descent so he stopped and tried to will himself to be calm and to think of how he could get out of this. Whatever it was.

The fingers seemed to twist and grip him more firmly now. The dirt was level with his eyes. He had to close them. He felt the earth cover them. Only his nose was exposed now. He tried to breathe in as much air as he could before he was pulled under. He felt the dirt cover his nose. The cold night air working through the mesh of his shoes and hitting his toes was gone. That's when he finally registered what Manchester had said about Heather. She was already below. And now Kyle was too.

# *Dunbar Lies Down*

An excerpt from
***Dunbar's Grove***
by Herbert Thomas

I was no longer protected by the canopy of the great white oaks that surrounded the graveyard, so the rain battered my skin mercilessly. I welcomed its tender flagellations. I stripped off my shirt, and then my slacks, and finally my underwear. I walked naked as the rain pelted me. It stung, and there was a sense of pleasure in the pain. It felt right. This felt like the first thing I'd done in so many years that was right. The rain was not cleansing. I could not be clean. It was punishing, and it was righteous. Brambles pierced the soles of my feet. Twigs tore at them. My blood mixed with the mud, and it was good.

Finally, I reached the center of the graveyard, and the large shattered gravestone I'd used to weigh her body down. I ran my hand gently over it as if it were her body and not just a weight that now crushed into her bones. The weight I'd placed on her. I closed my eyes and lay next to the black stone. It felt so smooth. I reached the back of my hand over and ran it along the edge of it. It reminded me of the day, so long ago, in the sunlit grove of my youth. When we lay next to each other, and I had traced the back of my hand along her spine. I had never felt anything so powerful and yet so delicate at the same time.

With this, the illusion shattered. I knew I was only scraping against unyielding stone. I withdrew my hand and crossed my arms. And then I began to sink, as she had all those years ago. I opened my mouth wide and welcomed the rain and the sloshing mud as it filled me. I greedily swallowed the earth, as the earth swallowed me.

# 35
# *Below*

Kyle Thomas was in the darkness of the ground. He could see nothing, not even his own body. The air was muggy and smelled of the same earthy and sweet smell as Manchester's breath, which made him want to vomit. But there was a cloth in his mouth. Until there wasn't. He felt it being pulled out. But he could not see who did it. Whoever it was barely made a sound. The only sound he could hear at all was a sort of unceasing rustling, as if someone was dragging wet logs across each other. There was no innate sense of someone else being there in the dark with him. But nevertheless, the cloth was gone.

He wiggled his feet but could not touch the ground. He felt like he was suspended, with only the strange grasping fingers at his back keeping him aloft. He heard a slow, dull rasping noise below him. It sounded familiar, but he could not place it. However, when he felt the pressure of the zip ties release from his hands, their sharp plastic edges no longer digging into his skin, he realized why the sound was so familiar. It was like a utility knife cutting through the plastic strips of a large package. Someone cut through the zip ties binding his hands. They followed soon after by doing the same for those around his feet.

His head felt foggy. Was it from the drugs that Max had pumped him full of? Except he'd felt more or less normal above ground. His thoughts were getting cloudier too, and he felt like the earthy sweet smell was getting stronger. He had the preposterous idea that he should thank whoever freed him. Even with the cloth removed from his mouth, he didn't dare to speak.

And then he felt them. The fingers.

They began to grasp at his shoulders, and then his side. Then they pulled on his hair. And then they wrapped around his legs, and his arms, and his neck and he knew they were not fingers at all. They felt so strange. They were wet and rubbery and covered in small knobby bumps. Kyle wondered if they were tentacles or vines, and both possibilities horrified him in a dull, far away way. It was as though his ability to process the horrible impossibility of his situation had fled him. Everything was muted and gray, even when he grasped behind him with his right hand and felt writhing strands of the stuff. He grasped with his other hand and felt the same thing. He had the sense that the walls were covered with the things.

He fought through the fog in his mind. He remembered he needed to know what was happening to him. He could not just accept it. He squeezed hard with both hands. The writhing tendrils in his hand resisted the pressure of his grip for a moment. But then the outside of them gave way, and his hands tore through them with stomach-churning ease. He clawed at them, and they tore apart with a dry sponginess he found incredibly satisfying. Something sharp dug into both of his shoulders, and he cried out in pain. He instantly understood that he'd done something wrong. And if he did it again, he'd be punished. The rubbery pieces of whatever gripped him fell from his hands, and he felt new tendrils of it cover the wall where he'd torn into it. He tried to think of why the sensation, as disturbing as it felt, seemed so familiar. He thought of a time, three years ago, when he was making his ex a salad. He'd gotten some portabella mushrooms to dice up and put on the mixture. And his ex had said he didn't like the gills. The gills creeped him out. So, Kyle scooped into the mushroom with his fingers and scraped the gills out. There was something distinctly fungal about the strands that were binding him. Even the smell was vaguely similar.

The air was so stuffy, and his moment of clarity and resistance passed as the fog settled on him once again. He could only note with curiosity the ripping and tearing sound at first. Then he felt his jacket, and then his shirt, fall away. His skin was exposed now to the humid blackness and its strangely sweet scent. There was more ripping and cutting, although soon he realized it sounded more precise than that. He thought of the noise his mom's shears made as she cut through the bolts of fabric she bought at Perry's. She'd bought cloth patterned with stars and galaxies for him. Made them into curtains. Kyle forced his mind back to the present, as his pants and his underwear fell away. His mind protested that the underwear had cost thirty dollars for the pair. It was a ridiculous thought. Why couldn't he focus? He was naked now, and the fungal tendrils wrapped around him more tightly and completely. They wrapped around his upper thighs and around his knees. They poked exploratorily at the slashes the fence had made in his chest. And a moment of panic broke through the haze.

"Not… not inside," he managed to slur out.

The tendrils withdrew, their smooth wet slickness sliding across his chest, the strange little knobby protuberances dotting the smoothness squeaking across his skin as they retreated. Then he heard the buzzing. And there was light. Terrible, terrible light. He looked away from what it revealed. Instead, he looked down and saw his cell phone. There was ground below, another two or three feet down. The phone must have fallen there, out of his pocket, when his pants were cut away. He could not see the name on the screen clearly, but he recognized the configuration of blurry shapes enough to know it said 'Janie.' He whimpered. She was looking for him. She'd be looking for him forever. He was in a different world now. He was below.

He could no longer deny the reality of what he saw around him and where he was. Some small part of his brain that still struggled knew that. He looked up as the blue-white light illuminated where he was. Some sort of chamber. He had no clue how large because it was covered in the writhing, slippery-looking tendrils of fungus. They flowed around and past each other in constant movement. They were a vivid shade of red that made Kyle want to retch. He could see they were somewhat segmented by darker brownish-red sections, and they did indeed have similarly colored polyps along the surface. There were thicker tendrils, too, that ended in engorged, club-like ends. They seemed to be more specialized than the others, and there were only a few of them that he could see. Most terrifying was what protruded from them. Thin projections that looked like thorns emanated from their ends. Kyle realized these must have been what cut the zip ties, cut away his clothes, and delivered the punishing cuts to his shoulders.

And then, on the far wall, the red tendrils shifted and parted. Slowly, a ghostly white figure began to emerge from them. Kyle remembered the woman in the dress, by the lake, and wondered how many ghosts he was going to see tonight.

The phone stopped buzzing, and the light was gone, and there was nothing but darkness again. His voicemail must have finally picked up. He knew it had only been thirty seconds. But it had felt like an eternity. Kyle thought he'd be relieved. But the darkness was worse. He could hear the tendrils moving. And there was someone else with him down here. There was a ghost. The buzzing began anew. The light of the phone filled the interior. Janie was still desperately trying to get a hold of him. He looked up and saw the pale figure of a woman, suspended in the air by the tendrils. She was naked like Kyle was. Her eyes were closed. Her arms were at her side, palms-up. She looked calm, her red hair cascading down her shoulders.

"H-Heather?" Kyle managed to choke out, his voice sounding far away. Her eyes fluttered open. She looked at him in confusion, at first. Then recognition.

"Kyle?" she asked, sounding exhausted.

"Yes. Heather, yes, it's me," Kyle said, trying to force some urgency into his words.

"I'm scared."

"Me... me too," Kyle said. He tried to strain against the tendrils. They'd been easy enough to tear into with his fingers. But his hands were securely fastened by them now, and they seemed to have no give as he pushed against them.

Kyle was about to say something else, to try to comfort Heather, although he knew whatever he said would be useless and hollow. That's when she cried out. But the phone stopped ringing again. He could not see why she was yelling.

"Heather!" he yelled into the darkness, although it felt like the word got swallowed up in the humid and thick air. The phone rang again. And then the real nightmare began.

The tendrils suspended Heather away from the wall now, wrapped around her wrists and ankles. One of the large cutting tendrils swayed and then struck her in the neck. She screamed as blood trickled out of the wound. And then the tendril swept downward in one swift stroke, and there was a new bloody seam along her back, exposing her spine. The phone stopped ringing, and she screamed in the darkness.

The phone rang again, and Kyle saw the wet and red tendrils invade her wound, sliding between her skin and her muscles and bones at the same time they pulled the wound wider. Heather still screamed, and Kyle wished she would pass out. Why hadn't she passed out? Why was the phone still ringing? One of the larger cutting tendrils worked its way into her neck, causing it to bulge obscenely as it wrapped around her. Her screams became choked, and then with a sickening snapping and a pop, she stopped screaming. Kyle, in his horror, could only feel relief. At least she wasn't suffering anymore. The phone stopped buzzing, and it was dark again.

But Kyle could hear the wet slurping and sloshing noises as the tendrils kept filling the body (Kyle could not think of it as Heather anymore, Heather was gone) followed by wet crunching and snapping sounds. Kyle could not decide which was worse—seeing it or hearing it—but the debate in his head was rendered pointless as the phone began to buzz again. In time to see the tendrils yank and tear the mangled muscles, organs, and bones of what had been his friend's wife free of its skin. Tears stung Kyle's eyes as the mess was carried away by the tendrils, and then disappeared into the writhing mass on the wall with a sound that Kyle could only think of as the smacking of lips. The phone stopped buzzing. Kyle felt more alert now. The adrenaline pumping into him finally fighting against the effect of the air down here.

The phone lit up again. The tendrils held the body's head, which seemed intact. The skin below it hung, flapping and loose. Kyle hoped that was the end of it. He hoped he could finally look away. But it was not. The fungal strands began to thrash and shake, and they streamed into the body. It began to inflate as it filled with them. The body was gently lowered to the ground, although it looked more like a sack of flesh with a head attached than anything human. Heather's face was captured mid-scream. Her eyes were wide with fear. One of the bulky tendrils with the cutting thorn swept down, slid along the long red line it had cut along the body's back, and deposited a thick stream of white fungal liquid. It reminded Kyle a little of the foam from a fire extinguisher, except it hardened quickly. It held the flesh together again, and the sack of flesh began to lengthen. The still writhing tendrils bulged through the skin in places as it filled the body up. The phone went dark.

"What are you?" Kyle managed to scream. "What are you? What are you!" Finally, he'd found his voice. He sounded and felt more like himself, his body fighting the stupor.

The phone lit up again. And Heather was back. She was facing him and smiling at him. She walked toward him. She swept her hair off her shoulder with her right hand as she reached out to touch his cheek with her left. Her movements were graceful, like a dancer's. Her small breasts moved only slightly as she walked. Her eyes were wide with warmth, and her face was full of humor. The light of the phone turned off.

"Don't be afraid Kyle," she said. Her voice was sweet and kind, as it had been. "We've gotten good at this after all this time. We keep the skull mostly intact. The mouth, teeth, and eyes—everything that opens to the world. It's much easier to keep it. We keep the brain too, so we can access the memories. No more forgetful returnees. It raised too many questions. But you won't be alive. You're not trapped in your own head, watching wordlessly as we use your skin. We're not cruel."

Kyle trembled as her soft hand brushed his cheek. He had so many questions. But he could only manage one.

"Why?" he asked. But the thing that used to be Heather did not answer. His phone began buzzing below again, and he saw her look at him with profound sadness.

"Now I need to rest. Give the sealant time to heal up the skin. And shaping ourselves to this form takes a lot out of us," she said, cocking her head to the side as if she were stretching her neck. The tendon in her neck rippled and slithered under the skin, before straightening once again.

Kyle watched as she backed away from him. The red fungal tendrils swirled down from the ceiling of the chamber, hooked themselves under her armpits gently as if caressing her. She tilted her head back and closed her eyes. She placed her hands by her sides, and the tendrils swept under her. They turned her until she was in a lying position again. And then they pulled her upward toward the chamber ceiling. The flowing tendrils there parted, a dusting of dirt falling through the opening for a second before the tendrils pushed the body up and out onto the surface again. And the light of the phone was gone.

Kyle felt the tendrils retreat from his body somewhat. Instead of wrapping so tightly around all of him, they only held him by the wrists and by the ankles. He felt himself turning. He knew what came next. He'd seen it. He thought of how he'd scolded himself for being childish. For being afraid of nameless things in the dark. Now he realized he wasn't suffering from an abundance of imagination, but a lack of it. He'd silenced the voice in his head that told him Essen was wrong somehow. That The Grove was wrong. And now here he was.

Adrenaline still surged through him. He yanked at the tendrils with all his might, but he couldn't get any leverage suspended in mid-air. He didn't fear the thorns anymore. It was going to rip through him at any moment anyway. But the tendrils only squeezed harder and more painfully around him. The phone buzzed again, and he could see his own shadow against the writhing red wall. He could see the shadow of one of the cutting tendrils, too, swaying behind him. Ready to strike. Kyle decided to close his eyes. He didn't want to see the walls anymore. He didn't want to have to watch the shadow puppet show that was about to play out before his neck was snapped and separated from his body. He closed his eyes.

And then the world was white. Even through his closed eyes, the searing white shone through his eyelids to make a rich orange blackness that glowed pink around the edges. He snapped his eyes open and saw a shaft of white light streaming down toward him. The tendrils hissed and scattered as the cool summer night air swept into the chamber. They loosened their grip as something curved and metallic thrust downward, widening the hole above him.

"Kyle! Kyle!" Janie cried from above.

The curved metal object was shoved further into the chamber, and Kyle saw that it was the head of a shovel. He wrapped his left hand around the tendrils that gripped his wrist on that side, and then thrust his right hand upward. But the tendrils on his right side, though weakened, pulled downward at the last second, so that his fingers only grazed the smooth curve of the back of the shovel.

"No, you don't, you bastards!" Kyle cried as he summoned every ounce of strength he had and thrust his hand up again, wrapping it around the handle above the shovel's head. "Pull!"

Most of the tendrils were spasming now, but one of the cutting tendrils swept toward him, its impossibly sharp thorn bearing down on him as he was pulled upward in one great lunge. He was dragged half out of the hole. Janie was there, with her phone's flashlight pointed downward, her face a horrified mask. On the end of the shovel was Patrick. He'd fallen on his butt as he pulled the shovel out with all the force he could muster. Kyle only managed a surprised smile before he felt the tendril's sharp thorn rip into his thigh. He screamed in pain and terror.

"Pull me out!" he cried. Janie dropped her phone, Patrick got to his feet, they both took one of his arms and heaved him out of the hole. The tendril withdrew before it would have been exposed to the surface. They still rattled with their strange screaming hiss until the hole in the ground repaired itself.

# 36
# *Above*

Kyle was sprawled naked on the ground of the graveyard. A chunk of gravestone or a rock was digging into his side. But he didn't care. He gasped and gulped the fresh air, unable to fathom that he was above ground again. He'd half fallen on top of Janie and Patrick, and he had his arms around them both. Janie was crying, one of her arms cradling the back of his neck. He looked up, and Patrick was staring at him, his green eyes gleaming with tears too.

"I'm so sorry," Kyle managed to croak at him.

"Shhh. It's okay. Janie explained everything. Once she realized I wasn't a part of… all of this," Patrick said. "What happened? Is your leg okay?"

Kyle looked down at his thigh. There was a fresh red cut that was bleeding profusely. He wasn't sure how bad it was, but it looked worse than it felt.

"I think I'm okay. How… how did you know where I was?" he asked. Janie and Patrick exchanged glances.

"We got here after you'd been tied up. We, uh,  heard what Max and Manchester said," said Janie.

"But we couldn't take all of them on. We waited until they cleared out. They said the 'process' would happen overnight. We hoped to God you were still alive down there somehow," Patrick said, his voice wavering slightly toward the end.

"Is that Max's wife?" Janie asked. Kyle swiveled his head to look at Janie, saw where she was staring, and then scrambled to his feet. There she was, sleeping on the other patch of earth. He picked the shovel up from where Patrick dropped it.

"No. It isn't," he said, his voice ragged. He walked toward Heather William's body, suddenly aware of the pain from the wounds in his chest and thigh. He stood over her. He gripped the shovel in both his hands and raised it up.

"What are you doing?" Janie cried. Both she and Patrick looked scared. But this time they were scared of him.

"She's not herself anymore," he said, spittle flying from his mouth and then dripping down the side of his chin. His tongue felt slow and dull. How could he explain? He couldn't tell. That was the truth of it. He had to show them. He rammed the shovel down toward her neck with as much force as he could, as Janie screamed.

But the end of the shovel didn't reach its goal. Heather's arms shot up and grabbed the edge of the shovel with both her hands. Her eyes snapped opened. She grinned and pushed upward. She was so strong, she sent Kyle tumbling backward and onto the ground. He let out a gasp as he hit the grass and the wind was knocked out of him.

"What the fuck?" Patrick gasped, scrambling to his feet. He

tried to hook his arms around Heather's, hoping to pin her. But she brought her foot up backward and kicked him painfully in the groin. She spun around, grabbed him by the neck, and flung him away.

"What are you?" Janie demanded. The thing that wore Heather's skin turned to look at her as if noticing her for the first time. It walked over to her slowly, never breaking its gaze from Janie's.

"We're the blood that courses through the veins of the Earth. We're the heart of the heartland," it said, its tone mocking and almost gleeful. It stalked toward Janie, its eyes flashing with menace. Janie didn't wait for the thing to reach her. She gripped her keys tightly in her fist and charged, aiming the makeshift claws right at the thing's face. The fungal mass that wore Heather's face stopped Janie's hand mid-lunge by grasping her wrist. Janie's momentum caused her to fall to one side, but Heather's grip was like a vice, twisting Janie's wrist unnaturally. Janie cried out as a terrible ripping and popping sound came from it.

Patrick bolted toward the thing, trying to go low and tackle it to the ground. He hit it square in the stomach and managed to knock it backward.

"Stay down," he said, his right palm pushing its chin up and away from him as he struggled to keep it pinned. Janie scrambled to the other side of the creature and tried to help pin it down with her good hand.

"Got you!" Janie screamed through gritted teeth.

At that second, Heather grinned while her body below the neck seemed to deflate as writhing tendrils underneath its skin fled the upper part of its body and rushed toward its lower half. Janie and Patrick, who were pressing all their weight onto the body, were caught off guard and tumbled forward into each other. They faltered for only a second, but it was enough. The thing arched its back to an impossible degree to pull its upper body out from underneath them the same instant the writhing fungus within it refilled Heather's body. It was Heather once again, at least in form. Janie tried to take advantage of the fact the thing's back was still turned, pushed off the ground, and slammed into Heather's back. But this time it was like hitting a wall since the creature was prepared for it. In one smooth motion, it grabbed a chunk of gravestone from the ground, twisted its waist two hundred degrees, and bashed the side of Janie's skull.

Patrick yelled in alarm as Janie fell and he saw the rock in the thing's hand was red with blood. He jumped onto its back, trying his best to get it in a headlock. But the thing gripped Patrick's arms and flung him forward with such force into the ground that dirt flew up into the air as he landed. The creature was on top of Patrick, now, pushing his face into the soil. Patrick realized then he was on the loose patch of dirt that they'd rescued Kyle from.

"Such a beautiful body," the thing that was Heather said. "We'll so look forward to filling it up." Patrick screamed as the thing pushed his head into the earth. He could feel the bizarre sensation of fingers caressing his face. Welcoming him from below.

Suddenly, there was a strange whistling sound—like an arrow parting the air, followed by a wet gurgle and the pressure of the thing's hands pushing him under was gone. Patrick turned, scrambling out from under her, and off the patch of earth and the horrific probing of whatever was under the ground. Heather William's body spasmed, her hands twitching and her fingers clawing at the air. Her head—its head—now rested mostly on its left shoulder. It was nearly severed, and thrashing red tendrils clawed at the air from the neck.

There was a look of shock in the eyes of the thing that was

once a sweet, smart, and kind woman. And then they spilled out from her. Ropey streams of red wriggled out from its neck. From the mouth and eyes and ears and nose. The fungal tendrils hissed and popped as they wriggled free from the compromised shell of the body, and back into the ground, leaving a deflated balloon of flesh behind. Janie, who managed to pick herself off the ground, trembled in shock. Kyle had the shovel in his hands. He crumpled to his knees, the last of his adrenaline spent. Patrick doubled over and vomited.

"What a waste," came a voice from behind them. Kyle turned and saw Alice Manchester stride back into the circle, still clad in her flowing blue robe with the silver trim, although her hood was pulled back to reveal the white curls of her hair.

# 37
# *Fair Trade*

"*L*ike father, like son I suppose," said Alice Manchester as she walked to the pile of pale flesh on the ground. "You've taken poor Max's wife away. And Zee has lost her mother. For what?"

"That wasn't Heather," Kyle said through gritted teeth. He gripped the shovel in both his hands. "Just like you're not Manchester."

"Mrs. Manchester to you, Kyle." She smiled at him with her wide grin. "And you might rethink your actions before you ram that shovel through me. For one thing, I've been in this body a while. I'd be harder to catch unaware. Also, there are fifty-three of my followers making their way to Darren Michael's house right now to catch a ride on the church bus back to Faith & Triumph. But I can have them back here in a second."

"Why are you here?" asked Janie, joining Patrick in sidling up next to Kyle. "Did you come to gloat?"

"I came back for my props," she said, glancing back at the makeshift altar. The silver cup and knife were still on it. "They're real silver. Not exactly cheap. They should have been safe here, but I figured there was no reason to chance it. Plus, the night is cool, and there's a storm on the wind. I thought some extra walking might be nice. So, imagine my surprise."

"All this shit about life forces and… Wah… Whaha… the Indian god—" Patrick began.

"All lies. Yes. In our minds, it's a fair trade. Your people want to be comfortable. They want nice houses and cars and to feel like they've carved out a little slice of stability in a chaotic world. We, on the other hand, need bodies. As you might have surmised, we don't do well in the highly oxygenated air above ground. One spouse out of two seems fair enough to us in return for the financial 'support' the Club provides. And we wait until they have at least one child, so there's plenty of stock for our future needs. But your kind still got so antsy about it. Thus, was born the Minty Green Club. And Wah'halesh and his need for 'life force.' The robes and the daggers and the secret meetings are all for show. But you all do love a good show."

"You were getting to the part about why I shouldn't smash your head in, I think," Kyle said. He felt so tired. But there was no way he was going to let Alice Manchester see that.

"Well, it'd be another body you'd have to explain. And considering your dad's mental breakdown, I don't think it'd be too much of a leap for people to believe you'd gone through the same. Mental instability runs in the family, doesn't it? Plus, I'm fairly well loved in the community. There would be quite a few people upset at the man who killed me."

"I wouldn't be killing you. You'd slither into the ground. You killed Alice Manchester… when? How long ago?" asked Kyle.

Manchester laughed.

"Very clever, Kyle. But no, she hadn't been replaced yet when you knew her as a child. That came much later. Her hatred for you was all her own. As for the reasons for her hatred… well, I don't think you deserve an explanation. Do you? But rest assured they were all small and human."

"Don't listen to it, Kyle," Janie said. But Kyle ignored her.

"What did you mean about me being like my father?" he questioned.

"Oh, have you not worked that out? Even now? Your father's little 'code?' It was far more literal than you supposed, I guess. He brought your mother here, to the circle. The earth swallowed her."

"You… replaced her?" asked Kyle, his grip tightening on his shovel.

"Oh yes. And your father was one of those rare cases that noticed something was wrong. It's one of the other reasons we like to induct people who have kids. They usually provide a good distraction, so the non-converted spouse doesn't notice their partner is acting a little off in the early days. But they'd already kicked you to the curb by then," said Manchester.

Janie thrust herself in front of Kyle."That's enough you meddling c—"

"Now, now, Janie. Whatever you were about to say, it didn't sound Christian," interrupted Manchester. Janie's face twisted into a snarl. She had a look in her eyes Kyle knew well.

"This good Christian has no trouble sending you back to Hell," snapped Janie.

"Janie, wait! I need to know," said Kyle.

"Are you sure you can believe anything that thing says?" asked Patrick. Kyle thought about this. He wasn't sure, but so far, everything she'd said made sense.

"That's what changed him. He could tell my mom wasn't herself anymore," Kyle said.

"Yes. Then he killed her for real. He saw a similar sight as you did with Mrs. Williams here. I don't think he handled it well. We were upset, of course, but we cleaned up the mess. And, Doctor Otto was happy to certify it was a heart attack. We considered getting rid of your father or even converting him. But, honestly, he was getting so old and wasn't in great shape with his busted liver. The conversion seemed like a waste. Those of us below wait so long to walk in the sun. Why give them a broken body? And what could he do? The suicide was a surprise. As was the book. I blame our own hubris more than I do him, really." Manchester walked to the altar and retrieved the silver cup and dagger.

"What now?" asked Kyle, trying to take everything in as well as he could, fighting back the tears.

"Now I make you an offer. I'd considered putting all three of you into the ground. But, to be honest, that seemed a little boring," said Manchester. "We wanted you, Kyle, because we thought an investigative reporter might be able to make up lies as well as he uncovered them. It's useful to have people who can whip up a good story to distract the meat. But the fact is we have plenty of people doing that already."

Kyle gripped the shovel firmly in his hands. He felt the uneven weight of it. He felt sure he could take Manchester out. He could have thought of nothing more satisfying than seeing it tear through Manchester's neck. The pleasure he derived from this thought scared him, although he reminded himself this thing wasn't Alice Manchester anymore.

"What's your offer? Spit it out," Janie demanded, before turning to Kyle and adding: "She certainly shares Manchester's love of hearing herself speak."

"I let you go," said Manchester.

"What's the catch?" asked Patrick.

"It's less of a catch and more of what I want in return. You say nothing about what you've seen here. Nothing about us. And you get to live your small and brief lives."

"We can't do that," said Janie. "Right, Kyle? We can't just… do nothing." Kyle hung his head and tried to think. He felt a little light-headed, possibly from blood loss.

"If it makes it easier, if you did try to say anything about it, people would probably think you were insane. Or, there's a high likelihood the police officer or FBI agent you were reporting it to would already be one of us." Manchester shrugged. Kyle loosened the grip on his shovel. He let it fall from his hands and clatter to the rocky ground.

"No!" Janie cried, reaching out for the shovel. But Kyle took her hand in his and looked into her eyes. He wiped a trickle of blood away from her forehead before it could dribble into them.

"What are we supposed to do, Janie? At least this way we live. You can go back to Sean and your kids," said Kyle. Tears started to stream down her face.

"You promise you won't touch them? Ever?" she asked Manchester.

"Of course," she said. "But there is one more condition. I want you to remember us. If the world ever gets too dark. If the bills are piling up, you can't pay rent, and everything feels like it's falling apart. It could be fixed with a little trade. And your family would be taken care of. We'd welcome you. Any of you." Manchester did not wait for a response. She lifted her hood up and walked to the edge of the circle. Kyle tried to process what she said. He wanted to call out to her. He wanted to ask her why she'd take such a huge risk with them. But he knew.

"You've been in her skin too long!" he called out to her. "You've been attached to her brain for so long, you're even thinking like her. You want to watch us suffer!"

Alice Manchester did not respond. But she stopped as she reached the edge of the cemetery and turned around.

"Oh, I'll leave the front gate open, so you don't have to crawl through the little hole we made for you. I'd suggest leaving town tonight."

# 38
# *Walking Away*

"Drop me off right here," Janie said. Patrick's car was still a few blocks from the Williams's house, where she'd left her Honda.

"Are you sure? I don't think we should split up," Kyle said.

Janie sighed. She didn't want to leave him, either."Max might be there, Kyle. He might already be home. I don't want to see him. But, I don't want to think of what you'd do if you saw him."

Janie got out of the backseat, and both Patrick and Kyle got out too. Kyle limped to her and gave her a hug. He was wearing Patrick's workout clothes. They'd tried to dress his wound, but she could see a line of blood starting to seep through the gray sweatpants.

"I still don't like this. We should stay together until we're out of town," Kyle said.

"I'm a big girl, Kyle," Janie said.

"I know. But what if I need you to save me again?" Kyle smiled at her sadly. Janie looked at Kyle and then looked at Patrick. The latter looked almost impossibly young to her. His green eyes had a certain haunted quality to them. But there was still an eagerness and innocence there she was suddenly bitterly jealous of.

"I need to take care of my family," Janie said. She squeezed both of their shoulders gently. "You should take care of yours."

Kyle nodded. Patrick gave her a slightly awkward hug, and they both climbed back into Patrick's truck. She waved at them as they made their way down the road. She felt her phone in her pocket. She ran her fingers over the now-cracked screen. She'd have to call Sean soon. She'd no idea how she was going to articulate what she had to say. And the throbbing of the wound on her head wasn't helping. But all of that would wait. She walked the last few blocks to Max's house. The lights were still dark. Maybe he hadn't come home right away. Perhaps he'd gone to the church with the others for some reason. She got into her car and turned the ignition. The lights in the house came on, and Max came charging out of the door with a smile on his face. The smile faded some when he saw her.

"Shit," she muttered under her breath. She turned the car off and got out.

"Janie? I thought you were Heather for a second," he said. "What're you doing here?"

"I was looking for Kyle. I got worried about him. He wasn't picking up his phone. I thought he'd be here," Janie said.

"Old habits die hard, huh?" Max said. Janie found she suddenly wanted nothing more than to walk up to him and claw his eyes out. Instead, she forced a smile as he continued to lie to her. "We had a little too much to drink, so we postponed our investigation into The Grove. I drove Kyle back to the farmhouse so he could sleep it off."

"Yeah, I guess I'm being silly. Sorry, I didn't come up and knock or anything. I didn't see your car, and the lights were off, so I figured I was out of luck." She said this partly to explain herself, and also because she wanted the man to squirm a little.

"Oh, yeah. I left the car, so Heather could drive it back," said Max. His eyes widened suddenly, and he quickly added: "I left it so she could take Zee to her mom's house, I mean."

"Where is Zee? Where is your daughter?" Janie asked, a little too frantically. Max looked at her like she'd sprouted an extra head.

"I just said. She's at her grandmother's for the week so Heather and I can get a little alone time." Max flashed his patented shit-eating grin, and Janie wanted to retch.

At least Zee was safe. She didn't think he'd lie about that. She couldn't help but think about the fact Max might not have liked what was going to come home to him. And then she remembered Heather was dead. She'd never come home. And no matter what Max had done, she didn't think he deserved that pain. Then, she realized Manchester had mentioned Heather's death would have to be explained. The Club was good at explaining away their dark deeds. No doubt they'd go with something easy, like a murdering husband. Suddenly her desire to see Max squirm felt petty and cruel.

"I'd better get going, Max. If you see Kyle, tell him I was looking for him," Janie said quickly.

"Will do. I have a feeling he'll show up tomorrow, good as new." Max waved goodbye as Janie quickly backed her Honda out of the drive. She had to get home. She had to get her family out of Essen.

# 39
# *Veins of the Earth*

"Damn it, I need gas," Kyle said.

Patrick looked over at him. Kyle could see in his eyes he didn't want to stop. Not this close to Essen. They'd stopped by the farmhouse. Kyle had grabbed his backpack, the box of childhood artifacts from his room, and the box of family photos. Everything else, he could leave behind. They'd debated whether to take Patrick's truck or the Prius, but the gas mileage was the deciding factor despite the Prius being more recognizable. They ran to the Kirby farm, and Patrick got his things. His mother and father had thankfully not come back from services at Faith & Triumph yet. It worried Kyle that Patrick seemed to have not processed the fact his parents were all a part of this. But he knew that'd come later. The one thing that had never been debated—that hadn't been talked about out loud at all—was whether they were leaving Essen together.

Patrick gripped Kyle's hand as they pulled into the Qwik-Fill station outside of town. Kyle could feel Patrick's pulse quicken, and a knot formed in his stomach. Rain pelted down onto the overhead metal canopy covering the pumps. It beat out a chaotic metallic rhythm as the drops came heavy and hard. If Kyle could have pushed the car further, he would have. But the last thing they wanted to do was end up on the side of the road anywhere near Essen. Despite what Manchester had said, Kyle didn't trust that she and her kind might not go after or hurt them. He tried not to think of the red lines on the map he'd found in his dad's dashboard. How they stretched and branched all over the Midwest like some sort of circulatory system.

We're the blood that pumps through the veins of the Earth.

"You could write a story," Patrick said suddenly. They'd barely said two words since leaving town.

"Even if anyone believed me, I'm pretty sure these creatures would consider writing a news story a breach of our agreement," Kyle said, shaking his head.

"But we can't let it win." Patrick's voice was pleading, and suddenly he seemed so young. Like a child protesting the fact the ice cream had fallen off his cone and onto the floor. Kyle ripped his hand away from Patrick's grip, although he regretted it immediately.

"Patrick, grow up! What are we supposed to do? How do you kill something that's everywhere?"

"The military—"

"Assuming they believed us, what are they going to do? And what if one of the generals or whatever is one of them?"

"We don't know they're everywhere," Patrick said. But he looked sullen. His voice was much quieter.

Kyle sighed, feeling like a total asshole. Patrick wasn't saying anything that hadn't been screaming through his brain since they left

The Grove. All they'd seen was one map, sure. But how literal had the Heather-thing been when it had said they were the blood that flowed through the veins of the earth? Earth as in dirt? Or was that through the Earth, as in the planet? Kyle looked out the window and saw the gas pumps were ancient and didn't even have card readers on them.

"I've got to pay inside," Kyle said, poking his head through the window. "Do you want a water or something?"

"How about a Mountain Dew?" Patrick asked.

Kyle nodded his head, and after he filled up, he headed inside. He walked into the gas station and selected a water and a Mountain Dew from the flatly lit refrigerated section at the back. The tile was yellowing, and the signage in the store looked like it hadn't been updated since the seventies. An older man in his fifties with short salt-and-pepper hair and a bushy beard to match sat behind the counter, watching cartoons on a little TV near the register and puffing away at a cigarette.

"That'll do ya?" he asked. Veins pulsed on the man's temples and he stared at Kyle intently.

"Just this and the gas, thanks. Pump two," Kyle said. The man looked out at pump two and Kyle's car with Patrick inside. He rang up the total.

"That'll be twenty-three seventy-five," he said. "You boys heading out of town?"

"Yeah. Here… visiting," Kyle replied, handing the man his debit card. The man swiped it.

"Good, good. That's good, I think." He handed Kyle back his card. Kyle fumbled it back into his wallet, and the wallet back into his pants, as the man continued. "I don't think it's too friendly around here anymore. Not for your kind. The cities, maybe. Might be your speed."

"Right," Kyle said flatly, grabbing the drinks off the counter. The veins on the man's temple moved. They did not pulse, but they writhed. One of them seemed to travel down the side of his head, and then disappear down into his cheek.

"We'll be seeing you around, then," said the man with a grin not reflected in his watery gray eyes. Kyle didn't respond. He clutched the two cold bottles in his hand, turned around, and walked as quickly as he could to his car. He said nothing as he climbed in and practically threw the bottles toward Patrick. He buckled, switched the car to drive, and took off. Patrick looked at him, an unsaid question and concern on his face. They got a few miles down the road before Kyle put his hand, palm up, on the middle console. Patrick understood, and took his hand.

Inside, Kyle was shaking. But the feel of Patrick's hand in his helped calm him a little. The storm was raging outside now, a gray sheet of rain obscuring Kyle's vision. Great cracks of lightning tore through the sky all around them. Inside the car's little shell of metal and plastic—a perilously thin membrane that protected them both—Kyle gripped Patrick's hand tighter. He pushed down on the gas pedal and raced against the storm.

# About the Author

In addition to his fiction work, Jon writes a variety of blogs, ebooks, video scripts, and more as Director of Marketing for a green cleaning product manufacturer. In addition to writing, he still enjoys illustration as a hobby, and still does the occasional bit of design work. His reading has expanded to all sorts of genres. His favorite things are books, movies, TV shows, video games, or comics that transport you to another world and place-real or imagined, past or present-and invite you to understand the people and their lives. The power of story is in the possibility of expanding empathy. He currently lives in Central Illinois with his partner, Paul where they spend their days making each other laugh a lot.

# Other Works

*Eon Quest*. Oblivion House. 2015.

*The Master of Shearhaven*. Oblivion House. 2024.

**For more information, visit Jon's website at:**

**www.jonwesleyhuff.com**

# *About the Typefaces*

URW Baskerville was used for the majority of the print. Based on Baskerville, designed by John Baskerville in 1757, was chosen both for its high readability and elegance, in an attempt to evoke the Modern Gothic sensibility of the Oblivion House release of *In The Dark of the Grove*.

Paragraph and section heads are set with Adobe Jenson Pro by designer Robert Slimbach. The typeface's elegance matches that of Baskerville but with bold, graphic versions for both display and subhead, which are used here.

Dropcaps use Saber by Zavier Cabarga from CarbagaType. It's a decadent, highly decorative typeface that hints at a history that is shared by many places. Again, this was chosen to evoke the Mondern Gothic sensibility.

This book uses a number of other typefaces to represent the "found" nature of the clues that Kyle and his friends gather along the way. The attempt here was to give these sources their own personality, without the book becoming a graphic designer's nightmare of a mish-mash of too many fonts. These include the classic Big Caslon for the excerpts from other (fictitious) books such as *Dunbar's Grove* and *Midwest Mysteries*. American Typewriter was used for the message from Kyle's father, and Banshee was used for the handwritten code.

Jon Wesley Huff

# *About Modern Gothic*

The Modern Gothic series of books from Oblivion House imagines a legacy of gothic literature that features openly recognized queer characters. "Queer" being a catch-all for a wide variety and mix of identities. Horror and queer identity has always been strongly interconnected, but for much of its history the queerness of horror characters had to be hidden in analog and codes.

By presenting these stories with a nod toward the past—especially the gothic literature of the 70s in its style, while featuring modern storytelling—the hope is to retroactively create more space for open queerness in this legacy. In its small way, it's the closest one can get to traveling back in time and slipping a book or two into history. To invite the reader, for a moment, to imagine what could have been and what could be.